"Sophie, if you're trying to open your store by spring, you're going to need a babysitter."

"Do you know one?" she asked, pushing her glasses in place.

Zeke opened his mouth, processed that hopeful expression of hers and closed it again, unwilling to disappoint her.

This is a really bad idea.

But it was the only idea he had to pay for truck repairs, so he pressed a thumb to his chest and said, *"Me."*

To Sophie's credit, she didn't laugh, but she did look at Zeke the way she'd looked at her twins when they'd tried to start a snowball fight indoors with snow smuggled in their jacket pockets. "My last nanny was trained at the Young's Academy."

Which sounded as snooty as Sophie's pedigree.

Still, Zeke wasn't a quitter. "I've been trained at the school of hard knocks. And better still..."

Sophie raised her slim brows above the rims of her lenses.

"...I'm here and available."

Dear Reader,

Harlan Monroe left a small town in Idaho to his twelve grandchildren. What did Second Chance mean to Harlan? His adult heirs are going to find out. And while they're at it, they'll get a second chance at love.

Sophie Monroe has her hands full. She's a single mom to twin four-year-old boys and she's decided to make a business out of selling her grandfather's collectibles in town. She needs a nanny, preferably someone who can continue to teach her boys how to read. Enter cowboy Zeke Roosevelt, who's recuperating from a broken leg suffered when his truck hit a patch of black ice and then a tree. He can't go back to work for at least a month, but he needs money to repair his truck and pay his bills. The nanny job seems perfect. He's used to wrangling a ton of beef on four hooves. How hard can it be to wrangle two little boys?

As with all the Monroe romances, there's a little laughter to go along with the journey to a happily-ever-after. I hope you come to love the Mountain Monroes as much as I do. Happy reading!

Melinda

HEARTWARMING

Rescued by the Perfect Cowboy

USA TODAY Bestselling Author

Melinda Curtis

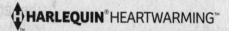

HARLEQUIN®HEARTWARMING™

Recycling programs
for this product may
not exist in your area.

ISBN-13: 978-1-335-51085-3

Rescued by the Perfect Cowboy

Copyright © 2019 by Melinda Wooten

HARLEQUIN®
www.Harlequin.com

Printed in U.S.A.

Prior to writing romance, award-winning *USA TODAY* bestselling author **Melinda Curtis** was a junior manager for a Fortune 500 company, which meant when she flew on the private jet she was relegated to the jump seat—otherwise known as the potty. After grabbing her pen (and a parachute) she made the leap to full-time writer. Melinda recently came to grips with the fact that she's an empty nester and a grandma, concepts easier to grasp than her father buying property in states he rarely visited or her former life jet-setting on a potty.

Brenda Novak says *Season of Change* "found a place on my keeper shelf."

Jayne Ann Krentz says of *Fool For Love*: "wonderfully entertaining."

Books by Melinda Curtis

Harlequin Heartwarming

The Mountain Monroes

Kissed by the Country Doc
Snowed in with the Single Dad

Return of the Blackwell Brothers

The Rancher's Redemption

Visit the Author Profile page
at Harlequin.com for more titles.

THE MOUNTAIN MONROES FAMILY TREE

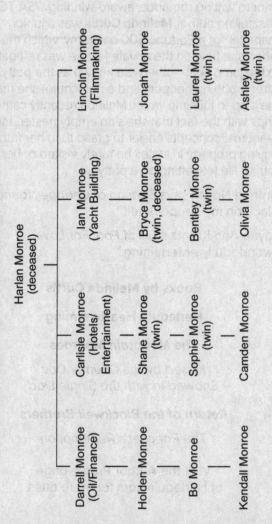

Harlan Monroe
(deceased)

Darrell Monroe
(Oil/Finance)

Holden Monroe

Bo Monroe

Kendall Monroe

Carlisle Monroe
(Hotels/
Entertainment)

Shane Monroe
(twin)

Sophie Monroe
(twin)

Camden Monroe

Ian Monroe
(Yacht Building)

Bryce Monroe
(twin, deceased)

Bentley Monroe
(twin)

Olivia Monroe

Lincoln Monroe
(Filmmaking)

Jonah Monroe

Laurel Monroe
(twin)

Ashley Monroe
(twin)

PROLOGUE

"As for my grandchildren, there is hope for their moral fiber. But only if they break free of the influence of my four failures and learn there is more to life than the bottom line… To that end, I leave the town of Second Chance, Idaho, to my grandchildren…"

Harlan Monroe
Father of four
Grandfather of twelve
Last will and testament

CHAPTER ONE

SOPHIE MONROE WAS COLD.

Her fingers. Her nose. Her toes. All as cold as ice.

"There's more to life than a working heater," Sophie mumbled. Since coming to Second Chance, Idaho, Sophie had taken to talking to herself. Well, that's what her twin brother, Shane, said. From Sophie's perspective, she was talking to her dearly departed grandpa Harlan, without whom she wouldn't be in Second Chance. "There's more to life than a high-rise apartment in Philadelphia."

"This is more fun than school," her son Andrew said. It wasn't a believable statement given he was four and hadn't been to school.

"Way more fun," Alexander, his twin brother, said.

The two boys were playing in a corner of the unheated log cabin Sophie was trying to clear. In the olden times, it'd been a trading post. The boys were out of sight behind a wall of boxes she'd stacked days earlier. Sophie considered it a wise choice since the boxes blocked the chilly gusts that whipped through the mountain cabin every time someone opened the front door. They'd been entertaining themselves for nearly an hour with something that occasionally groaned like two metal bars being pried apart.

"Boys? Show me all your fingers and toes," Sophie commanded, turning to their corner.

They scurried into sight, giggling and wiggling their fingers. They looked angelic, bundled up in yellow jackets and gray knit caps with their broad grins and dirt-smudged faces.

"You're not doing anything you shouldn't, right?" Sophie asked, because she may love her sons, but she knew them too well.

"No," they chorused, not entirely believably given they exchanged mischievous glances. But there was no blood or broken merchandise to suggest otherwise.

"Carry on." Sophie returned her attention to the assortment of 1:18 model cars circa the 1960s. The small cars were in pristine condition. The doors opened and closed. The wheels spun. These weren't made for toddler boys to play with.

The boys returned to their hidden playground unaware of her find.

Shane, Sophie's twin brother, opened the

door to the cabin, letting in the wintry wind. "How's it going in here?"

"Good." Sophie closed the box with the small cars, wrote a description on the top flap and set it on the stack behind her. She planned to sell collectibles inside the trading post when she opened in a few weeks and the cars would definitely make the cut. "Shut the door." Sophie righted her glasses, which had slipped down her nose, and tried to get her fingernail underneath the tape sealing the next box. Her cold fingers moved sluggishly.

Shane navigated the winding path between stacked boxes from the door to Sophie. "Did you take a break? This place looks the same as when I was in here earlier. There are still boxes everywhere."

"I've gone through those three stacks of boxes." Sophie pointed to the tall, wide heap behind her. "It's not like I have room to put anything on display."

The trading post had been built over one hundred years ago by Sophie's ancestors from thick round logs and had been a place for early settlers to trade furs for the essentials. From what Sophie could tell, it had been closed for several decades. The cash register was ancient, not electronic. The ceilings were high and open-beamed, which would have made the space seem large if it had more natural light and less clutter.

Someone—she suspected her grandpa Harlan, since he'd owned every building in town—had left boxes and boxes of their possessions. She was more respectful of a person's right to collect what they had heart for than she'd been a few years ago, when as a curator of the vast Monroe art collection, she'd used monetary value as a way to manage things.

"Look at you." Shane chuckled. "Trapped in piles of junk."

"Please don't call it that. I've told you, one man's junk is another man's gem."

"Seriously, Sophie. You're trapped in treasure," Shane revised his assessment.

Sophie stopped trying to open the box and glanced up. *"Oh."* She saw what Shane meant. Burrowing into the stacks, she'd blocked herself in a sea of stuff and had no way out. Kind of like her situation in Second Chance.

Metal snapped behind the wall of boxes where the twins were. They shrieked gleefully, which had to mean they had all fingers and toes unscathed.

"Boys," Sophie called, a little worried. "What are you doing?"

"Nothing," they chimed.

Shane moved to investigate. "What are you little heathens—"

"*Adorable* little heathens," Sophie hurriedly corrected him. Her sons were a rambunctious, but lovable, pair.

"—doing?" Shane rounded the wall of boxes, let out an oath and dropped out of sight.

Sophie's cold parts tingled with fear. *"Shane? Boys?"*

"No!" Shane firmly but gently reprimanded them.

Something metal clinked and slid across the wood floor, but the boxes were stacked so high Sophie couldn't see what it was.

Shane reappeared, guiding her adorable little heathens out from behind the box wall. "The boys can't be in here unsupervised."

"I'm right here." Sophie breathed easier at the sight of her children, who were free of blood drips. "I've been here the entire time, just a few feet away."

"Speaking of feet…" Shane leaned down to the twins' eye level. "You aren't to play with that bear trap ever again."

"Bear trap?" Sophie echoed weakly. Her entire body was cold now.

"Boys," Shane said firmly. "That fascinating thing you were playing with could have cut off your hand, your feet or your fingers."

He showed his nephews no mercy in his severe tone or stern expression. "Blood would've spurted out from whatever it snapped on, like water from a garden hose."

Sophie felt faint.

"And your mother couldn't have saved you because she's trapped in the midst of all those boxes." Shane didn't let up. He glowered at her, too. "And there's no doctor for a hundred miles, so once all your blood gushed out, you'd be dead. *Dead!*"

"Hey." That was extreme, even for Shane.

Even considering the boys had been playing with a death trap.

Sophie worked up enough saliva to swallow.

Alexander's and Andrew's brown eyes were open wide and unblinking. They looked as scared as Sophie felt.

Fingers and toes.

They were all accounted for, thankfully.

"Can you imagine going through the rest of your life without your twin?" Shane continued his campaign to shock the four-year-olds. "Can you imagine going through the rest of your life never talking to your brother again?"

"Surprisingly, I can," Sophie said sharply. "Enough already."

"That *is* enough for one day." Shane released her little rascals and began moving boxes out of Sophie's way. "Didn't you hear them playing with the jaws of death? Rattling chains like ghosts in a haunted mansion?"

Vaguely.

Guilt pooled at the base of her throat.

Good moms didn't let their kids play with sharp objects.

Good moms didn't become so distracted with work they lost sight of their kids.

Good moms raised their adorable little heathens full-time.

With effort, Sophie swallowed guilt back down. She loved Alexander and Andrew, but she also loved mental stimulation, being useful, accomplishing something. Good moms weren't just moms.

"That's enough, Shane." Sophie raised her chin and slid her glasses where they belonged. "I'm a working mom fostering independence."

Shane pressed his lips together and mumbled something about keepers.

"Is this place haunted?" Andrew asked Shane, face still frozen in shock.

"No, Andrew. It's not haunted," Sophie reassured her son, before turning her attention back to her brother. "And, Shane, I checked on them. They were fine a few minutes ago."

Famous last words.

Guilt came back. More bitter than before, congealing in her throat.

Good moms...

"But Uncle Shane said *ghosts*." Alexander glanced nervously over his shoulder to their play place.

"Do you see what you've done?" Sophie gestured toward the twins, grateful for the chance to toss irresponsibility back in Shane's court. "They aren't going to sleep tonight for fear of ghosts."

Until spring arrived in a few weeks' time, they were staying in the Lodgepole Inn across the narrow highway, which was about as old as the trading post and creaked with every breath of wind coming down from the mountains.

"Maybe a little fear will keep them alive and in one piece." Shane finished clearing a path for Sophie to get free. "Don't try to put this back on me."

There's more to life than being a helicopter parent.

Sophie couldn't face her twin.

They'll learn something from this.

Grandpa Harlan would've phrased her arguments differently: *They lived to tell the tale. What's wrong with that?*

She'd heard him say that to her father often enough when she was a kid.

But no matter what arguments Sophie made with herself, Shane was right. She'd endangered her children.

And she couldn't let it happen again.

CHAPTER TWO

ZEKE ROOSEVELT HAD often heard it said there
was nothing prettier to a cowboy than his horse.

Zeke was a cowboy, but he was going to have
to disagree.

Sophie Monroe was beautiful. She had short,
brown hair that tended to take a charge of elec-
tricity and float around her face like a halo. Her
brown eyes were big and soft and when she was
happy, they sparkled. She also had a sweet figure to match her sweet disposition.

In horse terms, she was a goer, always up
for whatever challenge her twin boys threw at
her, despite the fact that those kids were what
his grandmother would have called, "hell on
four-year-old wheels." Those twins operated
on batteries that never ran low. They were the
reason Sophie never sat still and always looked
exhausted.

"Careful now, boys." Sophie descended the
stairs at the Lodgepole Inn.

She and her sons were hidden from Zeke's

line of sight. It sounded like the twins were bunny hopping down the steps.

Sophie appeared, stopping on the first-floor landing in the stream of late-winter sunlight coming through the front windows. She pushed up those red-rimmed glasses of hers and turned to monitor the bunnies. "One hand on the rail, Andrew. That doesn't mean you can take yours off, Alexander." And then she smiled at Zeke.

There was no way to deflect that smile. It hit him square in the face and dared him not to think of shamrocks and rainbows and pots of gold—all the things he'd wished for when he was a kid.

Status of his childhood dreams? Abandoned.

But back to the business at hand...

Sophie was definitely pretty, but she was off-limits to a temporarily unemployed, nearly broke cowboy with a severely broken leg. He'd introduced his truck to a tree in January and broken more than the leg below his kneecap. His truck was incapacitated, sitting in the repair bay of the garage next to the Lodgepole Inn, waiting for Zeke to come up with money for parts. Only Zeke was no longer able to work at the Bucking Bull Ranch. Ever since, he'd been living off his savings and renting a room in Second Chance, Idaho.

Status of his bank account? Precariously low.

"Good morning, Zeke," Sophie said as if the day had already revealed its pot of gold.

Zeke replied in kind, but Sophie had already refocused her attention to the twins and their progress to the inn's common room. He ran a hand through his short hair, torn between being grateful Sophie didn't return his interest and wondering why he seemed invisible to her.

Women didn't use to ignore me.

Over the years, he'd been told he wasn't a hardship to look at. Zeke backed up in his wheelchair. His leg was in a bulky walking boot, propped parallel to the floor to encourage healing.

He wasn't looking his finest exactly.

Oh, yeah. That explained a lot.

He was missing his signature boots and a cowboy hat sitting firmly on his head.

Status of his pride? Precariously low.

It was hard to be studly when you could pull on only one boot. Although he'd graduated to a bulky walking brace, the doctor had recommended he keep his leg immobile as much as possible for another few days.

Patience for his injury? Next to none.

He was ready to make a run for it out of the Lodgepole Inn. Not that Zeke could afford to go anywhere. He had twenty-five dollars in his wallet. Precarious and pathetic, that's what he was.

Now, Sophie. She came from money. Her generation of Monroes owned the small town of Second Chance. The Monroe name was attached to a movie studio, a yacht building company, oil rigs and a string of luxury hotels. She was from Philadelphia and had probably never faced bankruptcy in her life. Even worse, Sophie had a college education. She'd earned two degrees in art history, of all things. She might just as well have majored in Russian. Both areas of study were foreign to him.

"Hurry up." Sophie gestured for her kids to reach the ground floor. "Come sit on the couch while I make your oatmeal."

"Oaty-meal." One of the boys took a flying leap from the stairs, stumbled and landed sprawling on his belly on the hardwood. He giggled, none the worse for wear, and glanced behind him. "I beat you."

His brother kept up the bunny hop. "You have to do *all* the steps." He stuck his landing from one step up, raising his arms like an Olympic gymnast. "I win."

"Both of you are winners." Sophie helped Twin Number One to his feet and herded both boys toward the couch. "Now sit."

Zeke nodded a greeting at the twins. They were brown-haired kids with sturdy legs and mischief in their eyes. Zeke had trouble telling them apart, seeing as how they were identical in both looks and temperament, at least to him. Alexander had a cowlick, but currently both boys had none. Their hair was wet and slicked back, and they were dressed in identical blue snow bib overalls.

Sophie veered toward the alcove and the inn's small kitchenette. The twins did the church walk toward the couch, looking as well behaved as altar boys. But as soon as their mother disappeared into the inn's small half kitchen, they poked each other and danced around like boxers in a ring.

"Boys," Sophie called sternly from the alcove. "I hear you."

Their arms paused midpoke.

"We aren't doing nothing," said one.

"You *aren't* doing *anything*," corrected Sophie.

"That's what Andrew said." Alexander, whose cowlick was making a comeback as his hair dried, grinned at Zeke before poking his twin in the belly.

"Oof." Andrew threw an elbow.

The boys danced to the opposite end of the couch near where Zeke sat in his wheelchair with his nearly healed leg propped up and vulnerable, trapped between them and the large, stone cooking fireplace.

"Sometimes kids need a little separation." Zeke said it as much to get the boys' attention as Sophie's.

"Thank you for the advice," Sophie called. "I've got everything under control."

"Yes, ma'am. I'm sure you do." Zeke rolled his chair back another couple of inches, eyed the boys, who were trying to tussle in silence, and wished he had a bit of rope to lasso these misbehaving little doggies. "You boys want to hear a story?"

The twins gave Zeke a look that managed to be half measuring and half rebellious.

Around the corner of the common room in the alcove, the microwave began to hum.

"Is it about pirates?" the boy who might have been Andrew asked, rubbing his nose.

"Nope."

"Is it about spacemen?" the boy who might have been Alexander asked, scratching his cowlick.

"Nope."

The boys exchanged glances that Zeke interpreted to be lack of interest. One of them raised a hand to get in another poke.

"It's about a bull," Zeke said quickly, trying not to sound desperate, even though he was. He didn't like to lose and yes, losing an audience when he'd offered to tell a story was a loss. He was also nearing the end of phase two of his recuperation, which meant he could progress from a walking boot to walking carefully in his own cowboy boot—as long as nothing set his knitting bones back, like tussling boys accidentally bumping into his leg.

The boys were silent, watching him, waiting to be mesmerized or to renew their tussle.

"You see, there was this bull named—"

"Ferdinand!" they chorused.

"We saw the movie with Aunt Laurel," said Andrew.

"And Mom read us the book," said Alexander.

"Nope. This story isn't about *that* bull." Leastwise, not anymore. "This bull's name was...*Buttercup*. And he was the biggest, meanest bull on the rodeo circuit this side of the Mississippi." Neither boy called him out on his story, so Zeke kept going. "Why, he killed a man and very nearly ate a rodeo clown."

"Nah-uh." Andrew dropped his butt on the couch cushion, brown eyes wide.

"Nah-huh." Zeke decided a little-boy language was in order. "Buttercup ate the clown's curly red hair before the poor guy could be rescued from the arena."

"Nah-uh." Alexander plopped next to his brother, brown eyes wide.

"Nah-huh," Zeke reiterated. "Buttercup was a killer."

Sophie returned with two paper bowls filled with instant oatmeal. She set them on the coffee table. "I don't suppose Buttercup happened to be ridden by a redheaded cowboy named Zeke."

There goes that angle.

"No, ma'am. I'd be too scared to attempt riding such a beast."

The boys got down on their knees and began eating their oaty-meal, but the majority of their attention was on Zeke, as was Sophie's.

Zeke's chest expanded with manly pride.

Sophie pushed her glasses up her slim nose and gave Zeke a look that might have said: *My boys are a tough audience but give it your best shot.*

She had spunk. She didn't always show it, but it was there if a man was willing to wait for it to make an appearance from behind those glasses.

He dipped his chin, hoping she wouldn't see him fighting a smile, and continued his story. "Now, you see, lots of rodeos are held at county fairs, which are filled with laughter. But Buttercup only ever saw the rodeo side of the event. No one laughed at the rodeo. Leastwise, not around him. The sounds he was used to were the ones he created. Big snorts of air." Zeke made a blustery, snorting sound. "And cowboy howls of pain." Zeke howled like a coyote. "So that bull? He sneaked out of his pen one night to see what all the hubbub at the fair was about."

"What's a fair?" Alexander asked.

Zeke gasped dramatically.

"It's part carnival, part museum," Sophie said.

"Museum?" Sophie's answer put a wrinkle in Zeke's brow.

We're as different as peas and carrots.

"At a fair, there are displays of local art." Sophie looked down her nose at Zeke, the way he knew someone with her education and social background should. And then she laughed. "Not that I've actually been to a fair since my grandfather took us when we were kids. He would've laughed at me calling a fair a sort of museum." She laughed again.

She laughed! At herself!

Tempted as Zeke was by the promise of pots of gold and rainbows, he very nearly lost his train of thought. He drew a deep breath and got back to business. "There are also displays of things farmers have grown, like vegetables and sheep." Zeke leaned toward those boys. "But the thing that makes everyone laugh is the carnival part."

"What's a car-knee-val?" Alexander asked, sounding out the word.

Alexander's question required another dramatic gasp from Zeke.

What were they teaching kids in Philadelphia?

His father would've scowled and made a snide remark about city folk.

Zeke rubbed out the wrinkle in his forehead. "A carnival has rides that go faster than that sled you've been riding down Sled Hill. It has rides that go really high and make it feel like you left your stomach on the ground. And it has games you play to win huge stuffed animals bigger than you, *pardner.*"

Oh, Ms. Heater from his high school drama class would be impressed with Zeke's performance.

And bonus! Sophie's gaze hadn't left Zeke since he'd begun talking about the carnival.

Was she impressed, too?

Zeke didn't know. He warmed to his tale anyway. "Well, ole Buttercup knocked over some milk bottles and made a little boy with a cowlick laugh." Zeke winked at Alexander, who poked Andrew. "Buttercup ran off, kind of scared of that laugh. He ran over the strength machine, kicked it and made the bell ring, which made a little boy wearing a pair of blue pants laugh and spill his popcorn." He winked at Andrew, who poked Alexander. Zeke continued telling the boys about the bull's made-up antics, including eating all the popcorn from the popcorn cart, keeping them entertained until their oatmeal was gone. "And then Buttercup trotted back to his corral and fell asleep dreaming about laughter and bells and popcorn."

"Is that the end?" Not only did Alexander have a cowlick, he seemed to be the future academic, like his mother, asking all kinds of questions.

Zeke sat taller in his wheelchair. "No, siree. Why, the very next day there was a contest to see how long someone could ride the killer bull named Buttercup. And do you know what?"

"What?" everyone chorused, including Sophie.

Zeke suppressed a smile. There was nothing he liked better than storytelling. Except maybe riding and roping. And kissing a pretty woman, of course.

"The cowboy who was unlucky enough to draw Buttercup for a ride was wearing blue jeans, had a cowlick in his brown hair and laughed—" Zeke let out a holiday-worthy ho-ho-ho "—just like all those carnival folks." Zeke slapped the thigh on his uninjured leg, feeling more like himself. "And old Buttercup? He was so full of popcorn that he didn't feel like eating anybody that day. That cowboy got on Buttercup and that old bull took him for a sweet ride around the arena, as gentle as an old pony."

"And did the cowboy win a big belt buckle?" Sophie smiled, but her gaze drifted toward the door and she didn't wait for Zeke to answer. "Do you need anything else to eat, boys? We've got to get over to the trading post." Which was the huge log cabin across the road she was trying to open as an antiques store.

"Mo-om." Andrew crossed his arms and pouted. "Can't we stay with Aunt Laurel?"

"Nope." Sophie shook her head. "Your aunt already left for Odette's." Where she was most likely stitching a quilt or knitting a scarf or something equally boring to boys on four-year-old wheels.

"Jackets on." Sophie gestured toward the hooks by the door where everyone hung their coats. "And don't ask if Uncle Shane can watch you today. He's helping around town."

Meaning Shane was going to spend the day talking to people he thought had known his grandfather, who'd left them the town in his will but hadn't said why. Shane fancied himself a detective, although as far as Zeke knew, he'd detected nothing about his grandfather's motives for bequeathing them a town.

Andrew thrust out his lip even farther. "But you don't let us do anything at the trading post."

"I nearly let you cut off your appendages in a bear trap." Sophie didn't seem to be joking.

Zeke's mouth dropped open.

"Mo-om." That was Alexander bouncing on the couch cushion. "Can't we stay with Gabby?" He pointed toward the innkeeper's closed apartment door behind the check-in desk.

"Nope." Sophie tsked. "Gabby left for school while you were in the shower this morning." She reached for her jacket. "There's no one else around but me."

"He's here." Andrew pointed at Zeke.

"No." Sophie dismissed Zeke the way her boys might refuse to acknowledge chopped liver on their dinner plate. "Come on."

So much for no longer feeling sorry for himself.

"But…Zeke's here." Alexander tilted his head and stared at Zeke. "He never goes anywhere."

"No," Sophie said again.

Zeke's ego was taking a shoulder-slumping beating today. He was lacking whatever Sophie saw as qualifications to babysit kids for a few hours.

"Please," the twins said, not taking no for an answer. When their mother didn't relent, they thrust their faces toward Zeke, trying to look like they'd be no trouble at all.

Which was about as believable as Zeke earning a college degree online.

He should just tell the boys, *Sorry, not today.* But there was nothing on morning television to interest him and the day was stretching out to be just like yesterday—as in boring. And there was Sophie… Sophie wasn't looking at him, not even to give him a polite smile. She obviously thought watching her boys was above Zeke's pay grade.

I've herded bulls more troublesome than these two.

"I *am* here," Zeke said tentatively. And then because that sounded wishy-washy, he added, "I can watch them for a few hours."

"I couldn't impose." Sophie glanced at Zeke's walking boot, which was impossible to miss stuck out from his body like a ladder over the tailgate of a pickup truck. And she might have taken in the wheelchair he'd been sitting in the past two months, too.

Somehow, I have to dig myself out of this pathetic, precarious hole.

Zeke wanted his mobility back. He wanted his bank account back. He wanted his manhood back. He might just as well start by wrangling two little boys. "I can watch them. I'm days away from getting out of this walking boot." It seemed important to get out of his wheelchair and support his credentials. It seemed essential to do so without catching his feet on anything and falling.

Mission accomplished.

Standing, Zeke smiled reassuringly. "It's not a problem." Or so he hoped.

Sophie scanned Zeke from head to toe, not saying anything but implying impending rejection. And then her gaze slid to the door, giving away she wouldn't mind accepting his help.

"Well, boys?" Zeke asked the little minions. "What do you say?"

The twins exchanged glances, silent messages, head nods.

"We'll be good, Mom," Andrew said.

"Yep." Alexander scratched his cowlick. "Good as gold."

Zeke didn't believe that for a minute. He'd witnessed their antics every day for nearly two months.

Sophie pushed her red glasses up her splendid nose. "Are you sure you want to do this, Zeke?"

"Yes, ma'am."

"Okay." He was the object of her complete

attention. "But if there's any trouble, any trouble at all—"

"There won't be any trouble." Zeke gave the twins hard looks.

They grinned wickedly.

"If there *is* any trouble," Sophie murmured, "there won't be any second chances."

CHAPTER THREE

"YOU LEFT YOUR adorable little heathens with Zeke?" Laurel cradled her barely there baby bump beneath her unzipped teal jacket and gaped at Sophie. "By choice?"

"Yes." Doubt about her mommy skills prickled along Sophie's skin as she faced her cousin midmorning at the trading post, holding a velvet painting of a redheaded clown and trying not to think about how cold she was.

For hours, it had been just Sophie and box after box of interesting plunder. She'd refused to worry about the boys since she was only a shout away and she hadn't heard any shouts. And then she'd come across the velvet painting and thought of rodeo clowns and Zeke.

"You left your boys with that cowboy?" Odette, a lifetime resident of Second Chance, stood on the front porch, holding on to Laurel's shoulder for balance as she stomped snow from her boots. The old woman wore red snow pants that rustled with every movement and three layers of sweaters beneath a big green jacket. "That's practically criminal. He's convalescing."

"It's not like Zeke is bedridden," Sophie argued, setting the clown painting aside. If not for the walking boot, any woman would look at Zeke and know he could handle anything in his path, be it bulls, boars or boys. "And my boys are well behaved."

"Well behaved?" Odette's bushy white brows rose up to meet the brim of her snow-dusted yellow knit cap. "That's what they said about the tigers in the circus before they devoured the ringmaster."

Mommy doubt was replaced by the heated need to defend the honor of her boys. "They're four. Of course they're going to be a handful." That didn't mean they were as dangerous as wild tigers.

Laurel came inside, gathering the ends of her red, wind-blown hair and twisting those locks over her shoulder. "Odette's joking. And what *I meant* was Zeke doesn't seem like the kind of man who has childcare experience."

"*Au contraire*, my little protégé." Odette stepped past the two younger women and rummaged in the nearest open box. "Before his accident, Zeke worked at the Bucking Bull Ranch. That Clark widow runs it now and she has three boys. I'd expect Zeke knows a thing or two about kids. But boys—" she picked up an old metal ice skate, the kind you strapped onto your shoe. She shook it at Sophie "—*especially your boys*, know a thing or two about testing authority, which is why you shouldn't take advantage of a man on the mend."

"Zeke offered. What was I supposed to do? *Turn him down?*" Bruise the poor man's ego?

"Yes!" Odette and Laurel said together on visible puffs of air.

"No." The clown in the painting seemed to be laughing *at* Sophie, not *with* her. "Besides, I need a sitter. Yesterday when I brought the boys here, they very nearly snapped a bear trap on each other." Sophie shuddered. "Zeke only offered to watch them because the boys begged him." She felt guilty about taking advantage of the man. "Zeke likes them."

"Zeke only offered because he likes *you*, Sophie." Laurel plucked the ice skate from Odette's hand and returned it to the box where she'd found it.

Odette huffed, although it wasn't clear if she huffed about the skate being taken away or because Laurel assumed Zeke liked Sophie.

"There's more to life than romance." Sophie wanted to roll her eyes. "And I accepted Zeke's offer because I trust him." Plus, with a walking boot on, Zeke wasn't likely to take the boys outside to Sled Hill or anywhere else they could run away from him and get into trouble. Because, frankly, Alexander and Andrew had a tendency to find trouble. "Zeke will be fine. He's been fine all morning. Look across the highway. I don't see any SOS flags flying."

Her two visitors dutifully glanced toward the inn.

Although it was early March, snow fell softly, adding to the few feet already blanketing Second Chance. Far across the valley, the snow-covered Sawtooth Mountains rose majestically above everything.

"Speaking of looking..." Laurel elbowed Sophie's arm. "Have you noticed the way Zeke looks at you?"

"Stop it." Sophie laughed Laurel's observation off and adjusted her glasses. The plastic was cold across the bridge of her nose. "If you mean he looks at me like I'm from another planet, of course I've noticed." Since they'd arrived in Second Chance, half the time Sophie felt as if she was running around with her head cut off. She was used to having a nanny help keep her life and her boys on track.

Odette tsked. "The only thing out of this world about the way Zeke looks at you is the way he makes moon eyes." The old woman opened her faded gray eyes and stared at Sophie without blinking.

"Agreed." Laurel mirrored Odette's ridiculous stare, but her mouth wobbled as if she was struggling not to smile. "Tell us you've noticed his interest."

Sophie kept her mouth shut.

Because she had noticed Zeke, just not any mooning stare. His eyes were green. His face and arms freckled from the sun. His hair was ginger, a color between the brash red of Laurel's and the light strawberry blonde of Gabby's. He talked more than preteen Gabby, which was saying something. And he joked more than her twin brother, Shane, which was hard to do. But Zeke was polite. He said, "Yes, ma'am," and "No, ma'am."

The boys could use a good influence like Zeke.

She didn't mind adding the cowboy to her growing circle of friends in Second Chance. But beyond that, Sophie wasn't interested in a romance, even if Zeke wasn't a hardship to look at or be with. Part of the reason her first marriage had failed was because her interests and Frank's were worlds apart. She loved studying the stories of artifacts from the past and Frank had interest only in the background pertaining to the next ball game.

Sophie had shaken her head so much in the last few minutes her glasses had drifted down her nose. She tilted her chin up to look at the two women. "I won't be drawn into this argument. Besides, I'm not the type of woman a cowboy finds interesting."

"You're breathing, aren't you?" Odette teased. "Cowboys find all sorts of women interesting."

"I mean, I have mama curves." Sophie had always meant to lose a few more pounds, but divorce and single parenthood made the gym inconvenient. "And I wear glasses." She shoved hers back up her nose.

"Zeke don't care about pounds and spectacles." Odette's bushy brows lowered, creasing her already creased brow.

"And where did you hear such nonsense?" Blue eyes blazing, Laurel looked ready to start a fight with someone. "If you tell me that deadbeat ex-husband of yours told you your mama curves and glasses weren't attractive, I might have to—"

"*Please*. Can we talk about something else?" Sophie had enough on her plate without complicating it with a side of man. "I'm assuming you're over here because you want me to help with the mercantile."

Which was next door, at least fifty years newer than the trading post and built of bricks.

Laurel planned to open her shop and sell quilts, local artwork and other handmade goods.

"I need something moved." Laurel smiled sheepishly. Being pregnant with twins meant she couldn't lift anything. "Odette can help, but I can't find Mitch." Mitch being Laurel's fiancé and the innkeeper, although he wasn't Laurel's baby daddy.

Sophie narrowed her eyes. "Is this the steamer trunk? The one with all those vintage Levi's you found?"

Laurel nodded, apologizing with her eyes.

"The same trunk I moved with Mitch yesterday?" Sophie planted her hands on her hips. "The same trunk I helped move three times in as many days?"

"Yes." Laurel wouldn't look at Sophie.

Who wasn't going to agree to help so easily. "Is there a reason you keep wanting it moved?"

Laurel stuck her chin out. "It never looks right."

"She's nesting," Odette said kindly. "She'll change her mind several more times before she has those babies."

Sophie didn't have the luxury of changing her mind. There was too much to do in the trading post, too many things to look at and think about and wonder if she could find them a good home. A home Grandpa Harlan would approve of.

"What's wrong?" Laurel laid a gloved hand on Sophie's shoulder.

"I thought this would be more like cleaning the boys' room." Sophie was horrified to find tears filling her eyes. "It's more like a hoarder's wormhole. I don't think I'll be able to open when you do." She could sort through the boxes for only a few hours a day because the boys couldn't be counted on to stay out of trouble. And she hadn't cleared boxes away from the fireplace in the back or from the few wall heaters, so she couldn't keep the place warm.

"No one says we have to open on a certain date." Laurel hugged her. "I'll wait for you. Odette is helping me create an amazing crazy quilt. And with wedding planning and babies on the way, I've got a lot to do."

"No one says you have to open at all," Odette grumbled. She was uncomfortable selling her wares, although her quilts and knitted items were of the highest quality. She'd agreed to feature her work in the mercantile only because she was fond of Laurel. "People don't need to stop in Second Chance. We've got enough people here already."

Despite Second Chance being located at a crossroads of two narrow mountain highways, few people found it interesting enough to stop and eat at the diner, buy snacks or gas at the general store, or stay the night at the inn. The town needed the commerce Sophie's and Laurel's stores would bring.

Ignoring the feisty woman, Sophie squeezed her cousin tight. "But we agreed—"

"Sophie?" Shane appeared in the doorway. He took one look at her and nudged his way past Laurel to give Sophie a hug. "You look like you need a break, a latte and a massage."

Sophie sighed. Her twin was good at reading her moods.

"If only there was a place in Second Chance to get a decent latte and a spa treatment." Sophie may have been whining, but she felt better after those two hugs.

Odette edged past Shane to get closer to Sophie. "Worries are nothing a nice hot bath won't solve." That might have been the kindest thing the old woman had ever said to Sophie. She brushed her gloved hand over Sophie's cheek and gave a curt nod. "That's better. I wasn't sure if you had a streak of dirt or a cobweb on your face. It was a cobweb."

Ew. Sophie scrubbed her face with her hands.

Shane had backed up to give Odette room to reach Sophie. He bumped into a stack of boxes, sending them tumbling back into another stack of boxes, and another stack, and another, and another. Boxes keeled over like well-placed dominoes.

Sophie's shoulders sank.

This is going to set me back.

When the thunder inside the fur trading post stopped rumbling, Sophie looked at what the collapse had revealed. Spilled contents. A jumble of loose items. And...

She whooped. Climbing over boxes, a wagon wheel and a pair of boat oars, Sophie reached the item that had caught her eye. Her find was so heavy, she couldn't lift it. "Shane, come get this."

She had to backtrack so that Shane could reach her newest treasure.

"I don't know why you're so excited." Shane reached into the jumbled mess. "It's just a big old bell."

"It's an Asian elephant bell." Uncaring of the cold, the mess or her image, Sophie danced with excitement. "They hung these around an elephant's neck, so they could locate them in the jungle when they were needed."

"Shouldn't that be in a museum?" Laurel asked, tracing the engraved markings on the rim.

Sophie shrugged. "Or featured in a private

collection. Regardless, it's going to find a new home where it can be loved."

That was Sophie's goal for everything she sold—to be cherished the way she wanted to be.

THE LAST TIME Zeke had wrangled a four-year-old, it'd weighed a ton and had four legs.

That bull had been easier to negotiate with than Sophie's twins.

"I want to be the red checker!" Alexander raised his voice loud enough to shake the timbers above them.

"I'm red!" Andrew was just as determined, but he had an advantage. He had all but one red checker hugged to his chest. "Red always wins."

"Not always." Zeke's murmured comment went unnoticed.

"I'm red!"

"No, I'm red!"

Sitting in a wingback chair at the end of the coffee table in the inn's common room, Zeke put his thumb and forefinger in his mouth and whistled.

That silenced both boys and sent four red checkers tumbling to the wood floor around the common room's coffee table. Andrew body-blocked his brother and scooped them back up.

Zeke sighed. If he hadn't broken his leg, he'd

be out riding and rounding up strays on this snowy day. Instead… "Do you boys know what taking turns means?"

"It means I go first!" Alexander clutched the one checker in his possession.

"It's not your turn to go first," Andrew said stubbornly.

"I guess we'll have to use my method to decide." Zeke scratched the back of his neck. "Which one of you is taller? The bigger twin can go first."

They both drew themselves up as tall as they could.

"That's a tie." Because Zeke couldn't count Alexander's cowlick. Zeke fought a smile. For all the boys were a handful, they were amusing, too. "Which one of you has a larger nose?"

They stared at each other's faces. Andrew might have giggled, but he caught himself quickly.

"That's a tie, too." They were identical and had the same button nose. "Okay, which one of you has bigger feet?"

They shoved their feet next to each other on the wide wood planks.

"They're the same." Alexander grinned.

"Because we're twins." Andrew grinned.

"Let me get this straight." Zeke grinned, too,

leaning forward in his chair. "You two scamps are alike in every way?"

They nodded, brown eyes wide.

"Well, then..." Zeke sat back, prepared to deliver a lesson his grandmother would've been proud of. "If neither one of you can share, then you both must be mean." Zeke sucked in a breath. Had he really meant to say that? He sounded like he was channeling his father, the bitter man whose wife had left him, rather than his kindhearted, dearly departed grandmother.

Before he could soften his words, the twins responded.

"I'm not mean." Andrew clutched his checkers closer to his chest.

"Me either." Alexander put his red checker on the board.

After a moment, Andrew dumped his red checkers on the board, as well. "Alexander should be red."

"You picked red first," Alexander said generously, using his indoor voice.

They slumped on the floor on either side of the coffee table as if spent.

"I don't think you boys want to play checkers. Now, Alexander..." That was a mouthful of a name for such a little guy.

The boy stared up at Zeke expectantly.

"Kid, I can't call you Alexander any longer.

Where I come from people have names like John and Mary, or nicknames like Bubba or Whiz."

"But…" His slender brows drew together. "I'm *Alexander*."

"I'm going to call you Alex," Zeke said firmly.

"Mom doesn't like—" Andrew frowned as he searched for the word *"—nicknames."*

"Andy," Zeke countered. "Your mother may give you a name, but your family and friends give you another one."

"Andy." Grinning, Alex pushed his brother in the shoulder.

"Alex." Andy pushed back, smile splitting his little cheeks.

"Now," Zeke said before things dissolved into another fight. "Alex and Andy, what do you say we play a game of hide-and-seek?"

The twins glanced around the room as avidly as if they were searching for presents beneath the Christmas tree. There weren't many places to hide. There was a long, low couch with a blue-and-brown quilt over the back, a couple wingback chairs that wouldn't provide much cover. The check-in desk was perpendicular to Zeke, offering no place to hide. Mitch, the innkeeper, had an apartment behind the desk, but that door was closed. There was a half kitchen around the corner of the fireplace wall. Slim pickings for a game of hide-and-seek.

"I've got rules," Zeke said, not that the boys would follow them. "Boundaries of where to hide. We can play hide-and-seek in my room." He gestured with his thumb to the doorway behind him. "Or in this room." He used both forefingers to point at the ceiling. "Or in your room upstairs."

"I call dibs on hiding behind our bed," Andy said to his brother.

Alex made a disappointed noise. "I wanted to hide there."

"I hope you both hide there, because it'll make it easier for me to find you." These boys were soft. And they lacked imagination. "I'm going to close my eyes and count to twenty, and then I'm going to come find you." Zeke covered his eyes with one hand and began counting slowly.

Two pairs of feet pounded up the stairs, most likely to hide on the far side of their bed. Two pairs of feet ran down the hall. A door opened and slammed shut.

Zeke finished counting and removed his hand from his eyes.

Gabby, Mitch's daughter and the inn's resident preteen, came out of her family's apartment and sat at the check-in desk with her laptop. "Aren't you going to go look for them?"

Her father appeared in the doorway behind her. "You're missing the point, Gabby." Mitch beamed. "Parents encourage kids to hide and then take their own sweet time finding them. It's called a parental breather."

"That's cruel." Gabby tucked a loose strand of strawberry blonde hair behind her ear and then narrowed her eyes. "Wait. Is that why it took you forever to find me, Dad? I thought I was practically unbeatable at hide-and-seek."

"I'd never crush your childhood belief, honey." Mitch flashed Zeke a conspiratorial smile that disappeared almost as quickly as it came. "You shouldn't have let them hide upstairs. You shouldn't be walking that far."

"I've got to start walking longer distances sometime." Zeke got to his feet and took a few steps. His cowboy boot had a short heel and a stiff sole. His walking boot had a thick flat sole. In theory, they should have been the same height. In theory. His walking boot seemed taller than his cowboy boot, making his gait uneven.

"Jeez, look at yourself. I'll go find them." Mitch crossed the room, glancing around. "Where's your wheelchair? You should be sitting with your leg propped up."

Zeke's pride had required him to put the chair away. "I thought you were a lawyer in a former life, not a doctor."

Mitch smirked. "Seeing as how our doctor left town and I've helped care for you since your hospital release, I'm allowed to ask."

"Ask all you want." Zeke walked a few more steps toward the stairs, feeling as graceful as a newborn steer. "I retired the chair. It was time."

"Have you both forgotten the twins are hiding and you finished counting?" Gabby sounded put out. "Never mind. I'll go *find* them."

"That doesn't seem fair," Zeke said, although he was relieved by her offer, given his unsteady gait and the steep staircase. "I'm the one who asked them to hide."

"After what my dad admitted to, I'm going to have to reevaluate my entire childhood." Gabby climbed the stairs with catlike feet. Likewise, she and Shane were able to traverse the stairs and the second floor like ninjas, having made a mental map of the squeaky floorboards.

"Now might be a good time to get a cup of coffee." Mitch nodded toward the alcove and the coffee maker. "Before they bunny hop back downstairs."

True that. Zeke limped toward the alcove.

Mackenzie Irving entered the inn, hanging

on to the doorknob to keep the wind from slamming it against the wall. "Zeke, I finally found the parts we need to fix your truck. Here's my estimate." Mack ran the general store and repair garage in town. She closed the door and crossed the room to hand Zeke a piece of paper.

He risked a glance at the total and swallowed. Other than word problems, he'd always been good at math. But he didn't like the way these numbers added up.

"Isn't your insurance paying for repairs?" Mitch peeked at the total.

"Not all of them. My truck is so old my insurance totaled it." They'd sent him a check, which had barely covered repairing the axle and drivetrain. That left him to pay for the radiator, grille, bumper and replacement airbag.

"I'll purchase the parts as soon as you give me a down payment," Mack said cheerfully. She could afford to be cheery. Between the Monroes in town for the winter and Zeke's accident, her business was up.

"Give me a few days." Zeke thanked Mack for her diligence. His truck was nearly two decades old and parts weren't easy to find.

"Twenty-five percent and I'll place that order." She tossed her thick brown braid over her shoulder and left.

Zeke stared at the estimate. "I need to get a

MELINDA CURTIS 51

job." Because the only things he had left to sell of any value were his horse and his saddle. Sell them? Not on his life! Zeke turned to Mitch. "I don't suppose you're hiring." Although the doctor had told Zeke he could remove the bulky walking boot this week if he wore his cowboy boots, Zeke knew his leg wasn't strong enough to return to the Bucking Bull and ride.

"I'm not hiring, but maybe Ivy needs help at the diner." Mitch didn't try to hide his skeptical glance at Zeke's walking boot. "Are you sure you're ready to reenter the workforce?"

Zeke shook the page with Mack's figures. "I can't afford to sit around any longer."

Sophie and Laurel entered the inn on a gust of wind. Snowflakes settled at their feet.

Sophie carried what looked like a large framed picture. The front was covered in a towel, possibly to protect it from the snow. "Where are the boys?" She glanced around, her gaze tinged with panic.

"Playing hide-and-seek upstairs with Gabby," Zeke reassured her, like the good sitter he was.

"I brought you something." Sophie removed the towel from the picture. It was a black velvet painting of a clown with neon orange curls. "This reminded me of your story about Buttercup the Bull."

It was what his grandmother would've called

awful. But Zeke graciously accepted the gift, wondering how much it might be worth and whom he might sell it to.

Sophie came to stand at his shoulder, admiring her gift. "Did you know that black velvet painting is an art form?"

If Zeke shifted on his bad leg, their arms would be touching.

Zeke didn't move.

But she did! Inching closer to touch the top corner of the frame with her fingers. "It began south of the border and requires a delicate stroke of a brush with just the right amount of paint. Not too much. Not too little." Sophie glanced up at him through those red-framed glasses that made her brown eyes look huge.

He made a noise that was supposed to indicate interest in her expertise, but it came out like the contented wheeze of a hog in a bog.

She moved away, not that he blamed her.

"You always know the weirdest things about things, Sophie." Laurel shed her jacket and knit cap, freeing her bright red hair. She gave Mitch a hug and kiss. Whispered terms of endearment were exchanged.

I'm not envious.

But Zeke's gaze strayed to Sophie, who was hanging her jacket on a hook by the door.

She straightened her glasses. "Mitch, can you

help me bring in a box and a bell? Shane left them on the porch."

"I'll get them." Zeke set his gift on the couch and tried not to stagger like a drunk on his way to the porch and Sophie's wares.

"Are you sure?" Sophie stared at Zeke as he hobbled past.

That look… No one had ever stared at Zeke that way before—as if he wasn't strong enough to lift a box and a bell!

And the same expression was on Mitch's face!

"Yes, I'm sure." Zeke limped to the door with as much pride as a man could muster given he wore a walking boot and had been reclining in a wheelchair for over two months.

Hobble. Quickstep. Hobble.

To prove he was still a Man of the West, Zeke didn't bother with a jacket. He opened the door, limped out and was bathed in a wind so cold it stole his breath. It sprang into his lungs and clung to his exposed toes in the dreaded walking brace. He lurched to pick up the cardboard box.

"Lift with your knees," Mitch called to him.

It was hard to lift with your knees when your ankle was held immobile in stiff plastic. Zeke heaved the box to his waist, twerking when his lower back twinged.

Strength grows when it's tested, son.

Strength? Zeke hadn't lifted a hay bale, hefted a saddle onto his horse's back or roped a heifer and tried to bring her around to his way of thinking in what seemed like forever.

Zeke elbowed the door closed, annoyed that he'd gone soft.

Quickstep. Hobble. Quickstep.

It seemed like it took forever to get the box to the large, sturdy coffee table in front of the fireplace. "What's in here? A collection of bells?" He straightened, back cracking loudly.

"Is someone making popcorn?" Mitch joked, earning a poke in the ribs from Laurel.

"Those are antique hood ornaments, including a flying lady from a Rolls Royce." Sophie dug out the iconic hood ornament—a winged woman tilting forward as if flying at high speed. "The bell is still outside."

To his credit, Zeke didn't hesitate. He turned and headed for the door.

Hobble. Quickstep. Hobble.

The bell was resting by the stairs. It was the size of a large cat. Thankfully, it had a handle. Zeke hefted it with his left hand, so he could favor his right leg. It hung from a bronze frame and clanked as Zeke lurched back through the door.

Quickstep. Hobble. Quickstep.

He placed the bell on the floor near the fireplace because he was afraid the minion twins would rush down and knock it onto their little toes.

"This ain't no cowbell," Zeke said goodnaturedly. "Or a bull bell." He thought he'd mention it, seeing as how he was an equalopportunity cowboy. "Was it hanging in the church down the road?"

Sophie got to her knees in front of the bell, explaining its use on elephants. "It's most likely from Thailand and at least a hundred years old. Can you imagine?"

"I can imagine." Zeke sat in a chair nearby, awestruck by her knowledge. "What I want to know is how you knew what it was."

"Ancient Asian culture is fascinating to me." Sophie lifted her gaze to Zeke's. Joy accented every nuance on her sweet face.

"I'm into cattle culture myself," Zeke murmured, although if she stared at him like that much longer, he'd ask Mitch if there were any audio books available online on ancient Asian culture. "We're just like two peas…"

Sophie continued to stare up at Zeke.

He could swear they were sharing a moment. She confessing her passion. He confessing his.

I should ask her to coffee.

"Cattle culture?" Sophie's brows nearly disappeared behind the rim of her glasses. "It's not quite the same as ancient Asian culture, is it?"

Zeke released a breathy laugh, one that sounded like steam escaping in that first moment when a kettle gets hot.

Behind Sophie at the check-in desk, Mitch put the heel of his hand on his forehead and Laurel shook her head.

"I was joking. You see…" Zeke started to explain, hesitated, and then started again. "I meant we each had a fascination with something we were passionate about. Me, with cattle. You, with ancient Asian culture."

"Oh." Her cheeks gathered color, pink contrasting with the red of her glasses.

The twin-mins came hopping down the stairs and ran around the corner into the common room.

"Mom!" they cried, knocking Sophie to the ground and piling on top of her.

"Boys!" Zeke hadn't moved so fast since before his accident. He stood and pried them off Sophie by the waistband of their snow bibs. "That's how people get hurt."

They stared up at him, wide-eyed, as if no one had ever pulled them away from something they wanted before.

"It's okay." Red-cheeked, Sophie got to her

feet, righting her glasses before drawing the twins to her side. "I'm fine."

"It's not okay," Zeke said in a hard voice too much like his father's. "Boys need to act like gentlemen before they turn into young men who don't know any better."

Sophie's mouth formed a little O.

"Can we go sledding, Mom?" Andy asked, completely recovered from Zeke's scolding.

"Oh, yeah. Can we?" Alex seconded.

"Sure." Sophie grabbed their jackets and gloves.

The boys spotted the delivery truck through the window and shouted, "Truck! Truck! Truck!" They were as excited as if it'd been Santa Claus. Since the Monroes had come to town, packages had been delivered with more frequency and were often for two little boys.

Sophie ushered them out the door as if she couldn't get away from Zeke fast enough.

After the door closed, Mitch made the sound of a rocket falling to earth and then exploding, emphasizing the crash and burn with his hands. "Magnificent fail, buddy."

"It wasn't a fail." Zeke scowled, because it most certainly had been. But he couldn't admit that, now could he? "It was a…a conversation. You can't fail at a conversation."

"You did." Gabby stood on the bottom step

of the stairs, nodding her head. "This is what I always imagined happened at middle school. The awkwardness. The conversations where two people are on different wavelengths. Pain so sharp you're left humiliated and speechless."

The truth hit him like a hot pie in the face. It was humiliating. Zeke didn't know what to say.

"Listen to her." Mitch grinned. "Gabby recognizes a crash and burn when she sees one."

"How?" Recovering, Zeke winced. "She's twelve and homeschooled."

Or at least on independent study. The town was lucky enough to be the homeschooling hub for the county. The teacher hung out in the diner most mornings during the week, so kids could stop by, get their work done, get help if they needed it and, more important, socialize.

"You two need to lighten up." Laurel took Zeke by the arm and guided him to the wingback chair, helping to lift his walking boot on a footrest. "If you need any advice regarding Sophie and making a move," she whispered, "come see me."

"Thanks," Zeke said to the lot of them. "Thanks a lot."

He had yet to regain his manly mojo. But he would. Soon.

Not that he planned to use it on Sophie.

CHAPTER FOUR

SOPHIE'S HEART POUNDED, and not because the twins were barreling down Sled Hill on a blue plastic toboggan.

Odette and Laurel had been right. Zeke looked at her the way a man looked at a woman before he asked her out—long and lingering. Sophie didn't want him to look at her that way.

Oh, yes I do.

Zeke's regard made Sophie remember she hadn't put on lipstick in weeks. It made her want to change out of her boxy cable-knit sweater and find something more figure flattering. It made her long for feminine dresses and hairstyles that weren't smashed beneath knit caps.

Darn right, she didn't want Zeke looking at her in all her flawed glory. She didn't want to feel like an adult who craved adult companionship. She was working on being a good mom and a successful entrepreneur. She had no time or energy for lingering looks and moon eyes. She didn't miss that part of her life at all.

Sophie's shoulders drooped, and she stared skyward.

Who am I kidding?

She missed having someone to share the joys and travails of the day with. She missed walking arm in arm and moonlit kisses. It was just...

Two peas in a pod.

Sophie scoffed. The divorce had made her pragmatic and the loss of her job as the Monroe art curator more so. What if the trading post couldn't support her? What if the pressure to provide her children with a top-notch education became too great? She'd have to return to Philadelphia and leave whatever connections she had here—Grandpa Harlan's possessions, newly made friends, cowboy acquaintances. It was safer to keep her distance where Zeke was concerned.

"Mom?" Andrew waved to her from the bottom of the hill. "Did you see me?"

"Yes," she called back, not having seen a thing. She clapped and applauded anyway.

A truck she didn't recognize stopped at the intersection from the west. It turned north and drove slowly past. The driver waved.

Would the man have stopped in town if the trading post was open for business? Would anyone be interested in buying bear traps and black velvet paintings? She'd found more of both.

A feeling of being overwhelmed washed over her, colder than the wind whipping down from the mountains. She slid her glasses back in place.

What in the world am I doing in Second Chance, Idaho?

She knew the answer. She was supporting Shane as he tried to unravel Grandpa Harlan's reason for leaving them the town. She was seeking closure concerning her grandfather. She was making a new life for herself and the boys.

Dragging the sled behind them, the twins reached the top of the incline. She helped them steady the sled on the crest of the hill as they prepared for another run.

"I like Zeke." Alexander took a seat on the front end. "He calls me Alex."

"He's cool." Andrew sat behind him. "He calls me Andy."

Together the boys used their hands to scoot over the edge of the hill, whooping as they picked up speed, while Sophie stewed.

Nicknames? It'd taken her months to land on the right names for her babies.

She and Zeke weren't alike.

They weren't alike at all!

ZEKE WAS GOING to eat at the Bent Nickel tonight if it killed him.

It had nothing to do with Sophie taking the boys there every night for dinner and everything to do with the possibility of a job working for Ivy washing dishes, slinging breakfast hash or scrubbing toilets. Whatever. He wasn't proud. He had bills that needed paying.

If he saw Sophie, there would be no moments, imagined or real.

Zeke put on his jacket, not looking forward to his bare toes being exposed to twenty-degree temperatures. He could put on his other cowboy boot, but his shin had given him a twinge after toting around Sophie's bell. Better safe than sorry.

He wasn't without options. Odette had knitted him a large sock to cover his exposed toes. She'd tossed it onto the coffee table the other day when she'd stopped by to see Laurel. He fingered the stretchy yarn. It was kind of the old woman to make something for him.

If he'd been ten years younger, he wouldn't have considered putting the sock on.

If he had a snowball's chance in Havana of being with Sophie, he wouldn't consider putting the sock on.

The wind shook the inn's timbers.

Zeke put the sock on, soaking in the sight of

a worn brown cowboy boot next to the bulky, red knit sock.

Ridiculous.

His toes wouldn't get frostbite on the walk to the diner. But before Zeke could remove the sock, Mitch came out of his apartment, a crease in his brow. "Going somewhere?"

"No offense," Zeke told him. "But if I don't get a burger, fries and a chocolate shake today, I may be hard to live with tomorrow."

Mitch was a nice guy, a fastidious inn-keeper, but an unimaginative cook. The same seven items graced his menu every week. Two months of Mitch's cooking and Zeke was ready for a change.

The innkeeper didn't argue. "You'll be ask-ing Ivy for a job. I'll grab my coat and walk you over."

"I'm thirty-five years old," Zeke said stiffly. "I think I can walk to the diner by myself."

Mitch stared at Zeke's red bootie, raising his brows.

"What's going on?" Gabby appeared be-hind Mitch, a concerned expression on her face. Thankfully, she'd gotten over her crush for Zeke. It'd been replaced by her adoration of actor Wyatt Halford, the sexiest man alive, ac-cording to a gossip magazine she'd shown Zeke.

"Our guest needs to spread his red culinary wings," Mitch said, no ounce of sarcasm spared.

Gabby peered at Zeke's knit sock. "If Shane were here, he'd place a bet on how likely it'd be that Zeke would land in a snowdrift on his way to the Bent Nickel."

Mitch and Shane were frenemies, thanks to the Monroes' uncertainty about what to do about the town, so it wasn't surprising when Mitch grinned. "And then I'd wager Zeke would fall in the snowdrift at the bottom of the stairs."

Gabby stared at Zeke's bootie again. "I'd bet he'd fall in the snowdrift between the general store and the Bent Nickel."

"Not that we'd ever bet with Shane." Mitch laid a hand over his heart.

"Never," Gabby added solemnly.

"Or wish Zeke ill." Mitch slung his arm over his daughter's shoulders and drew her close. "Because we like Zeke and we're going to miss him for dinner."

"But that means we'll have leftover chili and corn bread tomorrow," Gabby singsonged, offering her hand for a father-daughter high five that had the pair chortling.

"This is why I need to get out of here," Zeke said over the sound of their laughter. He left the inn, bootie on, and made his way carefully down the stairs.

There was a patch of ice near the bottom step next to the snowdrift Mitch had predicted he'd fall into. Zeke walked carefully around it and followed the path to the Bent Nickel Mitch had made with his snowblower that morning.

The sun dipped behind the mountains. It would be dark on the way back.

The wind. Zeke hadn't missed it during his convalescence. It chilled his toes through Odette's knit sock. It blew beneath his jacket, puffing it up until he felt like a marshmallow.

Soon, Zeke's left calf threatened to cramp. His hips, unused to so many strides in a row, threatened to freeze up. Didn't matter. There was no going back. He made it past the general store without incident. He was going to reach the Bent Nickel without tumbling into the snow. He wanted to whoop and holler.

Don't squat with your spurs on, Roosevelt.

Because he wasn't there yet and the return journey was going to be another story.

Cowboys don't quit, Roosevelt.

The door to the Bent Nickel was in sight. Little Alex stood at the window and spotted Zeke, turning to shout at someone. He was joined by his twin and they both pressed their noses to the glass.

Zeke wasn't used to being a spectacle. He

quickened his steps before everyone in the Bent Nickel put their schnozzes to the window.

And that's when it happened.

Shwoop.

Zeke's cowboy boot slipped on the ice. He plunged into a snowdrift just outside the door to the diner.

Snow cradled Zeke's fall in its chilly arms. It wrapped its icy fingers around his neck and over his ears. It packed him tighter than a crystal vase being shipped by a fancy department store at Christmas.

On a positive note, neither Gabby nor Mitch had predicted where he'd take a tumble.

"Holy mackerel." Sophie appeared before him without so much as a jacket or a glove. "Cowboy down."

And then Shane was there, too. "Come on. Let's get you inside."

They each grabbed hold of one of Zeke's arms and pulled him to his feet.

Sophie brushed snow from Zeke's back. Her efforts caused her glasses to slip down her thin nose. "Should you be out here, Zeke? Are you licensed to walk in that thing?"

Zeke began to laugh, because the intelligent answer would be no, but Zeke had never been known for his intelligence.

"Is he in shock?" Sophie asked Shane, worry

clouding her brow. "Should we take him back to the inn?"

"Ignore the laughter." Shane helped Zeke forward. "It's cabin fever. If we took him back, he'd just sneak out again."

"I suppose we should've expected it long before this." Sophie shivered and put her hands back on Zeke's arm as if afraid he'd slip once more.

Her touch evaporated his laughter. "Hardy-har. Everybody wants to be a comedian," Zeke grumbled, trying to reclaim his appendages. "I've got this, folks."

"Humor us." Shane kept one hand on Zeke's arm and opened the door with the other. "I was there the day of your accident, remember? It wasn't pretty."

"I can make it a few feet more," Zeke said, sounding like a wounded marine limping toward the rescue chopper.

Despite his protests, the adult Monroe twins helped him inside the diner and to a chair near the wood-burning stove.

Zeke gently shrugged their hands off and sat down. "I feel old." And annoyed.

"Hey, I resemble that remark." Roy Stout, the town handyman, pulled up a second chair to sit next to him. "And I didn't fall in the snow." He slapped Zeke on the shoulder. "That said, you got nerve, cowboy. Not much in the brains department, but you got nerve walking over here. You could have fallen and rebroken that leg."

"Or broken the other one," Shane pointed out, ever the optimist.

"Give it a rest." Zeke glanced around at the familiar sights in the diner.

Green pleather bench seats in the booths. Formica tables. Photos on the walls of Second Chance in its early years. And there—behind the counter—was the milkshake machine.

He heaved a contented sigh.

Sophie and Shane flanked Zeke. A warm mug of coffee was pressed into his hands by Ivy, who ran the diner. Roy was recounting his fix of a burst pipe in the empty medical cabin. There was talk, joking, laughter. Some at Zeke's expense.

It was worth the fall.

Sophie didn't laugh. Instead, she adjusted her glasses and bent to look Zeke in the eyes. She waited for Roy to take a breath to ask, "Are you okay?"

Zeke had the strongest urge to laugh again. He wasn't okay. He might never be okay again, because Sophie was looking at him with concern and perhaps something else, something he couldn't identify with certainty, because her lenses had fogged or perhaps the snow hadn't been all powder and he'd hit his head on ice.

He felt the base of his skull. There was no bump, which meant—

"Did you hit your head?" Immediately, Sophie's fingers skimmed through his hair, her touch emptying air from his lungs. "Shane, why haven't you hired another town doctor?"

"Yes, why?" Ivy's voice, somewhere near. She had young kids in that awkward stage where things got cut or broken because growth spurts stole their grace.

"I'm not the mayor." Shane tossed his hands. "Hiring a new doctor is Mitch's responsibility."

"But you're an honorary council member," Roy countered, smacking his lips. "Maybe we should vote you off."

"I didn't get voted in!" Shane's eye twitched. "That's why I'm *honorary*."

Shane and Roy's argument moved deeper into the diner.

Or maybe Zeke couldn't hear them over the roaring in his ears, because Sophie was still touching him.

She finished her inspection, removing her hands from Zeke's hair but bringing her face closer and staring into his eyes. "How many fingers am I holding up?"

"Two," Andy said, wriggling between them.

Sophie chuckled.

Air filled Zeke's lungs. "What Andy said."

"Andrew," Sophie corrected. She smiled, but there was a stiffness to her lips that hadn't been there before.

"Can we argue about nicknames some other time?" Zeke much preferred Sophie's concerned smile to her annoyed one.

"I'm glad Ivy invited me to dinner tonight." Odette gently propped Zeke's injured leg on another chair and pulled off the red bootie, which was crusted with ice. "I wouldn't have wanted to miss your swan dive. Besides, I knew this would come in handy." She beat the bootie against her thigh until all the ice had tumbled to the checkered linoleum. "I'm going to make you another."

"No need," Zeke assured her. "I'm retiring the brace in a few days." Sooner if he lost his patience.

"That's a shame." Odette turned the bootie over and around, inspecting it. "Do you think there's a market for knit socks at the mercantile?"

"It's worth a shot." Who knew what was going to sell?

"Seriously." Sophie touched Zeke's knee, deflating air from his lungs as quickly as they had filled. "Are you okay?"

"I will be." *If you kiss me.*

Come on, Roosevelt. Get a grip.

"I'll be fine." Zeke carefully modulated his smile, so it was no wider than the one he'd given Odette. "Just as soon as Ivy makes me the meal of my dreams." Zeke placed his order with Ivy, reminding himself to ask her about employment opportunities.

"You can eat with us." Andy glanced up at his mother. "Can't he?"

"Sure." Sophie gestured toward the back booth, but she still hadn't recovered her easy-going smile. "When you warm up, why don't you join us?"

"Isn't that sweet?" Odette clasped Zeke's hand. "In my day, women waited for men to ask them out."

Sophie's cheeks flamed with color and she retreated to her booth, dragging Andy with her.

"It's not what you think," Zeke said to Odette.

"Young people nowadays." Odette tsked. "Can't be truthful with themselves." The old woman got to her feet. "I best be off. I've got to get home before it's completely dark. I want to start right away on my knitting. You need a sock for every day of the week."

Zeke tried to protest, but Odette would have none of it. He gave up. She looked so happy…

"Zeke, come sit with us." Andy waved frantically.

Roy claimed the seat Odette had vacated and placed a hand on Zeke's arm, holding him in place. "If that fine lady doesn't walk you home after dinner, I will."

"She's not my—"

"I don't care what she is to you," Roy said, uncharacteristically firm. "I saw your leg the day of the accident. You need to be careful."

Zeke didn't want to admit he shared Roy's concern, but he nodded. "Okay."

"Smart man." Roy got to his feet with none of his usual spryness. For a moment, he looked… as old as his years. "Hey, Ivy. Order up one bowl of chili."

"That always gives you heartburn," Ivy snapped back from the kitchen.

Roy rubbed his breastbone. "I have heartburn all the time anyway."

Instead of joining Sophie and the twins, Zeke walked to the kitchen like a cowboy who'd ridden too long. He leaned against the door frame and poked his head in. "Hey, Ivy. I was wondering if you needed any help."

"Help?" Ivy's brown hair was pulled back in a firm bun. She flipped his burger and then shook the basket with his fries, draining the grease in the deep fryer. "Help cooking your burger?"

"No." Why did everything have to be so difficult today? "I meant, do you need any paid help? Another cook? A dishwasher? Help cleaning?"

"I thought you were returning to the Bucking Bull." Ivy had a warming tray set up with green beans, mashed potatoes and gravy. She slung them on plates with practiced precision.

The good news was, she hadn't said no.

"It'll be another month at least before I'm cleared to ride." Zeke reached down and tapped the stiff plastic brace at his calf. "I lose the walking boot this week."

Ivy made a noncommittal noise as she dished portions of meat loaf from a large pan onto plates. "I'm flattered you'd want to work for me, but I don't think I can afford help. Laurel isn't eating here anymore, and I heard Sophie might be moving to a cabin with her own kitchen soon." She paused to look him in the eye. "I'm sorry."

Not as sorry as Zeke was. He thanked Ivy for her time and went to join Sophie and the twins.

How was he going to raise the cash he needed to repair his truck?

"Sit with me. Sit with me." Andy wiggled

over to make room. "We're having meaty loaf for dinner. You can have a bite of mine."

"You can have my broccoli," Alex said, as serious as Roy had been a few minutes ago.

"That's very kind of you." Zeke maneuvered his walking boot beneath the table and out of the aisle. "But I ordered my own dinner. I've been dreaming about this meal for nearly two months."

"A burger and fries?" Sophie's smile seemed forced. "You could have ordered takeout."

"When has takeout ever been as good as sitting in a restaurant and eating at a table?" Ivy wasn't the best chef around, but he'd had worse. And today, after months of Mitch's cooking, her burger was going to taste like a culinary delight.

"I like eating at the Bent Nickel." Alex had risen up on his knees on the bench seat. "Sometimes they have school here." He pointed to the booths and tables in the corner.

"We sit when we're at a restaurant, Alex." Zeke patted the green pleather and waited for the boy to get down before praising him. "I know they have school here. I've driven Davey Clark and his brothers into town a couple of times."

"I know Davey," Alex said solemnly. "He's missing a hand."

"He is," Andy confirmed, just as solemnly.

"Birth defect." Zeke nodded when Sophie looked doubtful. "You'd never know if you saw him. He does everything a boy with two hands does. He rides. He ropes. He fishes." Stomach growling, Zeke glanced over his shoulder, checking on Ivy's progress.

She had her head down in the kitchen, but her arms were moving quickly.

Alex waved a folded piece of paper toward Zeke. "Wanna see the card I made for Mom today?"

"Want to see," Zeke corrected softly. "Sure."

The paper had been colored with broad-stroke crayon doodles in blue, red and yellow.

"It says I love you, Mom." Alex frowned. "I don't write letters so good."

"So well," Zeke corrected again, just as gently. "Don't worry. I don't either."

"It'll come, Alexander." Sophie slid several folded bills across the table.

"What's that for?" Alex asked.

"How much money is that?" Andy levered himself back to his knees. "A million-trillion dollars?"

From a booth across the room, Shane glanced over. From his chair near the front windows, Roy craned his neck.

Zeke gave Andy a gentle tug on his T-shirt

to encourage him to sit down, and then slid the money back toward Sophie. "You don't owe me anything. It was a favor. Besides, you gave me a very valuable painting."

One could hope.

"I want to do this." Sophie gave him a small smile. "The boys raved about you all the way over. Plus, I hear you need money to fix your truck."

A thought flashed through Zeke's brain. It wasn't the most sensible of thoughts. But it was an idea. And it refused to go away. "Sophie, if you're trying to open your store by spring, you're going to need a babysitter."

"Do you know one?" she asked hopefully, pushing her glasses in place.

He opened his mouth, processed that hopeful expression of hers and closed it again, unwilling to disappoint her.

This is a really bad idea.

But it was the only idea he had to pay for truck repairs, so he pressed a thumb to his chest and said, *"Me."*

To Sophie's credit, she didn't laugh, but she did look at Zeke the way she'd looked at her twins last week when they'd tried to start a snowball fight in the common room with snowballs they'd hidden in their jacket pockets. "My last nanny was trained at Young's Academy."

Which sounded as snooty as Sophie's pedigree.

Still, Zeke wasn't a quitter. "I've been trained at the School of Hard Knocks. And better still—"

Sophie raised her slim brown brows above the rims of her lenses.

"—I'm here and available." He sat up taller. "And I'm mobile. My walking boot is officially off in two days." It was a risk, suggesting he babysit so soon after he'd slipped on the ice. But Zeke had no choice. He had bills and no way to pay them. "Think of all the work you could get done."

She considered his words longer than he deemed necessary. "You really want to watch my kids?"

Alex and Andy encouraged Zeke to say yes with vigorous head nods.

Okay. "Yes."

"We could give it a test run." Sophie mentioned an hourly rate that was more than Zeke had made working at the Bucking Bull. "But I have a few stipulations. I don't want them to play all day." She laughed self-consciously. "I mean, that's what they've been doing, but I'd like them to read more. When we lived in Philadelphia, they were at a preschool that used the Kelvington Immersion method. I can't let them fall too far behind scholastically. They start kindergarten in the fall."

Reading? Scholastics?

A tremor of unease shifted in Zeke's belly, stealing his appetite.

"It would only be until I find a more qualified nanny." Sophie sat back as Ivy delivered their food. "Four weeks, tops."

He'd likely be cleared to ride by then and could return to work at the Bucking Bull.

"Qualified nannies are hard to come by," she added.

"By qualified nanny, you mean one who was trained at Young's Academy," Zeke murmured.

"Yes." She glowed.

Graduates of Young's Academy most likely frowned on babysitters who couldn't read at an age-appropriate level. Sophie would frown on him, too, if she knew the truth.

Not that he planned on telling her.

CHAPTER FIVE

YOU'RE REALLY GOING to hire that beefcake as your nanny?

That was Shane's voice in Sophie's head.

Not that he'd said anything out loud. They'd never been the kind of siblings well versed in twin-speak. That's just what Sophie assumed her brother was thinking as she and her twin exchanged glances across the diner.

"Are you still interested in being my nanny?" Sophie forced herself to ask Zeke. She was half hoping he'd come to his senses and turn her down. But the other half… The other half believed if she had help she could make the trading post support her little family.

Ivy delivered their meals and quickly returned to the kitchen.

Alexander and Andrew stared at Zeke, wide-eyed and waiting.

"Yes." Zeke's gruff voice sounded about as enthused as she felt offering him the job.

"Woo-hoo!" Andrew cried.

"Yay!" Alexander shouted.

Zeke ruffled Andrew's hair next to him and high-fived Alexander across the table. "Eat your dinners before they get cold." He was a stickler for good manners.

"Meaty loaf." Andrew dug in.

"Cheesey-burger," Zeke murmured with a half smile, dressing his bun with ketchup and mustard. "I can start after the boys eat their *oaty-meal* in the morning."

"Perfect." It should have been perfect. They had a business relationship now. There would be no more moon eyes from him and no more answering tug of longing from her. She'd have more time to think about what to sell and how to sell it. She should feel excited.

So why did she feel disappointed?

"Sophie." Roy ambled over to their table, carrying his coffee mug. "Odette told me earlier that your progress clearing out the trading post has been slow. I've been thinking about how to help you."

"Really?" Sophie set down her silverware and smiled up at the old man. She hadn't thought to ask the town handyman for help. This, combined with having a sitter, would make a world of difference. "Another pair of hands would be great. There's so much to go through, categorize, research and price."

"Oh, I…" Roy cleared his throat, looking

apologetic. "I was thinking more along the lines of helping you empty the place of junk." He pulled up a chair and straddled it. "The way I see it, you gotta get things outta there before you can make it attractive for shoppers and the like."

"Yes." But that was only one thing on a very long list of tasks that needed to be done. She stared across the diner at Shane.

Don't look at me. The trading post is a tear-down.

Sophie returned her attention to Roy. "I'd love the help." Any help.

"I can rig a system so you can get boxes out the door and down to the highway. From there, you can put them on a sled and tow them to the inn's porch." Roy patted Zeke's shoulder. "Any old yahoo can carry them up the stairs from there."

That was a lot of *yous*.

"Apparently—" Zeke smiled "—I'm any old yahoo."

Apparently, Roy was offering only to do the rigging.

"I thought Zeke was our nanny." Alexander looked confused.

"I thought Zeke was working for the Bucking Bull?" Roy stared from one adult at the table to the other.

"I'm Sophie's nanny until I'm cleared to ride again," Zeke clarified, smiling at Sophie as if they shared a secret. "Or until Sophie hires a fancier nanny."

A fancier nanny was less appealing when stacked up against Zeke's handsome smile beaming at her from across the booth.

Sophie stared at her untouched meat loaf, reminding herself Zeke was her employee, reminding herself Roy had just made a generous gesture, reminding herself her twin had done very little to help her.

She glanced over at Shane, who shrugged almost imperceptibly, as if to say: *I have more important things to do.*

Sophie reached over and squeezed Roy's hand. "I'd be honored to have your help."

"I'll work on it in the morning," Roy promised with a proud smile, getting to his feet with a wobble. "Didn't mean to interrupt your dinner."

Sophie and Zeke watched him walk away.

"Shane or Mitch should give him a hand." Zeke tapped the table near Andrew's plate. "Eat your broccoli." He lifted his green gaze to Sophie's. "Roy's not as invincible as he, or anyone else in town, thinks he is."

Images of Roy tumbling down the short slope

to the highway had Sophie dropping her fork. "Should I have turned him down?"

"If you did—" Zeke pointed at her with a french fry "—you'd wake up in the morning and he'd have done it anyway."

She supposed that was true.

"Do you need a room to sort through things?" Zeke swirled his fry through a puddle of ketchup. "There's a room at the inn next to mine that's vacant. I bet Mitch will rent it to you."

A warm room to sort through Grandpa Harlan's collection? Heaven.

"That's a great idea." Sophie grinned and glanced around the diner. A nanny? A quick way to empty the trading post? A warm workroom? After so much good luck, something else had to land in her lap.

She looked around the diner. All she saw was Shane's head bent over his cell phone and Ivy's five-year-old son, Nick, poking his head out of the kitchen.

Andrew saw him, too. He stuffed a broccoli crown in his mouth and asked to be excused. When Alexander noticed Nick, he crammed broccoli in both cheeks and asked to be excused, too.

"When you chew and swallow," Zeke said before Sophie could, increasing his cachet in the nanny department.

They bolted down their vegetables, leaving half the meat loaf, a few green beans and some mashed potatoes on their plates. Both adults had to move to let them out.

And just like that, Sophie and Zeke were alone in a crowded restaurant.

Sophie shoved a bite of meat loaf in her mouth, wondering what they should talk about. Rules she had for the boys? His passion for cattle? Her passion for ancient Asian culture?

She shouldn't have worried.

Zeke still had fries on his plate and was intent upon eating them rather than making idle conversation or swooning at Sophie. When he finally spoke, it wasn't at all what she'd expected. "About support for Roy…"

"Shane's out." Sophie knew her brother too well. He'd been a CEO. He wasn't one who liked to get his hands dirty. "Mitch might help for a little bit. Maybe an hour?"

"You could pay Mitch to make it worth his while." Zeke finished his fries and scanned the boys' plates, as if he was still hungry.

Sophie pushed Alexander's dish his way. "I'm not wealthy, you know." That came out testier than Sophie might have liked. "I have money saved, but I'm not a trust fund baby. None of us are." None of her Monroe siblings and cousins, that is.

Zeke didn't fall over in surprise, possibly because he was more intent upon eating. "I thought Harlan was rich."

Sophie nodded. "My grandfather was wealthy. And our family made sure everyone in my generation went to college without worrying about expenses."

He flicked a glance at her before cutting up Alexander's meat loaf. "And…"

Perhaps she should have left it there. But if Zeke was going to be her employee, he needed to know she wasn't made of money. "And…we all worked for the Monroe Holding Company and lived rent free as part of our employment contract." She picked at her meat loaf, wishing it had jalapeños in it or anything else to make it more interesting. "My ex pays child support and I sock away what I can—or could—into retirement." She didn't have much in available cash. "I have to pay our room and board until Roy can ready one of the empty cabins for us."

The town handyman had promised her a cabin after the snow in town melted. Apparently, it was his job to winterize all town buildings that were vacant. And since the Monroes owned every building in town, she could pick and choose. Any. Cabin. She. Wanted.

"Sweet deal." Zeke had cleaned Alexander's plate and started on Andrew's.

"It was a sweet deal," Sophie said, unable to keep herself from sounding defensive. "My grandfather doted on us. He was very generous. But it's over now. Per Grandpa Harlan's will, my father and uncles couldn't inherit a dime unless they fired my brothers and cousins, not to mention evict us, which is how I ended up here as part of the advance team to decide what to do with the town. And then I fell a little in love with Second Chance." Enough in love to agree to stay and open a store.

She stopped staring at Zeke's firm jaw, which had a five o'clock shadow.

"Your grandfather—" Zeke salted Andrew's potatoes "—seems to have had some radical ideas in order to get his point across to his family."

Sophie smiled. "You catch on quick, cowboy."

"Things are much more streamlined with us poor folk." He drank the last of his milkshake, probably not worrying if it would go straight to his hips. "My grandfather left my father the family ranch and a mountain of debt. Thankfully, he didn't leave me anything."

"I don't resent my grandfather." She just needed to make peace with the past.

"Me either."

"Grandpa Harlan wanted us to come to Second Chance to find our own paths." Sophie leaned forward and lowered her voice. Earlier at the inn, he'd said they were like two peas in a pod. Sophie wanted to make sure Zeke realized they weren't. They were boss and employee. City girl and cowpoke. "When we were growing up, Shane was out on the lawn having sword fights with our younger brother, while I was inside with the nanny having tea parties with the antique silver set." She sat back in her seat, comforted that she'd established a boundary between them.

"Cowboying is more of a twisted path with lots of breaks in it," Zeke said with that endearing half smile of his. "Pun intended." He took stock of the food left on the table and then took stock of Sophie.

Something that shouldn't have fluttered, fluttered in her chest.

"So, you were forced to leave behind your silver spoon and take a new path," he said, still looking in her eyes. "What about the life you left behind?"

Her chest panged with something that wasn't attraction. "I miss the art world." Normally, she'd keep discordant thoughts to herself, but she hoped her confession would add to the impression that they were different.

Zeke's expression didn't change. "Any resentment toward your dad or granddad?"

"I won't lie." How could she under his direct gaze? "I'm disappointed my father chose money over me."

"What child wouldn't be?" That half smile of his turned into a sly grin. It was his turn to lean forward and lower his voice. "Makes you wonder what your father is going to put in his will, doesn't it?"

"I hadn't thought about that." Sophie was glad she had the stiff bench seat at her back. Zeke's intense regard made her want to melt. "I mean, I haven't talked to my dad since he fired me."

"Feeling a little—" his eyes were a warm, understanding green "—cut off? Afraid about having to live from paycheck to paycheck?"

Sophie nodded.

"And your mom?"

"My mother calls, but all she wants to talk about is how disappointed she is with my father." Sophie may have been upset with her father, but she didn't want her parents' marriage to fall apart. "Honestly? I miss my dad. I'd never have believed..." How had the conversation turned so personal? And yet, she didn't feel as if Zeke had shared much about himself. "Are you close with your father?"

"We're good." Zeke's gaze turned distant. "He gave me my first horse, a long time ago. His name was Tank. What a goer that chestnut was. All Tank wanted to do was hurry up and get there—across the pasture, out on the range, out of the gate at the rodeo."

The world of working horses and working cowboys was as alien to Sophie as missions to Mars. "Why did you call him Tank?"

"He was barrel-chested." Zeke drew himself up, expanding his chest. "Broad, like a tank."

"Your father sounds…" She didn't know why she pushed. She had a feeling Zeke was holding something back, that's all. "I'm not sure you said anything about your father."

Zeke shrugged, his gaze focusing elsewhere. "Other than giving me a roof over my head and food in my belly until I was eighteen, what should I say?"

Alexander returned, scooting into Zeke's lap. "Do you have a favorite book? We can read it tomorrow."

"When I was a kid," Zeke said. "I liked *Under the Big Bright Moon*."

Alexander laughed. "That's a baby book."

Sophie blinked. *Under the Big Bright Moon* was indeed a baby book.

"I liked it." Zeke shrugged. "Besides, I liked playing jacks when I was little, even though my cousin told me it was a girl's game. It gave me good hand-eye coordination, which made me better at roping." He made a lasso motion with one hand, tossing his imaginary rope toward Sophie.

Sophie felt as if he'd caught her and was reeling her in. Her lips began a smile she had no right giving.

Employee-employee-employee.

Zeke ruffled Alexander's cowlick. "The moral of the story is not to judge someone by what they like, not the books they read or the clothes they wear or the education they've had."

"Oh." Alexander rested his head beneath Zeke's chin.

Sophie's breath caught in her throat. Zeke was a natural with kids. The fluttering returned, more urgent than before.

"As I live and breathe." Roy rose from his spindle-backed chair near the woodstove. "It's Egbert." He hurried to the door and opened it for a bearded old man who'd gotten out of a dated gray SUV covered in road grime. "It's March, Egbert. What are you doing here?"

"You called me, you reprobate." The older man went straight to the chair Roy had just vacated, ignoring Roy's weak protests about having called him two months ago. "I got bored in Houston. My grandchildren don't care about the past. They're only interested in the latest video game."

Ivy brought the man ice water and coffee, setting them on a nearby table and fussing over him.

"Who is Egbert?" Sophie asked Zeke.

Zeke scratched his head as if trying to decide what to say. "He runs a rental business here in town. I heard he used to rent snowmobiles in winter, but he hasn't wintered here since I came to Second Chance. In spring and summer, he rents inner tubes and fishing gear to tourists. Oh. And he has a hobby that might interest you." Zeke's eyes flashed as bright as his smile. "Egbert collects blacksmith paraphernalia. He set up a blacksmith shop in the cabin next to his rental business."

"Egbert set up a blacksmith shop? Like an interactive museum?" The old man sounded like her kind of people.

"I think so," Zeke said.

Andrew returned to their table, but instead of sliding in with Sophie, he leaned against Zeke.

Used to being their favorite person in the whole wide world, Sophie experienced an unexpected pang of jealousy. They'd never loved on their nannies the way they were loving on Zeke. And their father... He treated them like an afterthought.

"What's a blacksmith?" Alexander asked, twining his hands around Zeke's neck.

"In the olden days," Zeke began, checking the inside of his metal milkshake cup wistfully, "they made everything people needed to survive. Horseshoes, hammers, axes, knives."

All things little boys might think they needed to live in the wilderness.

"They also made axles, wagon wheels, nails and frying pans." Sophie added more practical items. "It was nearly impossible to establish a town in the frontier without a blacksmith."

"Nowadays," Zeke continued with that half smile, "instead of having a shop of their own, most blacksmiths travel to their clients in a big truck."

"We had food trucks back home." Alexander rubbed his stomach. "Cheesesteak. Yum."

"Sushi." Andrew sighed. "Yummy-yum."

"Is Egbert's collection private or does he give tours?" Without waiting for an answer, Sophie got out of the booth and went over to introduce herself, expressing interest in the old man's blacksmith collection almost immediately.

"Do you like history?" Egbert's blue eyes sparkled beneath his white bushy brows.

Sophie nodded.

"I'm out." Roy scurried to the diner's counter. "Tell me when it's over."

Egbert chuckled. "Roy is tired of hearing what I have to say about Second Chance's past."

"That's because we've heard all your recollections for years." Roy may have retreated to the counter, but the dinner crowd had thinned out enough that he remained within hearing distance.

Shane, who was interested in any and all information about the town, carried chairs over for himself and Sophie. "We'd love to learn more about Second Chance's history."

Roy frowned, shifting his weight, as if considering returning to Egbert's side. "Eggie can't tell you anything about Harlan specifically."

Because everyone who'd accepted a buyout from Grandpa Harlan had signed a confidentiality agreement that expired a year after his death, which made it near impossible to understand why he'd left his grandchildren a town or why he'd bought it in the first place. Barring anyone breaking the agreement, the Monroe heirs would have to wait until New Year's Day to get their answers.

"I'd never ask you anything about my grandfather specifically," Shane murmured with a look at Roy that said otherwise.

Sophie sat down and leaned forward eagerly. "Are you the town historian? Would you know anything about the items left in the trading post?"

"I'm interested in everything about the past and what my grandchildren might call junk, although I'm not sure what was stored in the trading post." Egbert gave her a cagey stare, before redirecting it at her twin. "I signed one of Harlan's legal documents, but I know plenty of what happened prior to Harlan buying the town."

"Egbert..." Ivy warned.

Shane's smile was wider than a clam's at high tide. "I love hearing stories about my grandfather's youth."

"He was a ladies' man," Egbert said.

"I love hearing stories that don't involve his romantic conquests," Shane amended.

"Duly noted." The old man winked.

"Would you be willing to show me your blacksmith shop?" Sophie asked.

"Would he be willing?" Roy hooted. "Eggie would pay you to see it."

"Ignore the man in the cheap seats." Egbert grinned, looking much like Santa with his full white beard and rolling white locks. "Come see me tomorrow morning."

Alexander appeared at Sophie's elbow. "Me, too?"

"You, too." Egbert gave Alexander's belly

a gentle poke. "What would we do if the new generation didn't want to hear about the past?"

Zeke said something softly to Andrew, something Sophie couldn't hear from this distance. They both got to their feet. Zeke left a few dollars on the table for Ivy and then pulled that red knit sock from a jacket pocket and slid it over his walking boot.

Sophie stood, taking Alexander's hand. "We'll see you tomorrow, bright and early." She instructed Ivy to put her meal and Zeke's on her tab. And then she handed Zeke back his cash.

The cowboy didn't look happy, but after some hesitation he accepted.

He looked even less pleased when Sophie insisted on taking his arm during the walk back to the inn.

Which was great because with him stewing there was no fluttering.

No fluttering at all.

CHAPTER SIX

"But, Mom, Zeke has to come with us to see Mr. Egbert. He's our nanny."

Shane Monroe had been drinking his morning coffee on the couch in the common room when Sophie and her twins came downstairs. His gaze dropped to Zeke's walking boot, currently covered by a big red knit sock, like an old woman's tea cozy. "You up for a walk, big guy?"

"Lead the way." Zeke got up from a chair in the corner, gulping the last of his coffee. "What good is a babysitter who isn't mobile?"

"My thoughts exactly," Shane murmured, but he wasn't going to argue if the man wanted to prove himself.

Shane had asked Sophie last night why she'd hired a cowboy nanny, telling his twin that convenience wasn't a good enough reason. Surprisingly, she'd admitted she'd accepted Zeke's offer to watch them because he was available and breathing. But she seemed to think Zeke had skills in the child care department. Shane was more inclined to believe Zeke had worked that cowboy charm on his sister.

Sophie had fallen once before for the wrong guy. Her ex had taken one look at Sophie and seen a gravy train. Shane wasn't going to let a man who wasn't their financial equal win his sister's heart again.

"Are you sure you want to go, Zeke?" If the doubt on Sophie's brow was meant to discourage Zeke from joining them, her question left open the door. She'd never mastered the art of putting others in their place. "It's snowing outside."

"Egbert doesn't share the blacksmith shop with just anybody." Zeke seemed excited. There was pep to his lopsided step. "I've looked through the window but I've never been inside. Heck, yeah, I want to see it."

Shane had peered through the windows, as well. He'd thought it was an old, abandoned blacksmith shop—the real thing, not some private museum. Now that he and Mitch were working together to prove the town had historical significance, Shane had a renewed interest in the cabin.

"Zeke's coming, Mom." Andrew ran over and took Zeke's hand. "I won't let him fall."

Shane suppressed a smile, knowing his nephew was too little to prevent the tall cowboy from taking a tumble, but appreciating his desire to protect someone from getting hurt.

"And when Mom goes to work, we're going to read books." Alexander put his favorite book—*Mama Duck, Papa Duck*—on the coffee table.

"Yep." Zeke stared at the children's book with a guarded expression the innocuous book didn't warrant.

"Don't let go of my hand," Alexander said solemnly, taking Zeke's. "Some snow isn't soft."

"Truer words were never spoken." Zeke stared down at Shane's nephews as if they'd found a soft spot in his heart, much the same way Shane imagined he looked at the boisterous twins. When they were being good, that is.

Maybe Zeke did have skills when it came to wrangling little cowpokes.

Shane bit back a smile.

"You'll have to let the poor man go while you put on your coats." Sophie bundled up the twins, who reclaimed Zeke's hands as soon as their jackets were zipped.

But when the twins descended the porch stairs, all bets were off. They raced ahead into the gently falling snow at a four-year-old's pace. Sophie scurried after them, leaving Shane and Zeke to bring up the rear.

Shane slowed to match his pace to Zeke's. The wind coming down the mountain wasn't as biting as it had been the past two months, which made moving slowly easier to bear. "So, you're a nanny now."

"Temporarily and part-time," Zeke clarified. Unlike Shane and the rest of the Monroes, he hadn't closed his jacket. "Just until I'm cleared to get back on a horse or until Sophie finds a qualified candidate from Young's Academy. Whichever comes first."

"You and I both know no one from the prestigious Young's Academy is going to leave a big city on the East Coast for the snowy mountains of Idaho." Shane pointed out an icy patch on the sidewalk for Zeke to avoid. "That means my sister is going to be relying on you."

"Just until I return to the Bucking Bull Ranch." Zeke slowed near the slick part of the sidewalk. "I'm not qualified to be a tutor."

"And Sophie's overqualified to run a junk shop."

"Antiques store," Zeke corrected him.

"Potato, *poh-tah-toe*."

"I'm only looking for a job to tide me over." There was nothing in Zeke's expression to suggest he had a romantic interest in Sophie.

"Good." Shane was satisfied Zeke had received his message. He was fine with the cowboy watching his nephews. He wasn't fine with Zeke watching his sister. "Do you know what takes guts?"

"Riding a bull bareback?" Zeke chuckled softly.

Shane supposed that was cowboy humor. "It takes courage to wear that red sock out in public."

"Ah." Zeke paused to look Shane up and down. "And I suppose wearing chinos and penny loafers in the Idaho mountains takes no courage whatsoever. It's more like an act of foolishness."

"My father always taught me to live the leader look." And Shane had struggled with letting go of his CEO persona. "I've conceded snow boots are a requirement to live in the mountains." He wore a pair today.

"The leader look?" Zeke scoffed. "You still follow the principles of a man who chose to inherit millions and disinherit you?"

"One and the same."

Was that a trace of bitterness in Shane's voice? He held back a sigh. It was.

His cousin Holden chose that moment to text Shane and demand an update on what had been learned about the town's financial potential. Investment banker Holden would love to develop Second Chance into something like Aspen or even Ketchum, a place for the wealthy to escape their busy urban lives. Holden would cackle gleefully as real estate prices skyrocketed and the town turned from a one-stop-sign dot on the map to a place with stoplights, rush-hour traffic and French chefs. Holden was the reason Shane wanted to gain historical significance for the town. That way, no one could turn it into a playground for the rich and famous. But to do so, Shane had to prove Second Chance's history was important in the development of Idaho or the United States.

No easy feat. He'd been talking to residents, trying to glean what was special about Second Chance to determine why it held such importance to his grandfather.

Shane's answer to Holden? *Nothing has changed.*

Sad, but true. Shane and Mitch were sorting out the best way to apply for historical significance, determining which buildings to include, and generally getting nowhere. They needed a break. In the meantime, Shane had hired a consultant to evaluate the best course for the town's future and that report was due any day now.

They reached the end of the cleared walkway. Egbert's property was another four doors down.

Sophie held on to the twins, who tugged her

toward Egbert's place and the sidewalk buried in four feet of snow. "How do we get there from here?"

"We walk on the highway." Zeke pointed to the two-lane road that had been plowed earlier by the county.

There was no traffic, but there seldom was. They walked along the deserted highway to reach Egbert's rental shop. The old man lived in an apartment above it. That building might have been built midcentury. It had big windows and shake shingle siding. Next to that was a round log cabin with the blacksmith shop. The cabin looked as if it'd been built at the turn of the last century.

"What do you hope Egbert will tell you?" Zeke asked Shane.

"Something about the Lees." His ancestors who'd founded the town. "Something about my grandfather." People often let something slip once he got them talking. "Something that might let me leave Second Chance feeling like whatever it was my grandfather thought I needed to learn here was learned here."

"Huh." Zeke took a couple of limping steps. "You ought to be able to do that in twenty questions."

Shane scowled at him.

"Start with what's the meaning of life and go from there."

"The cowboy is a comedian." Shane shook his head.

When they were even with Egbert's place, there was no avoiding the facts: they were going to have to walk through waist-deep snow to reach the porch.

Without waiting for permission, Alexander and Andrew blazed a trail. Or at least attempted to. For every step forward, they'd sink down a foot or two, laugh uproariously and roll around until their feet found purchase and they got up. At their pace, it'd take an hour to reach the door.

Or, more realistically, at least fifteen minutes Shane wasn't willing to burn.

Shane looked at Sophie and Zeke. What were the chances one of them would volunteer to plow a path to the door?

Reading his mind, Sophie frowned and pushed her glasses higher on her nose, apparently content to wait for the twins to clear a path. "I'll wait."

"I'm *not it* either," Zeke murmured, a rueful expression on his face, as if were he to have two good legs, he'd have jumped right in.

"Hey, guys." Shane gently pulled one twin

back, and then another. "Let your big, strong uncle make a path first."

Easier said than done. It was like wading through quicksand.

When he reached the porch steps, Egbert came out the front door. He leaned one hand on his cane and one on a shovel. "Someone needs to be a good sport and shovel a path to the smithie."

"I'll do it! I'll do it!" the twins cried, falling in the snow on either side of Shane and raising their hands toward the old man.

Egbert smiled and chuckled, a dead ringer for Old Saint Nick. "*Somebody* meaning one of you two men."

The twins chorused their disappointment and glanced back at the adults making their way through the snow.

"I'll take a rain check," Zeke said. Reality was, he was probably good for it.

Accepting the inevitable, Shane took on shoveling duty. But he wasn't doing manual labor without reaping some intellectual reward. "Hey, Egbert, I hear you rent snowmobiles in the winter." And yet, he hadn't been here during January or February this year.

"It's a declining market in Second Chance." On the porch, Egbert walked slowly next to Shane. Slowly because Shane wasn't the speediest of snow shovelers. "So few people stop in Second Chance that I was only renting one or two hours to passersby a month." He scratched his full white beard. "Kind of hard to justify staying in town in winter for that, wouldn't you say?"

Shane hated that the old man had a good argument. "And if we attract more tourists here in winter?"

"That's a tall order." Egbert's frown was fleeting. "Not that it can't be done. The Monroes… You have a strong history of commerce here. Hobart Monroe was a fine man."

Shane stopped shoveling. "You mean *Harlan*?"

The old man pointed to the shovel in Shane's hands. "If you have enough gumption to finish that job you took on, I'd have enough stories to tell to make it worth your while."

Shane put his heart into shoveling. Alexander and Andrew followed him as closely as they could without getting in the way, which meant Shane had to be careful about not hitting them while he worked.

Finally, the path was clear. Shane and the twins waited on the narrow porch for the others to join them, stamping their boots free of snow.

"Egbert," Zeke said slyly, "Shane is curious

about the meaning of life from the perspective of Second Chance's historian."

"Love is the meaning of life," Egbert said without hesitation. "Even Harlan knew that."

"Of course he did." Shane exchanged a glance with Sophie, hoping she'd understand the irony of those words, given their grandfather had essentially chosen the most drastic option over love when it came to his grandchildren.

Egbert used a skeleton key on a big lock hanging from a rusty latch. "This was the original blacksmith shop in Second Chance." He pushed open the door, which creaked like it belonged in a haunted mansion. "It was built by a man named Jebediah Clark, a man whose sons would eventually start the Bucking Bull Ranch." He flipped a light switch.

Two industrial lights hanging from the ceiling came on as Shane closed the door behind them, shutting out the wind. The cabin was small, maybe fifteen by fifteen. The forge was in the middle of the room. There was a rudimentary cot in one corner and various implements hanging from the wall on another. The front door was large enough for a horse to walk through.

"Now, our Jebediah Clark was a hardworking man, a well-respected man about town." Egbert leaned down until his face was even with Alexander's and Andrew's. He pitched his gravelly voice low. "But he was no match for the desperado Merciless Mike Moody."

The twins gasped, which distracted them from the hammer and anvil they'd been inching toward.

Egbert straightened, laughing heartily. He lumbered over to a stool in the corner, a seat well positioned to have an audience gather around.

Shane hoped this Merciless Mike Moody was more than a fictional character. That would help Second Chance earn historical landmark status and protect the town from development by his cousin Holden. The sooner the town was protected, the sooner Shane could return to Las Vegas and find a job worthy of his executive skills.

The boys gaped at Egbert, unsure what to make of him.

Zeke herded them toward Egbert. "Listen up, boys. This is a popular local myth."

"*Myth?* Jebediah and Merciless Mike Moody were *real*." The old man stared down his nose at them all. "Merciless Mike Moody was a villain in these parts, a robber of trains and stagecoaches and always on the run from the deputies in Aspen and Ketchum." Egbert pointed over his shoulder to wanted posters that featured a poor drawing of a man called Merciless Mike Moody.

If Shane squinted, the outlaw looked like his cousin Holden.

Egbert continued his tale. "Being wanted didn't stop Merciless Mike Moody from furthering his life of crime. But not everyone was willing to throw down their money at the first sight of a gun barrel. Merciless Mike Moody shot a brave stagecoach driver near Iron Creek and tried to escape with his chest of gold through Second Chance. On the way to his hideout, his horse threw a shoe. So, he stopped here—*in this shop*—and demanded Jebediah shoe his horse. Right then and there!"

"Was there a queue?" Shane shrugged deeper into his jacket. "Were people taking numbers and waiting their turn?"

Sophie elbowed him. Egbert eyeballed him. The twins shushed him. And Zeke ignored him.

"Now, Old Jeb was busy that day," Egbert continued in that slightly superior tone tour guides used. "He told that desperado he'd have to wait until he fixed Eldred Lee's wagon wheel."

Eldred Lee. Shane stored the name in his memory. "Do you know more about Eldred Lee?"

"He was the son of Seymore. Please don't

interrupt," the old man chastised. "This is the good part, because a tussle broke out and Old Jeb ended up on the wrong side of a Bowie knife." Egbert waved a hand over the dirt at his feet. "Why, he was minutes away from dyin'."

Alexander's and Andrew's eyes were huge. Sophie frowned, looking like she wanted to send them back to the inn. Shane didn't blame her. This wasn't exactly a G-rated story.

"What happened?" Alexander asked breathlessly.

"Did he use that thingy to kill Merciless Mike Moody?" Andrew pointed to a coiled bull whip on the wall. He was the more bloodthirsty of the boys.

"The posse from Ketchum rode up just in time and Merciless Mike sneaked out the back." Egbert pointed to the smaller door at the rear of the smithie.

"But…" Alexander's forehead wrinkled. "What happened to Jeba…Jeba…Jeb?"

"Did his guts spill out all over the floor?" Andrew glanced around, presumably looking for bloodstains. "Did he die?"

Shane and Zeke exchanged smiles, amused at the little heathen.

"Old Jeb lived, but only because Doc Weber was called. He closed Jebediah's wound with the hot poker from this very forge." Egbert spread his hands like a ringmaster. "Now. Some of the equipment you see here was Jebediah's." The old man pointed out the anvil, a set of huge bellows whose leather had deteriorated to ribbons and a large hammer. "Other items, like the wagon wheel and axle, are period-specific pieces I picked up elsewhere."

"Why don't you charge admission for people to see this?" Sophie poked around, tilting a wooden barrel with rusted metal rings, and then peering at a set of fire tongs. "It would make an interesting stop for people driving through. They could get out and stretch their legs."

The boys took cues from their mother, touching things, ooing and aahing, testing how far they could go before someone told them to stop. Egbert apparently considered this a hands-on museum. He didn't prohibit anyone from touching his stuff.

Shane kept an eye on his nephews. "Hoping they'd visit your junk store, sister dear?"

"You mean my shop full of *treasures*?" Sophie gave him a hard look over the top of her glasses. "Yes."

Mostly immune to his sister's moods, Shane simply smiled.

"Why don't I charge admission?" Egbert

wondered aloud. "I suppose I was torn between the rental business and my hobby."

While Sophie was busy examining a collection of square nails, Andrew picked up the blacksmith hammer with two hands and tried to brandish it at his brother.

"No," Zeke told him firmly, before Shane could. The cowboy took the hammer and placed it back on top of the anvil.

"When you say hobby, do you mean this place?" Shane stood near the door. He'd talked to enough people in Second Chance to know a dead end. And Egbert was definitely a dead end when it came to his grandfather. The story about Old Jeb was interesting when considering historical significance, but only if Merciless Mike Moody had made it on the list of America's most-wanted desperados. A fact that would require investigation and validation to be of any use to Shane.

"My hobby is collecting artifacts." There was pride in the old man's voice. "I accumulate treasure, just like Merciless Mike Moody did. For that matter, just like Hobart did."

"Harlan," Shane mumbled. The old guy couldn't even get his grandfather's name right.

"Did my grandfather show you some of his collection?" Sophie asked excitedly. "There's an elephant bell…"

"Hobart and his wife found that one year when they went to Thailand."

Too interested in this bit of information to correct the old man, Shane returned to Egbert's side. "My grandfather went with Ruth to Thailand?"

"I'm familiar with my grandfather's taste when it came to traditional art." Sophie spoke over Shane. "What kind of collector was he when it came to other pieces?"

"He bought things that interested him." Egbert got up from his stool and picked up the hammer Andrew had been fascinated with. "Now, this hammer... This hammer was used to drive railroad spikes into the Northern Pacific line. Jebediah brought it with him. And those nails? A traveler traded them for shoeing one of the horses that pulled his wagon."

"How do you know that?" Sophie asked. "These are details people lose track of."

Shane didn't care about Old Jeb's details or Merciless Mike Moody's exploits. "About Ruth—"

"I have Jebediah's diary." Egbert walked over to a steamer trunk, lifted the lid and removed a small, leather-bound book from the top tray.

Sophie and Shane followed the old man. Zeke stayed where he was across the room, near the twins.

"Jebediah was a well-educated man." Egbert flipped through the pages, stopping somewhere in the middle. "He didn't start out that way. When he became literate, he began keeping detailed records, like who he worked for that day or who passed through town."

"Or who stabbed him with a knife," Zeke murmured.

Sophie looked as if she barely contained herself from grabbing the book. Her hands were extended palm up. Shane was itching to read the journal, too. There had to be something inside that would validate Second Chance; it deserved to grow but be preserved rather than destroyed and then developed.

Egbert didn't seem to notice their interest. He was flipping through yellowed pages. "Here it is. 'Hammersmith from Boston needed a horse shod. Lacked the coin. Traded for nails, one kettle, one dozen eggs. He left for Sacramento the next morning with the wagon train.'" The old man pointed toward the steamer trunk. "I found those nails in a small burlap bag in there."

Which proved nothing. For all Shane knew, the nails could've been made by Old Jeb at a later date.

And speaking of later dates… "What about Ruth?" Shane demanded.

"Ruth?" Egbert didn't try to hide his annoyance. "Whoever Ruth is, she wasn't in this book."

"Ruth was my grandfather's first wife!" Shane shouted, having lost all patience with Egbert and Second Chance, for that matter.

"Irene went with Hobart to Thailand."

"*Harlan*. It's Harlan," Shane fumed.

Roy burst into the cabin. "I'm ready to install that pulley system, Sophie." He gave Zeke and Shane a quick once-over. "I could use your help, too, Shane."

"Who is Irene?" Shane's words bounced off the exposed rafters. "Give me that diary."

Egbert wrapped his arms around the old book.

Dead end.

Anger thrummed in Shane's veins. "I'll get my own answers." He stormed out with no idea how to back up his statement.

CHAPTER SEVEN

IF THERE WAS one thing Zeke didn't miss about his family, it was the drama.

"We loved Grandpa Harlan." Sophie righted her glasses over tear-filled eyes and gave the two older men disapproving glances. "There's no reason *not* to tell us about Irene."

Had Zeke known anything about Harlan, Irene or Ruth, he'd have cracked like a struck piñata beneath Sophie's wounded stare, spilling all his information, just to see her smile again.

Looking paler than usual, Roy turned on his heel and left.

Egbert, on the other hand, remained. He opened his mouth to speak and then thought better of it and closed it, staring at his boots.

"Secrets are rarely worth keeping," Sophie announced, nose thrust in the air. Which might have been more impactful if she hadn't cast one last longing glance at Old Jeb's journal in Egbert's hands. But then she was gone, following Roy and Shane out the door, her boots crunching on the snow.

Outside, Shane and Roy exchanged verbal volleys, their angry voices echoing through Second Chance. They both ignored Sophie's attempts to make peace.

"Let's fight like Old Jeb and Merciless Mike Moody." Andy danced around the forge. "I'll be Merciless Mike Moody." He karate chopped the air with his hand. "Give my horse some shoes!"

"How did Old Jeb fight?" Alex asked Egbert, brown eyes alight with mischief.

"With his fists." Egbert stared at the front door, not helping Zeke in any way, because his answer fed into a little boy's imagination.

Predictably, Alex raised his fists and let out a primal battle cry, charging his twin.

Zeke stepped in Alex's path and held the twins apart, longing for the days before he'd been their sitter when the boys pretended to be cannonballs and somersaulted across the inn's floor. He frowned at Egbert. "I don't see the harm in telling the Monroes about Irene."

"Really?" Egbert's gaze swung around to Zeke. "If a man didn't mention his past to his relatives, what right do I have to do so? Especially when I signed a document saying I'd hold my silence."

Although Zeke could respect the man's moral code, he didn't want to see Sophie unhappy.

The boys struggled to punch and stab each

other. Zeke continued to keep them out of each other's reach. "It's going to get mighty unpleasant around here if the Monroes don't start getting answers."

"Would you like to read Jebediah's diary?" Egbert held it out as if it was a peace offering.

Hell to the no.

"Sophie would love to read it," Zeke said, gut churning with his secret weakness. "And Shane is working with Mitch to establish that Second Chance has historical significance in Idaho or the United States. Both men would love to read it."

The boys continued to try to reenact the fight between Old Jeb and Merciless Mike Moody.

"Perhaps I'll offer this to one of them some other time." Egbert put the journal back in the chest. "When tempers have cooled."

Wise man.

"If you're interested, there are instructions on how to shoe a horse on the back wall." Egbert tried to salvage his tour.

"Pass." There were too many words. Zeke considered heading back to the inn but remembered Alexander's books awaited. "How about you rent us some fishing poles, Egbert?"

"Fishing?" Alex lowered his fists.

"We've never been fishing." Andy quit slicing the air.

"Fishing helped Second Chance residents survive the harsh winters." Egbert walked toward the door in that slow gait of his, leaning heavily on his cane. "I'll get you boys some gear. On the house. I couldn't charge Harlan's great-grandchildren."

"Are there fish in the snow?" Alex trotted ahead of the old man.

"It doesn't matter if there's ice and snow on top of the water," Egbert said grandly. "There are fish in this river longer than your arm."

There might have been fish that big in the Salmon River forty or fifty years ago. Zeke doubted there were anymore. The biggest fish he'd heard caught since he'd been in town was about twelve inches long. Locals blamed man-made dams and the government practice of stocking mountain lakes with nonnative trout for the change in the fish population.

Andy ran after his brother. "I'm hooking the first fish."

"I'm hooking the biggest," Alex called back.

"I'm keeping mine," Andy countered. "My fish is going to have a big tail. And I'm going to call him Fred."

"We'll be lucky to catch a fish, fellas, much less keep one." Zeke followed at Egbert's pace, excited despite himself. Fishing. There was a solid, nonreading activity. Zeke was on the road to recovery, walking easier and now angling for an evening meal.

They followed the path Shane had shoveled to Egbert's place. The old man led them inside his store. There were chairs for customers and a glass counter with all kinds of fishing gear on display. "I've got poles your size, boys. Zeke, do you know how to tie a fly?"

"No, sir. I can bait a hook, though."

"No bait," Egbert said. "I'll tie flies on for the boys. Winter fish prefer a stone fly nymph."

"Flies?" Andy giggled, pressing his nose against the glass case.

But Alex shadowed Egbert, ready to learn. "Do we have to catch our own flies?"

"No. I've got some pretty ones that were made to look like real flies." Egbert pulled out a tackle box and opened it up, revealing several flies with hooks disguised in the fluff. Egbert had fishing poles hung on the back wall. He took one and beckoned Zeke closer. "I'll show Zeke how to tie a fly on and maybe next time he can do it for you. Fish are hungry in winter and less discriminating about what bait they bite."

A few minutes later, Zeke and the twins exited the back of Egbert's shop. Zeke shoveled a narrow path to the bank. The river curved around a bend, creating deep water, which Zeke assumed was where the fish were since that's where Egbert had directed them to go. Ice and snow lined the banks, but not midstream.

"Do you know how to fish?" Alex reached for a pole.

Zeke handed it to him. "I've fished before, but not fly-fishing."

Andy removed his glove and immersed his hand in the snow and ice of the river, yanking it back almost immediately. "How can fish live in the cold?"

"I guess they like it." Zeke planted Andy's pole handle in the snow.

"What do we do if we catch a fish?" Alex stared at the top of his pole, high above his head.

"We cut it into pieces and eat it." Zeke expected them to say *ew*. The Clark boys over at the Bucking Bull were staunch meat eaters and turned up their noses at fish.

"I love fish," Alex said, completely serious. "Salmon is my favorite."

"I love chicken nuggets more," Andy said in the same matter-of-fact tone. "But fish is good, too."

Their disliking fish would've made not catching any less of a disappointment. And Zeke was sure they weren't going to catch anything, especially given the four-year-olds didn't have a long attention span. He'd give this activity a thirty-minute timeline, perhaps less.

Zeke showed each boy how to cast, using only his observations from seeing men fish along the river over the years. "Pole in your right hand. A little slack on the line with your left. And then you cast it out to the water."

"I missed." Andy stomped his foot. His fly sat on top of the ice midstream. "What do I do now?"

"Reel it back in." Zeke showed him how to do it and then stepped out of the way so he wouldn't get snagged by Andy's fly when he cast out again. Which meant he was snagged by Alex's hook instead. "Hey."

The boy hadn't realized he'd caught Zeke by the sleeve of his jacket. He kept trying to cast. Tug-tug-tug.

"Stop, Alex." When the boy paused, Zeke removed the hook. It left a small tear in his thick maroon jacket. A white feather poked out, resisted the wind briefly, only to be taken on a ride across the river.

"I missed again." Andy got impatient and flicked his fly back and forth in the air, momentarily mesmerized by the action.

"Stop that, Andy." Zeke helped Alex cast, dodged Andy's fly because the kid didn't stop and then ducked to dodge Alex's fly when he began waving his pole through the air. "Stop it! Both of you."

They let their poles drop, but not before Alex's fly snagged the red knit sock on Zeke's foot.

"Nobody move." The last thing Zeke needed was Alex to flick his line again and tear out a bit of his toe. He bent to free himself.

"You're doing great!" Egbert called from his back patio.

Heartened, both boys lifted their poles and flung them about like bull whips.

Still hooked, Zeke's foot was pulled out from under him. For the second time in two days, Zeke plopped into the snow. His caught red bootie was flung toward the river on Alex's fly.

Just his luck. This time the boy's cast reached the water.

The bootie sank.

"Reel those flies in," Zeke said sternly in a voice reminiscent of his father's. "Both of you."

Andy's fly had also reached the river and as he spun his rod's wheel a very large trout lunged for the fly, rising out of the water with predatory intent.

Both boys shrieked and dropped their poles. Andy's pole shot toward the river, towed by the hooked fish.

Zeke leaped to his feet and lunged after Andy's fishing pole. He landed facedown in the snow but managed to get his fingers around the pole's handle. The line zinged out of the reel.

Who knew a fish that big could travel so fast? Or so far?

The twins stood on either side of him, more concerned with the fish than in helping him up.

Zeke got to his feet, not bothering to wipe the snow off his poor exposed toes. He wanted to catch this fish.

"Don't use brute force." Egbert may not be willing to spill his Monroe secrets, but he was more than willing to share his fishing advice. "That fish isn't a bull you're trying to lasso. Play with the tension."

Zeke had reeled in a fish only a time or two, and that'd been when he was a kid fishing with a bobber and a worm for bait. He tried starting and stopping reeling the fish in. Starting and stopping. The end of the line danced in the water as the trout contorted about, straining to gain its freedom.

Zeke's toes stung with cold. The wind chapped his cheeks. He didn't care. He was determined to land this fish.

"That's it. Bring him in now." From the porch above them, Egbert must have seen something Zeke couldn't. "Give him a jerk when he jumps."

The fish couldn't be that close.

Proving him wrong, the fish leaped out of the water just a few feet away.

Reflexively, Zeke jerked the pole back. The fish flew toward Andy, landing against his chest.

Andy screamed. Alex screamed.

The fish flopped around in the snow at their feet as if trying to jump back in the water.

"Grab him! Grab him!" Zeke tried to find solid footing, tried to bend—nearly impossible with his walking boot—tried to get his hands around the surprisingly agile fish.

Finally, something went right. Zeke straightened, holding the fish solidly with both hands.

"Fish tonight for dinner," Andy singsonged, raising his hands in victory.

"Nope." Egbert destroyed that notion. "Remove that hook and toss him back."

"Toss him back?" The fish struggled to free himself from Zeke's grip.

"You heard me." The old man was full of bad news today. "You can't keep him. That's a bull trout. The population is too low in Idaho. He's protected by law. Get that hook out of his mouth and release him."

"But he looks tasty." Alex rubbed his tummy and then glanced up at Egbert. "If we eat him, will Zeke go to jail?"

"With my luck, yes." Zeke had to put the fish

down on the snow so he could remove the fly. After a few unsuccessful tries, the fish was free, and Zeke tossed him into the water.

The bull trout disappeared, seemingly none the worse for the experience.

"You're bleeding." Alex pointed to Zeke's walking boot.

"That's fish blood." Andy peered at Zeke's toes and then at the snow around their feet. "It's all over the snow."

Zeke's big toe began throbbing, contradicting Andy's fish theory.

"No." Alex knelt near Zeke's walking boot. "Zeke's toes are bloody."

Sure enough, red blood dripped from Zeke's big toe where Alex had yanked a hook through his flesh. Suddenly, Zeke was grateful for the cold. It was like Mother Nature's bracing ice pack.

So much for a quiet pastime.

"Are you gonna cry?" Andy bent to examine Zeke's toes. And then he looked up at Zeke. "Mom says it's okay to cry."

"I'd cry if I were you." Alex patted Zeke's walking boot.

Both boys stared at Zeke as if waiting to see if he'd break down.

"There's not enough blood here to move this cowboy to tears." Zeke wiggled his toes, eliciting a sharp reaction. He stopped wiggling. "This is nothing. Why, one time I was gored in the backside by a bull. Couldn't sit down for a week." He reeled in Alex's fly. There was no red bootie on the boy's hook. "I think we deserve fish sticks for lunch at the diner. Who's with me?"

The twins cheered.

CHAPTER EIGHT

"IRENE DIDN'T HAVE an affair with your grand-dad." Stifling a belch, Roy excused himself and fed out lengths of rope down the slope to the highway more judiciously than he fed Shane information.

"So, you knew Irene?" Shane was like a dog with a bone about this Irene thing. He paced on the road beneath them.

Sophie sat in an old ladder-back chair on the porch of the trading post, occasionally playing referee to the two men while Roy built his pulley system. She waved to the boys when they went into the Bent Nickel for lunch, her gaze lingering on Zeke. He took his responsibility seriously, but he also cared for her boys. The proof was there in the way he tilted his head when they spoke, and the way he knew what they were up to almost before they knew it themselves.

"Sophie, do you hear this?" Shane was saying.

"Yes. Of course." With effort, Sophie returned her attention to Roy and Shane, but not completely. She wasn't as concerned with her grandfather's love life as she was with learning more about what he valued in these boxes. Should she keep the bell? Or the collection of silver souvenir spoons?

You sold what? Grandpa Harlan had been livid when she'd taken the initiative and sold a painting in his collection.

Her stomach lurched. She'd managed his collection. She had every right to sell, but she'd felt guilty after witnessing his reaction. And still did. What if she sold something he'd loved?

But if he loved any of this stuff that much— as much as the painting she'd divested—why had he left it here?

"Yes, I knew Irene." Roy threaded the rope through block and tackle, breaking into Sophie's doubts. He'd rigged a system from the trading post's porch to a tree below and attached a large sled to the other end of the rope. At the bottom of the hill was Gabby's old red wagon, which Roy recommended they use to haul boxes across the road to the inn.

Sophie had given up understanding what ends of the rope went where and for what purpose long ago. She turned her face to the sun, which was making a rare appearance.

"Irene was older than I was." Roy gave away

tiny details as if they were crumbs big enough to satisfy curious mice. "But in Second Chance, everybody knows everybody."

"I didn't know Irene," Shane grumbled. "But now I know she went to Thailand with my grandfather."

Roy scowled, but didn't look up from the knot he was tying. "Sophie, do you have anything unbreakable for a test run?"

"No." The most likely item she thought of first was the black velvet painting she'd taken to the inn last night. The rest of the black velvet paintings were unboxed, meaning unprotected.

"Well, then, find me something almost unbreakable to strap onto that sled so we can give it a shot."

Sophie went inside the trading post and opened the nearest box. It contained the old ice skates. They qualified as not easily breakable. She folded the flaps, carried the box outside and set it on the sled. Roy had provided bungee cords. She used them to strap it to the sled.

Roy adjusted the box before pointing at Shane. "Don't move."

"Why?" Sophie's brother was in a snit, not that she blamed him.

"Because if this box breaks free, I want someone in its path to stop it." For the first time since they'd arrived at the trading post,

Roy met Shane's gaze squarely. "Now if you're the kind of man who thinks that's a true statement, you deserve what you get." He blew out a frustrated breath. "Reality is, I want someone below in case the sled breaks free. Someone who can flag down a vehicle before there's a collision."

Shane frowned at Roy. And then he frowned at Sophie. "I'm only doing this because you need it done."

"I appreciate you, brother dear," Sophie said with faux brightness, before whispering to Roy, "Are you sure this is going to work?"

"I said I had an idea," Roy hedged. "I didn't say for sure it'd work." Roy tugged on the rope, making sure it held. "Let's give this a try."

Hand over hand, Roy lowered the sled to the bottom of the slope. Shane transferred the box to the wagon. Mitch had crossed the highway and wheeled the wagon to the inn, where he handed the box to Gabby. Gabby carried it to the front door, which Laurel opened. Gabby disappeared inside. Laurel waved to Sophie, and then shut the door.

Roy applauded. "I'd say it works."

Over an hour later, they had most of the room shuttled across the road and some of the unsalvageable furniture—a few tables and poorly made bookshelves—moved outside.

Roy planned to load them into his truck and take them the sixty miles to the nearest dump.

Sophie wanted to celebrate. While Roy disassembled the pulley, she and Shane inspected the nearly empty trading post. The six-inch-wide planked floors looked solid. The fluorescent lighting worked, even if it was hideous. There was a fireplace and it was ready for fuel.

"It's still dark in here." Especially in the corner farthest from the door and opposite the hallway that led to the small half bath and kitchen at the rear of the cabin.

"You can put a window on this front wall." Shane pounded the round log with a fist.

Sophie imagined it sounded as solid as the day it'd been built.

"I can order you a window," Roy offered, coming inside with a coil of rope looped over his shoulder like a mountain climber. "Might take a week to get here. But I can install it, too."

The town handyman was proving to be very handy.

That didn't mean Shane was cutting him any slack. "And what would you charge Sophie for that?"

Roy frowned. "I'm paid to keep up these cabins. I even have a budget for minor repairs. I can get you a window."

Shane wanted to argue, but Sophie thanked

Roy before her brother could dig at the old man some more. Their grandfather had made sure the town he'd bought would be cared for. It wasn't Roy's fault Grandpa Harlan had secrets.

There were just a few larger pieces left in the space, the most unusual of which was the front end of a car. Someone had taken a saw or blow torch and cut the front off two feet from the bumper.

Shane kept returning to it, unable to keep from touching the gracefully sloping metal. "This is from a Ford Edsel."

"Did Grandpa Harlan ever own one of those?"

"Intact, you mean?" Shane shrugged.

The wide grille looked like a face. An olive green and rusted-chrome face. "Wasn't the Edsel a big failure?"

Her brother nodded. "I think you should mount this on the wall outside, as if a car was crashing through the wall to get out."

"Uh…" The art enthusiast inside Sophie recoiled. "That's kind of…"

"Quirky? Unique?" He ran a hand over the bumper, smiling.

"Tacky." Although looking around the cabin… Well, the trading post wasn't exactly Bergdorf's.

Shane ignored her assessment, having a love

affair with the newfound Detroit metal and chrome. "Alexander and Andrew would love it. Think of all the other kids who'd drive by and ask their parents to stop. Including the kids at heart with wallets and credit cards."

Shane was right. "It's just… It's not very classy."

"Soph." Shane led her toward the doorway and the light, peering at her face. "You're not going to run an art gallery here. You know that, right?"

"I know. I know." But a part of her clung to the culture and sophistication of the art world, a world she'd studied for six years. A world she'd worked in for nearly nine years. "This will be good for the town. It'll add value to the property and help other businesses. I get it."

What she didn't get—what she refused to tell her twin—was how important running the trading post the way her grandfather would've wanted her to was.

Unaware of her indecision, Shane turned her to look at what she had to work with. "Do you remember how you couldn't take the boys to work in Philadelphia because they might break something worth hundreds of thousands of dollars?" Shane grinned. He dragged her over to a pedal car fashioned as a fire truck. "They can't do much to devalue this old thing."

He was right. The fire truck had no wheels. No pedals. And had more dings and dents than a demolition derby entrant.

Shane hugged her. "This is a different life. Kudos to you for wanting to try it." He released her, holding her at arm's length. "But don't forget, you can quit at any time."

"Really?" It was tempting.

He nodded. "I miss Las Vegas. I miss Starbucks and five-star dining. I miss my sports car. I miss days so hot the pavement steams."

"I miss my condo," Sophie admitted. "I miss parks with fences where the boys can run around safely. I miss shopping and traveling first-class. I miss my nanny."

He gently nudged her shoulder with his fist. "You have a new nanny."

Sophie shrugged. She was still finding it hard to reconcile that the big, attractive cowboy was her nanny. "My old nanny cooked dinner." And spoke French.

They both stared across the road at the Bent Nickel, probably thinking the same thing—microwaved trays of food weren't the same as a homemade meal.

Shane sighed. "But the fact remains we agreed to help this town get back on track."

Sophie heaved a sigh bigger than her twin's. "There's more to life than five-star dining."

And she couldn't leave without knowing she'd honored her grandfather's memory. If she didn't find a new home for all his stuff, Shane would rent a dumpster.

"There's more to life than uncovering Grandpa Harlan's secrets," Shane huffed. "How could a man who we know was married four times actually have been married a fifth time?"

And they were back to Irene.

"I'm sure that wasn't why he left us Second Chance or why everyone in town sold their property to him." Sophie checked her phone. She had a few more hours left of nanny time, but she was grimy and cold, and there were boxes to be gone through in the comfort of the inn. "Shane, you've talked to everyone in town about Grandpa Harlan, so I guess we'll have to be patient and wait for the new year."

"Patience isn't my strong suit." Shane headed for the door and she followed, locking it behind her. "We have a short window of opportunity to defend this small town before the rest of the family votes to sell. And all I have to work with is a bunch of hundred-year-old cabins and a tall tale of a stagecoach robber." He walked down the short slope dotted with melting snow to the highway. "Although...I've just remembered the Clarks over at the Bucking Bull didn't sell to Grandpa Harlan." He grinned. "I've never talked to them. And they're related to Old Jeb the blacksmith. Their relatives must have been in town as long as our descendants, the Lee family."

"They might know something that will help."

"They might." Shane sounded more hopeful than he had in a long time.

They reached the highway and crossed, heading for the inn, which always had a nice warm fire in the fireplace.

"You think the Clarks will welcome you with open arms?" Shane was too nosy for the likes of some.

"I have an ace in the hole." Shane walked swiftly. "That cowboy nanny of yours has a horse. I think he needs to pay Hi-Ho Silver a visit. We'll take the twins."

"You might want to ask me permission," Sophie grumbled.

"Can I borrow your children, sister dear?" Shane indicated she should go up the porch stairs first.

Of course she was going to let him. "Can you make sure they come back with all their fingers and toes?"

"No worries. I'm taking your cowboy nanny to make sure they stay safe."

When they got inside, the boys were still at the diner with Zeke. Shane approached Mitch for an update of Second Chance history, asking him what he knew about Old Jeb and Merciless Mike Moody. Sophie took a quick shower and changed clothes, returning downstairs as Andrew and Alexander came through the door with Zeke. Shane and Mitch were nowhere to be seen.

"Mom!" they cried, chasing away the worry that Zeke was replacing her as their favorite adult. They ran to give her hugs.

"I caught a fish!" Andrew held out his hands as if measuring a big fish.

"And I caught Zeke!" Alexander pointed to his nanny.

Zeke walked past Sophie, his pace slower now than it had been this morning. His red bootie was missing and there was a bandage on his big toe. He sat down on the couch and eased into the cushions until his head rested on the back. "I'm due a ten-minute break."

"You caught a fish *and* Zeke?" Sophie gathered the twins close. "What happened?"

The boys were quick to fill her in. When they were done with the telling, they ran upstairs to go to the potty and retrieve books for Zeke to read, perhaps forgetting one of their favorites was already on the coffee table.

"I'm so sorry you got hooked." Sophie tried to keep a straight face the way any good employer would. "Can I get you anything? Pain reliever? Ice pack?" Legal counsel.

Zeke was going to sue her, for sure.

"I've been trampled on by horses and cattle." Zeke had his head tilted back and his eyes closed. "I'll survive being hooked by a four-year-old."

"Still, I feel guilty." There was the bandage and Andy was adamant there'd been lots of blood.

"Why? I'm their nanny and fishing was my idea." Zeke opened his eyes and patted the empty couch cushion to his left. "Sit. You look like you worked too hard this morning."

Sophie bristled in her sparkly princess sweater. "I can work a full day."

"I'm sure you can," he said, eyes closing once more. "But with sons like yours, you need to conserve your strength. Sit. I won't bite."

She sat next to him. After a moment, she settled back more comfortably against the cushions and sighed wearily.

"I take it Roy's idea worked?"

"Yes. We put everything in the room there." She listened to the murmur of her children's voices as they drifted to her from upstairs.

Zeke gestured toward the extra room she was renting. "Those boxes are stacked taller than you are."

She sighed again. "I really should get started cataloging things." But she didn't move. Her body felt heavy and the cushions were so soft.

"Rest." Zeke patted her knee as if he'd done it a hundred times before.

Sophie fought the flutters.

He withdrew his hand. "For five minutes, just rest. I've got the boys taken care of."

He didn't have them taken care of. They were taking care of themselves upstairs, most likely building a fort on their bed using all the pillows and sneaking her tablet to watch one of the Disney movies they were so fond of. She closed her eyes, but listened with half an ear, just in case they got out of hand.

She woke up to her two angels climbing into her lap. They snuggled close. Alexander pressed his worn copy of *Mama Duck, Papa Duck* into her hands. But neither one of them was in the mood for a story. They melted against her and dozed.

She soaked up their love like a sponge, drawing her arms around them and breathing in the scent of boy.

There was a sound to her right.

Zeke had several boxes open and lined up along the wall. "I thought I'd help you start sorting."

"How long was I out?" she asked softly.

"About forty-five minutes. I think the boys fell asleep, too. They came down with eyes barely open, as if they'd realized they'd fallen asleep without you."

"Or they remembered their uncle's talk of ghosts." Sophie rested her head against the cushions and stared at the planked ceiling, briefly explaining the bear trap fiasco. Now that she was waking up, she wanted to be sorting. But she knew better than to wake the boys. She didn't move. Well, her eyes followed Zeke. Tall, broad-shouldered Zeke, who was lifting boxes and lowering them along the wall.

He turned and caught her gawking.

She didn't look away. "I'm so tired, I'm staring at you like a zombie would." There was a half-truth. She was exhausted, but she was staring at Zeke because he was her kind of attractive—inside and out.

"Don't get up." He didn't call her out on the classification of her stare. "I'll tell you what's in each box." Zeke brought one over to the coffee table. "This looks like an antique coffee grinder." He lifted the red cast-iron piece from the box.

"I'm impressed you know what that is."

"I cheated." He gave her a half smile without quite looking her in the eye. "It smells like coffee and there are coffee grounds on the bottom of the box."

He was cute when he was trying to be humble.

Zeke removed that box and returned with another. "These are baby cups, right?" He lifted several small silver mugs. "They have names and birth dates. Scrap metal?"

She shook her head. "I went to a baby shower last fall where they used old baby cups like that to serve punch."

"They used someone else's baby cups?"

He looked so baffled, she laughed. "I've also seen them garnished with velvet bows and used as Christmas tree decorations, too." They'd be the perfect item for the online version of her store. Easily shippable.

Zeke washed a hand over his face. "City folk amaze me."

"Do any of those baby cups say Monroe or Lee or Clark?"

Zeke dug through the box. "No. Does it matter?"

"I don't suppose it does. I just keep hoping I'll find a box that is a clue as to why we were left this town or why Grandpa Harlan collected the things he did."

"Who knows why anyone collects anything," Zeke said sagely. "My grandmother had a fondness for old chamber pots. She planted geraniums in them."

"I managed my grandfather's fine art collection and I…I used to think I knew what he liked and what was best for the collection." Her voice soured as she admitted, "And then at my father's urging I sold a piece Grandpa Harlan *loved*." He wouldn't have parted with that painting for any amount of money, not that she knew it at the time.

"You sold it without his permission?"

"Without his permission." She nodded. "My father suspected the Rubens market had hit its peak. To his credit, he was right. But my grandfather was furious. When he died… We hadn't spoken for months. Every box I go through makes me wonder…"

"If it had emotional significance to him," Zeke guessed. Or maybe it wasn't a guess. He seemed to have a bead on who Sophie was as a person. He considered her for a moment, and then the stacks behind him. "I haven't gone through many boxes, but everything is alike in each box, as if it was carefully stored. That implies—"

"Someone cared greatly." Sophie nodded. "I've gone to estate sales where there's no rhyme or reason as to how things are displayed."

"I suppose what's in the boxes should tell you

more about your grandfather..." Zeke held out his hands in surrender. "But I'll be darned if I know what it all means."

She didn't know either. "Grandpa Harlan used to say every dollar he earned was hard-won and every dollar he spent was a careful investment."

"So...he kept everything? He liked log cabins. Did he buy other towns?"

"Don't even joke about that!"

Zeke put the baby cups back and returned with another box. "This one has a different kind of cup." He pulled out several tall, slender trophies that had elegant lines like champagne flutes. "Scrap?"

"Flower vases," she said simply.

He raised one ginger brow. "Seriously?"

She shrugged, almost dislodging Alexander. "What's old is new again. Designers snap that stuff up."

Zeke shook his head in amazement and put the box away. "Is this something they teach you at art history school?"

"I suppose it's part of running with a certain crowd in Philadelphia." Her high society friends who wore designer labels, had educated interests and favorite charities.

They continued exploring boxes. Zeke often assumed it was nothing she'd want to sell in the shop. Sophie often felt it would bring someone pleasure even as she marveled at the idea of her grandfather assembling such a collection of... well...collections.

While Zeke was returning a set of miniature children's books to the pile, she spotted a box on the far end with writing on the side. She pointed to it. "What does that say?"

"I can't read that scrawl," he said brusquely, setting the box on the coffee table and stepping back as if singed.

"I owe yous." Sophie wished she could open up the flaps. "What's inside?"

Zeke pulled out an odd assortment of items. Torn boxing gloves. A worn baseball mitt. A small brass basketball engraved with the words *First Place*.

"How odd." Sophie drew the boys closer. "That's the first box we've come across that makes no sense. Grandpa Harlan wasn't an athlete."

"Give it time." Zeke shrugged. "If anyone can make a connection between these items and Harlan, you can."

His faith in her pleased Sophie.

Zeke surveyed what they'd gone through. "I can't take more boxes out without putting some of these back in." Boxes were stacked nearly blocking the door to his room.

"Let's stop. I know what I'm doing tomorrow." Sophie rubbed Alexander's and Andrew's backs. "Cleaning the trading post and getting it ready for merchandising."

"I can help you clean," Zeke offered.

"Or you can watch the boys."

"There is that." He stared at the fire. Cleared his throat. Shifted around to face her. "Can I ask when payday is?" He rushed on, "Mack needs an advance on the parts to repair my truck."

"I can spot you. How much do you need?"

He drew back, horrified. "I don't want anything I haven't earned. I just wanted to know if you'd pay me weekly, biweekly or monthly."

He was so different from her ex-husband. Different in a good way—better ethics, bigger heart, broader shoulders.

But still…

She and Zeke were different. And different meant incompatible. And incompatible meant broken hearts.

Not to mention, I might not stay in Second Chance.

Sophie returned her attention to the children asleep in her lap. They were getting so big. It seemed like only yesterday they were babies. That their fingers curled around her thumb when she placed it in their palms. That their eyes sought hers as they worked their mouths into toothless grins.

"They're a lot like you." Zeke settled into the wingback chair next to the couch.

"They have my coloring, but they don't look anything like me." Sophie smoothed Alexander's cowlick. The twins had the promise of Frank's sturdy frame.

"They're like you in personality and temperament," Zeke insisted. "They're both curious. They're both brave. They're both smart."

Oh, that was flattering. "When I was their age, my nanny left me for hours at a time. I'd be playing—"

"With your antique silver tea set."

He remembered.

Her smile settled in to stay as she nodded. "And staying out of trouble by reading books."

"Which they both enjoy." He leaned forward and patted Alexander's shoulder. "Alex more than Andy." His gaze came up to meet hers in a way that made things flutter inside her, not to mention her aversion to nicknames. "Andy is always on the lookout for an adventure."

Zeke knew how to tell her identical twins apart. He knew their personalities. How could she not sigh and admit, "I was a boring child. My nanny would chase after Shane and Camden, and then poke her head in the door to my room and ask if I still had all my fingers and all my toes."

"Which had never been in danger."

"Maybe just once."

He chuckled, a deep sound that scoffed at the differences and incompatibility between them. The warmth in his green eyes encompassed her. "I should have guessed they'd have been at risk a time or two. It was your curiosity, wasn't it? You went too far in your study of something… Ancient Asian culture?"

He was sharp. She was impressed. "How did you know?"

His gaze didn't shy away from hers. "When you spend the majority of your time with animals, you start to pick up subtle clues to behavior. That swivel of ears. That stomp of their foot. That swish of their tail."

None of which she'd exhibited. "Really. How did you know?"

That stare. Those weren't moon eyes. That was genuine interest. In her, not her money or her influence. "Sophie, you have a way of looking at things as if you want to absorb them into your very being."

"I do not." Sophie hoped she wasn't looking at Zeke as if she wanted to absorb him. Good moms didn't get lost in the eyes of men who worked for them. She shifted Andrew's rump farther from the edge of the couch cushion. "That sounds too...too...greedy."

He shook his head. "It's not a possessive look. It's more like an expression yearning for understanding. You want to know the history behind each object, like that bell. If it had been on display in a steeple, you'd have climbed in the belfry to study it. And Alex would do the same."

His words rang inside her the way truths do. Expanding, warming, comforting.

He knows me.

She wanted to absorb Zeke into that place where things fluttered. She wanted to know what made him tick. She wanted to learn the feel of his lips on hers.

Her heart beat faster.

Good moms...

Good moms kissed. How else could she explain how women ended up with housefuls of children?

Suddenly, Sophie wanted a houseful of little ones. A little redheaded girl with intelligent green eyes. A tall slender boy with ginger hair and a quiet confidence.

"You aren't going to tell me how you risked those delicate fingers and toes?" Zeke teased, hopefully unaware she was mentally nesting worse than Laurel.

"Some secrets are meant to stay secret." In that moment, she understood why her grandfather wanted his private life kept private. Divulging secrets was intimate. It made her feel vulnerable. Getting close to Zeke was just as risky as her behavior the day she'd almost lost her digits.

Because hearts couldn't be sewn back together.

CHAPTER NINE

"CAN WE GO sledding today?" Andy hopped up and down in front of Zeke the morning after the fishing expedition. "Mr. Nanny. Mr. Nanny. Mr. Nanny. Can we?"

Andy may not have had big feet, but he'd already put on his snow boots.

Better safe than sorry, Zeke drew his feet beneath the chair and held his coffee mug with both hands. "I suppose we should get in that sledding before the snow is too thin for the sport."

The day had dawned sunny, promising spring really was on the horizon. Through the front windows, patches of earth were visible in places on the hill above them, like dark brown splotches on a paint horse.

There were other things being revealed. Sophie's intelligence. Her intriguing past where she'd taken a physical risk. Her love for her sons. Not that anything he'd learned about Sophie would move them past an employer-employee relationship. He didn't need romantic risks. He needed four weeks of paychecks.

Alex ran up carrying a green book with a big duck on the front. "Can we read a story first?"

"What happened to you?" Zeke ruffled Alex's cowlick. "You weren't much of a reader before."

"We didn't have a nanny here before you." Andy kept on bouncing, shaking the old inn with each landing. "Our old nanny read to us all the time. Sometimes in French."

Zeke's stomach turned. After their nap yesterday, he'd taken them out to sled, dodging reading time the way a frisky colt dodged the halter. How was he going to get out of reading today?

"Boys, your oatmeal is almost ready," Sophie called above the hum of the microwave.

"Oaty-meal! Oaty-meal!" Andy hopped over to the couch and collapsed on the cushions, finally spent.

"Read to us before we have breakfast," Alex begged. He climbed into Zeke's lap, tucked his knees to his shoulders and opened the book.

Not to be outdone, Andy rolled off the couch and scrambled into Zeke's lap, resting his snow boots on Zeke's thigh.

The brown delivery truck rumbled past, pulling into a space in front of the diner.

"There's the truck," Alex said with half his usual delivery truck enthusiasm.

"It's not coming here," Andy said with his big-boy voice.

The twins settled more fully against Zeke, more interested in the reading of a book than in magically appearing packages.

The chair hadn't been made for one big man and two little boys. Zeke wrapped his arms around them so they wouldn't fall. The book Alex placed in Zeke's hands completed the circle.

"This book is *Mama Duck, Papa Duck*." Alex emphasized each word by tapping his finger on the cover.

Zeke's mouth went dry. He didn't remember ever reading that book. Like any good babysitter, he opened it and began turning the pages. Words registered—*the, duck, home*. Letter combinations registered—*ed, ing, 's*. But this wasn't as simple as reading beginner books like *See Jane Run* or street signs like No Parking Anytime.

These boys expected him to read the story, to assemble the words smoothly, to act like an adult who'd actually graduated from high school.

Zeke's body began to overheat. It was the warmth of their little bodies. His proximity to the fire. The sunlight streaming through the windows on his shoulder.

Who am I kidding? I'm having a hot flash because I can't read!

What would happen when Sophie discovered his secret?

She'll fire me.

And who could blame her? Kids deserved good role models and nannies trained at highfalutin places like Young's Academy.

"What's the holdup on that story?" Sophie called from the alcove.

The bitterness of Zeke's morning coffee crept up the back of his throat.

He tried to turn the first page over—the fewer pages to read the better—but Alex was having none of it.

"No. Start here." The thoughtful little tyke pulled the book pages open as wide as they could go. "Mama Duck wanted a safe home for her ducklings."

I'm going to have to read the book.

The words on the page faded. Zeke thought he might be sick.

Alex turned the page and waited for Zeke to read the next line.

Look at the words and read.

Dust motes danced on sunlight.

Zeke's gaze flickered to the page and then

back to the dust motes. Why draw this out? It was the perfect time to make a fool of himself. Only the twins and Sophie would hear. No one else was downstairs in the common room. Not Shane or Mitch.

Sophie would fire him, but she'd do it in a classy, private way that saved a bit of his pride. As long as he avoided the look of disappointment he expected in her eyes.

Look at the words and read.

Zeke's gaze flickered to the page and then away. He stared at a spot on the coffee table where a red string from someone's sweater had found a resting place. It was out of place and should be thrown away. He was out of place and...

Mitch opened the door to his apartment behind the check-in desk. Laurel stood behind him, hard to miss with all that fiery red hair and a gray sweater with shiny silver wrist ruffles.

"Zeke is going to read us a story," Andy announced, fidgeting as if he'd much rather be down on the wood planks hopping around.

"Mama Duck, Papa Duck." Alex nodded, squirming as if he couldn't wait for the story to start.

"I love stories." Mitch slung his arm over Laurel's shoulders and waited.

Zeke swallowed. Yes, his downfall was going to be a public thing.

Words blurred on the page: *Duck? Wolf? Home?*

Words gunked in his throat: *Duck? Wolf? Home?*

Words roared in his ears: *Stupid! Ridiculous! Loser!*

Roughly thirty years ago, his mother had tried to teach Zeke to read. "Take your cues from the pictures," she'd said. "Find words you know and fill in the blanks."

Sweat dampened the base of his neck.

What if I fill in the blanks wrong?

There were people waiting for him to begin, the same way they'd been waiting for him to tell the story about Buttercup the other morning.

They'd enjoyed his story about that bull.

He'd enjoyed making up that story.

The pictures rose up off the page—two mallards, a wolf's snout in the bushes.

Zeke swallowed the rising coffee back down.

And then words came blurting out of him like spring hail on the prairie. "Once upon a time, there were two ducks who were very much in love. They got married and thought everything would be hunky-dory." They weren't the words on the page—not even close! But the fidgeting

boys stilled, so he turned the page and continued. "But there was a big stinky wolf, one who
had loud parties every night and didn't clean
up after his pet raccoon."

The boys giggled. Andy stopped fidgeting.

Maybe Zeke didn't have to fill in the blanks.
Maybe he could fill in an entire page, an entire
book. All the way to the end!

"Those newlywed duckies had a filling
breakfast of grubs and water grass and wad-
dled their way to a neighboring farm." At least,
the picture looked like a farm. "But the rooster
there kept cock-a-doodle-doing, so they took
to the air and flew around the neighborhood,
looking for a quiet home." Zeke turned a page.

Sophie leaned around the corner to look at
him with raised brows. If she'd been a horse,
she'd have snorted her disbelief.

Alex stared up at him in openmouthed shock.
"But…"

"Let me finish." Zeke didn't have the luxury
of time. He kept making stuff up and turning
pages, hoping the microwave would ding and
Sophie would announce they had to stop so the
boys could eat their breakfast. "These ducks
went about the country looking for a new home.
They wanted lakefront property, which is very
expensive, but full of big, hungry, fly-eating

fish protected by the law. There had to be pro-
tections for ducks there, too, right?"

The microwave beeped, and Sophie disappeared.

Alex jabbed his finger into Zeke's chest.
"But…"

"Almost done." Zeke turned another page.
"But these ducks settled on an island in a park,
one without partying wolves or crowing roost-
ers, one that curious boys couldn't stomp to,
one with pink swan boats—"

"Swans aren't pink," Alex said staunchly,
thrusting his finger toward the book's artwork
and gumming up the works when it came to
page turning. "Look. They're white."

"—and friendly people who threw them
cracked corn and lettuce." Zeke pushed on.

"Peanuts," Alex insisted. "They threw the
ducks peanuts."

Is that what that said?

Zeke frowned, losing his storytelling rhythm
as he searched for the P-word.

Meanwhile, Andy continued to stare up at
him. "Why would they feed ducks salad?"

"Because it's better than peanuts," Zeke said
matter-of-factly. "Who's telling this story?"
Better yet, who'd written this story? You didn't
feed ducks peanuts!

Alex scrunched his face.

"Okay, where were we?" Zeke stared at the drawings on the page. No swan boat. No male mallard. Just the female sitting in a nest in the reeds. "Mama Duck went off to be alone and lay her eggs. She found a spot along a river." Zeke turned the page. "The eggs hatched. The ducklings had a quiet childhood, able to nap whenever they wanted."

Andy giggled.

"And when the ducklings were old enough, Mama Duck took her babies to swim with the pink swan boats."

Alex drew a breath as if he was going to argue the swan color again, but Andy shushed him.

The book was almost done. Zeke was almost home free. He stared at the last page, confused. "Wait a minute. I thought there were five ducklings." Zeke turned the last page back and forth.

"He's right there." Andy pointed to the shrubbery at the bookbinding.

"I see him now." Zeke nodded. "Behind Mr. Rooster."

"They aren't going to end *Mama Duck, Papa Duck* with a lost duckling," Sophie called from the alcove.

Zeke caught Andy's eye and whispered, "I wonder what that adventurous duckling has been up to."

Andy giggled.

Alex didn't. *"Mo-om!"*

"The end." Zeke closed the book, brimming with relief. "Time for breakfast."

"You are a very silly man." Alex scowled. And then he tossed his hands and shouted, "You didn't read a word in that book!"

"Shh," Zeke said softly. "Use your indoor voice."

Better yet, don't point out I didn't read at all.

"You're wearing two cowboy boots?" Andy stared down at Zeke's footwear.

"Yep." His cowboy boot wasn't as supportive of his leg as the walking boot, but he felt sturdier on his feet, the better to chase after young boys.

Andy grinned. "Now you can hop-race the stairs with us. I bet I beat you."

"I like Andrew's odds." Mitch took a seat on a stool at the check-in desk.

Laurel disappeared in their apartment.

"Breakfast is ready." Sophie deposited two bowls on the coffee table, saving Zeke from letting Andy down about any racing.

"Oaty-meal!" Andy scrambled off Zeke's lap.

Alex lingered, brown eyes serious. "You do know that's not how the book goes."

Zeke nodded. "I was just having fun."

"Okay." Alex slid to the floor. "But next time you read it for real."

Zeke's stomach turned as if he'd eaten bad oaty-meal.

Shane appeared, having sneaked his way down the stairs on silent boards. "Zeke. Get up out of your chair and come with me." Sophie's brother didn't wait for Zeke's answer. He crossed the room and grabbed his coat.

"Where are you going?" Zeke didn't get up. "Sophie's leaving for work after the boys eat."

Shane thrust his arms in his jacket. "The Bucking Bull Ranch. You work there, right?"

"I'm on hiatus. I work for Sophie now." At least until she realized he couldn't read. Franny Clark, his boss at the Bucking Bull, knew Zeke couldn't read.

"Shane." Sophie looked nonplussed. "You can't just steal my nanny."

Was it wrong to feel flattered that Sophie fought for him?

It was. Zeke smiled nonetheless.

"We talked about this yesterday, sister dear." Shane pulled his car key from his pocket. "You said I could take the boys."

"I suppose I did." Sophie didn't look happy about it. She held a slip of paper in her hand and stared at it.

"To a ranch?" Andy beamed at Shane, oatmeal on his chin. "Where they have horses?"

"Do they have bulls, too? Like Ferdinand and Buttercup?" Alex had oatmeal drips on his chest.

"The bulls are in the high pasture this time of year." Except for old Buttercup, who had his own stall. Zeke wiped both boys clean with a napkin Sophie had left on the coffee table. "We had other plans, Shane. We were going to go sledding. Kids need routine." Plus if they went to the ranch, Franny might let on he couldn't read. Shane wouldn't be as kind as Sophie with his secret.

"He's got a point." Sophie earned another smile from Zeke.

Shane's brows lowered. "Hang on—"

"Shane," Mitch interrupted, his expression darker than Shane's. "I thought we agreed now that we're working together and you're an honorary town council member that you'd stop your interrogation of people in town."

"I said I'd stop *interviewing* people who *sold* their property to my grandfather." Shane's smile gave away he knew he'd taken advantage of a technicality in their truce. "Don't get uptight, Kincaid. The Clarks didn't sell, and Gertie Clark is a descendent of Old Jeb. Wasn't it just yesterday you agreed the fight between

Old Jeb and Merciless Mike Moody might add color to our application for historical significance? I can get more details from Gertie."

"I doubt that." Mitch exchanged a knowing look with Zeke. "Gertie isn't—"

"No need for you to fret or come with me." Shane cut Mitch off at the pass. Not surprising given Shane wasn't exactly a team player. "I'll be on my best behavior and report back if I learn anything we can use. Besides, aren't you doing a phone interview with a doctor this morning? You know how important it is to get a doctor up here."

"Your timing becomes clear." Mitch gave Shane a hard stare. "We'll go *after* my interview."

"Sorry," Shane said. "I can't wait. I'm going to be helping Sophie stage the trading post later."

"You are?" Sophie laughed but it seemed strained. "By all means, take my boys and my nanny. I'm coming out ahead on this deal."

Zeke's mouth dropped open. Forget that Gertie's condition wasn't conducive to an interview. "What would Young's Academy say about broken routine?"

"They'd say disruption is balanced by new experiences, I suppose." Sophie handed Zeke a slip of paper. "Here's a list of activities I approve of when you're in the town proper."

"Not that I'll need the list today." Zeke folded the paper and shoved it in the back pocket of his jeans without attempting to read it.

Sophie stared at him, adjusting her glasses. "You might need it later."

"Then I'll look at it later," Zeke lied.

"Let Shane go visit the Clarks, babe." Laurel wrapped her arms around Mitch, her sparkly engagement ring flashing in the light. "You can trust him."

Mitch laid a hand over Laurel's. "Everyone says that, but Shane's still a maverick where your grandfather is concerned. And Gertie is—"

"Now that that's settled." Shane drew his nephews to their feet. "Let's get a move on. I'll warm up the SUV. Zeke, you get the twins bundled up."

Zeke exchanged another glance with Mitch. Yep, presumptuous Shane was going to get what he deserved when he met Gertie.

"Can you come here a minute, Zeke?" Sophie called from the kitchen alcove.

"Sure." Zeke came to stand in the doorway.

Sophie tugged him close enough that he could smell her delicate perfume. "I told Shane yesterday he could take the boys but I'm having second thoughts about bulls and…" She lowered her voice to a whisper. "You know they can find trouble in an empty room. You'll keep them safe, won't you?" Her brown eyes were wide and pleading.

"I'll return them with all their fingers and toes." It seemed natural to run a hand through the curls near her ear, to cup his palm at the base of her neck, to move close enough to kiss. "I promise."

He shouldn't kiss her. He wouldn't kiss her. Except he didn't seem to be stepping back and her gaze dropped to his lips and—

"Come on, Zeke!" one of the twins called, saving him from crossing a line.

"Everything's under control," he said, more for his benefit than Sophie's as he made his retreat and tried to appear as if nothing out of the ordinary had happened.

It didn't take long for them to get strapped into Shane's big black Hummer.

They hadn't even passed the Bent Nickel when Shane asked, "How's Sophie doing?"

"Is this a trick question?" Zeke tugged his seat belt as Shane accelerated toward the first bend in the road. "You just saw her."

And I nearly kissed her.

"She looked fine, but she's always such a trouper that it's hard to tell." Shane appeared unconcerned that he was about to take a corner too fast for such a tall vehicle.

Reflexively, Zeke pumped an imaginary brake, making Shane laugh.

"My sister is too softhearted. And she's a team player. Not that she likes sports. I mean, she'd go to a game if I asked her, but she'd much rather be at a museum." Shane cast Zeke another glance as they emerged safely out of the curve. "She wouldn't be opening the trading post if Laurel hadn't asked. And she probably wouldn't have hired you if you hadn't offered."

His punch landed and stung. Zeke jabbed back. "You don't give her enough credit. She lights up when she's digging through all that—"

"Careful," Shane warned. And he wasn't cautioning himself about accelerating into another bend. The man would have made an excellent barrel racer, if he could ride and it had been a man's sport. "Don't call it junk."

"I was going to say *history*." Zeke kept a firm grip on the door handle and glanced back to the twins, who seemed immune to their uncle's poor driving skills. "History is her passion, not just art. Managing all that stuff Harlan left behind… She's in her element."

"And what happens when all his junk is gone?"

Shane's words chilled Zeke. It was a timely

reminder that kisses and Sophie shouldn't occupy the same thought in his head.

Shane turned onto the Bucking Bull's drive and slowed down to a more reasonable speed. And then he stopped completely next to a large fir tree with a huge gash in front. "Is that where you had your wreck?"

"Yeah." Zeke gave it a cursory glance. His healed leg throbbed. "We don't need to stop and take selfies."

Shane gave him an assessing glance and then gave the SUV some gas, but not much. The road hadn't been plowed and had more than a foot of accumulated snow on it.

They drove past a small frozen lake and several cabins that used to house a summer camp. The road switched back and forth, ascending the mountain, snow deeper and deeper on the road. But nothing was stopping Shane or his Hummer.

Finally, they pulled up in front of the ranch house, safe and sound. Zeke unbuckled the twins and together the foursome climbed the porch steps.

Davey Clark opened the door before they could ring the bell. The family Labrador, Bolt, stood next to him. "It's Zeke and those little Monroe boys." His gray eyes caught sight of

Shane. "And one of them big Monroes. Should I let him in?"

"Your reputation precedes you," Zeke murmured to Shane, who was frowning.

"Davey, show some manners." That was Franny Clark, Davey's mom, and the woman who ran the Bucking Bull. Footsteps echoed on the hardwood and then there was Zeke's old boss, wearing a chunky knit beige sweater and a welcoming smile. She stepped onto the porch, took Zeke by the arm and led him inside as if he was fragile. "You should have told me you were coming, Zeke. I would've plowed the road." She kept a plow attachment on one of the ranch trucks during winter.

Franny didn't let go of Zeke until she had him settled in a chair next to her grandmother-in-law, Gertie. Bolt rested his head on Zeke's knee and stared at him with dark, love-me eyes. The twins followed Davey to a small desk in the corner with the family computer. His two younger brothers were playing a video game.

Zeke leaned over and kissed Gertie's wrinkled cheek. "Where's Emily?" Franny's sister-in-law.

"She's breaking ice at the lake so the herd has water." Franny retrieved a stack of envelopes from the desk. "I have your mail. Do you need any help—"

Reading it?

"No." Zeke shot out of his seat, stuffing his mail in his jacket pocket and ignoring Franny's worried glance. "How is Pandora? Boys, do you want to see my horse?"

Five pairs of boyish feet ran for the door.

CHAPTER TEN

SHANE HAD NEVER seen Zeke move so fast.

The cowboy was out the door before Shane could rib him for missing his horse. He was followed by all the kids in the house—the three Clark boys and Shane's two nephews. The old Labrador curled up on a rug in the foyer.

Shane was left with Francis Clark and a woman who appeared to be her grandmother. It was better than he'd hoped. They could talk freely about Grandpa Harlan. Perhaps he'd finally understand why the fate of Second Chance was in his hands.

Shane introduced himself to both women, reminding Francis, "We met the day Zeke was hurt."

Francis had driven Zeke into town—they'd had a doctor back then—and Shane had called 911 while Doc had stanched the bleeding, administered antibiotics and stabilized Zeke's broken leg for transport. Francis had a bump on her head, having struck the steering wheel when she rear-ended Zeke on the icy road. Today, she looked none the worse for wear.

"I remember you." Francis was a slender woman about Shane's age. She was wiry, perhaps from the physical demands of working a ranch. She wore no makeup and her brown hair was pulled back in a messy knot at the base of her neck. She was dressed in leggings beneath a chunky sweater and thick wool socks that were pulled midcalf. All in all, she was dressed for a day at home without visitors. "You didn't drive all this way for Zeke to visit Pandora."

Add *blunt* to the list of words describing her.

"Second Chance is a small town. You can guess why I'm here." Shane gazed around at the living area of the ranch house. The high ceilings and barnwood walls, the comfortable, outdated furnishings, the large, scarred oak table. The home spoke of better times for the Clarks. "I wanted to meet the family who turned down a buyout offer from my grandfather."

Both women made scoffing noises, but neither elaborated. Or smiled.

Shane wasn't deterred. If there was one constant in Second Chance, it was the imprint of Harlan Monroe. Shane had found pictures of his grandfather in several homes. His baby quilt was on display above Odette's fireplace. She claimed to be a relative, although she'd refused to admit to Shane how she was related. What tie did the Clarks have to Grandpa Harlan? And how could Shane use that to his advantage?

He glanced around once more. There were family photographs on the mantel. He moved closer. There were three wedding photos on one side, each of a different couple.

"Those are my grandparents. And that's my husband's parents—Gertie and Percy. And me." Francis stroked a finger down the side of a pearl frame encasing her wedding photograph.

Her husband wore a white military uniform. Francis wore a simple white gown and had glowed with happiness. Today, she seemed to carry grief on her shoulders.

Shane felt a tug inside, a compulsion to stare at her face a bit longer. He ignored it.

The other side of the mantel held photographs of two smiling girls, their arms roped around each other, three young boys sitting on the back of an old swayback horse and a huge bull with a faded blue ribbon stuck to the simple wood frame.

Again, Francis explained, "That's my sister-in-law, Emily, and me. We were best friends as kids. My boys—Davey, Charlie and Adam. And the bull is Buttercup. He's our main breeder and was my husband's pride and joy. Buttercup is a retired bucking bull rodeo champion, a legend on the circuit."

"I thought only cowboys got to be rodeo legends."

Gertie snorted.

"We make our bread and butter off angry bulls only the elite can stay on for eight seconds." Her voice rang with pride. "Everyone on the rodeo circuit knows the kind of stock the Bucking Bull can provide."

"That's a big task for a handful of women alone in the mountains."

Gertie snorted again.

"Clarks don't give up," Francis said tightly. "Nothing can break us."

Shane looked at her, not knowing what to say. Her eyes were a soft gray and filled with equal measures of pain and strength. Francis still hurt, and she didn't care if he, a stranger, knew it.

"I'm sorry for your loss," Shane said gruffly. It was time he got down to business. No telling how long it would take Zeke to visit his horse. He sat to Gertie's right. "I'd like to talk to you about my grandfather."

Gertie gave him an odd look. Her white hair was cropped short and her expression pulled down on one side in disapproval.

"Granny Gertie suffered a stroke a few days

after Christmas," Francis explained, rubbing the old woman's back. "She's going to be fine, but she's working on her speech."

That explained the half frown and the silence, as well as Mitch's attempt to warn Shane about Gertie.

Shane nodded. "Will it frustrate Gertie to be asked questions?"

"Pfft." Gertie grabbed his forearm and squeezed. She had a strong grip. "You. A-a-ask."

"Thank you." Shane grinned. "Just because I ask, I don't expect you to answer." He glanced up at Francis. "Very few people like to talk about my grandfather."

"I never met him." Francis had the most amazing eyes.

The more Shane looked into them, the more he felt curious about their depths. "Why did you turn his buyout offer down?"

"He didn't make us an offer," Francis said flatly, gaze drifting to her wedding photograph.

"Pfft," Gertie said again, narrowing her faded gray eyes. She made a fist with her right hand and pounded the chair arm. "Arruft."

"Ha." Shane smiled at the older woman, interpreting her reaction. "Wounded your pride, did he? By not making an offer?" Maybe Shane needed to swallow his pride and talk to Egbert again.

"No." Gertie didn't want to discuss it. She sliced her right hand through the air.

Not wanting to upset her, Shane switched tactics. "Gertie, you must have known my grandfather."

"Hhhandsa." Gertie pointed to Shane.

Not that again. "You ladies in Second Chance all seem to think my grandfather was handsome and slick with the ladies." Shane hoped he was reading the old woman's signals right. "Did you ever go on a date with my grandfather?" He leaned closer and whispered, "You can tell me. I won't tell Francis."

"Ha!" Gertie beamed. She'd been a looker when she was younger. It was there in the delicate curve of her cheekbone and her petite features.

"Granny Gertie!" Francis sounded shocked.

"No." Gertie waved off her granddaughter-in-law's shock. *"Ho..."* She swallowed and tried again. *"Ha..."*

"I know who you mean." His grandfather. Shane patted her arm. "Did he break your heart?"

"No... Yes." Her smile fell. She waved a hand around Shane's face and then pointed out the window. She gave an exaggerated half shrug and tapped hand over her heart. "Left."

Shane tried to interpret her message. "You were friends. And he went off to see the world. And you missed him."

"Yes." Gertie blew out a breath. "No." She rolled her eyes again. "Mon-*roes*."

Francis stood next to Gertie reminding him of a guard dog, one with messy hair and soulful eyes. "This is more than Granny has spoken at one time since the stroke. I don't want you to tire her out."

"Argh." Gertie's lopsided frown deepened.

"Are you tired, Granny? Have you had enough questions for one day?"

"Pfft." Eye roll. Significant glance to Shane.

The old woman wanted to talk some more.

Shane turned toward his hostess. "Do you think I could trouble you for a cup of coffee?"

Francis had a frown as fierce as Gertie's, but she had small-town hospitality. She didn't refuse.

When she disappeared into the kitchen, Shane faced Gertie once more. "Now we can talk in private. Would you have sold if Harlan had offered?"

"No." Gertie swirled her hand over her head. "Home."

"Yes, it's your home. But I bet the money would have made things easier on your family."

"Li-fee har-rd." Gertie's wrinkled face reddened with the effort to speak.

Shane agreed. "Yes, life is hard." He leaned toward Gertie and took her hand. It was both soft and leathery at the same time, the hands of a woman who'd spent her life working outdoors. "Everyone who sold their property to my grandfather signed a legal document forbidding them to discuss anything about my grandfather."

She nodded. She knew.

"That means legally they can't answer my questions. But you aren't bound to silence."

Gertie tapped her lips. She may not legally have been sworn to silence, but there were physical bonds to break through.

Shane shook his head. "You're smarter than that."

"Pish." She gave him that fierce half scowl.

He sat back. "I'm not sure if you just told me off or just vented your frustration."

Gertie held up two fingers.

"Both." Shane laughed.

The old woman smiled.

The sounds of coffee dripping into a pot drifted from the kitchen. Time was running out.

"My grandfather didn't tell us why he left us Second Chance. Do you know?"

She hesitated a moment, and then nodded.

He'd need more time to interpret her limited vocabulary to get his answers. "Can you write it out?"

She shook her head, made a fist and pounded it gently on the arm of the chair. He took that to be frustration over her inability to communicate with the ease she had prior to her stroke.

"Francis said you were on the mend. You'll get your speech back." He hoped, for both her sake and his.

The old woman stared at the ceiling, irritation evident in every line on her face.

"In the meantime, I can come visit."

Gertie laughed. And then she leaned forward and patted Shane's knee.

"I guess you just got yourself a regular gentleman caller." Shane smiled.

"We're much too busy to regularly entertain." Francis gave him a cup of coffee and a go-away frown.

"Don't." Gertie stared up at her granddaughter-in-law.

"Do you need help around the ranch?" Putting on his most easy-going smile, Shane glanced at Francis, steeling himself not to get sucked into the depths of her eyes.

Francis pointed at Shane's snow boots. "I

couldn't in good conscience accept help from a man who didn't have the right gear."

"I can buy cowboy boots."

"Zeke will be back," Francis said confidently. The grief was gone from her eyes and in its place was an unshakable confidence. This was the woman who handled the responsibilities of the ranch.

Shane felt the need to prod her. "Zeke has a job. He's babysitting my nephews for my sister."

Gertie laughed.

His adversary's gaze hardened. "Zeke's baby-sitting?"

"Yeah. You know. He plays games, makes sure they get fed and reads books to them."

Francis said nothing. She probably didn't approve, possibly because the Monroes had stolen her cowhand.

Shane tried again. "I could help out a little in his place. Perhaps in exchange for some information about my grandfather?" He'd seldom found first rounds of negotiations to be indicative of eventual agreements. "Is this something we can negotiate over a cup of coffee?" He raised his mug and his smile.

"No." Francis shifted her weight and gave her grandmother a hard stare. "My grandmother can't alienate the town by telling you anything. It's best you don't come around anymore."

"Pfft." Gertie didn't agree.

"That's my final word on the subject." Francis crossed her arms and stared at the door.

They were at an impasse.

CHAPTER ELEVEN

"THIS IS REALLY your horse?" Standing next to Pandora, Alex tilted his head upward. "She's huge."

"To you, maybe," Davey said from the top of the metal stall door. He rested the elbow of his left arm on his thigh, stub at the end of his wrist on display.

At only fifteen and a half hands, Pandora wasn't what any cowboy would call tall. But she was a lot taller than either Davey or Andy.

"Manners, Davey," Zeke reminded the oldest Clark boy absently. He was distracted, wondering if Sophie would leave when her inventory ran out. Even odds. That was about as likely as Franny telling Shane he couldn't read. Franny liked to butt in when she thought folks needed taking care of.

I don't need anyone.

Zeke shrugged deeper in his jacket. The barn wasn't heated.

"Manners," Davey huffed. "That's what my mom always says."

"Granny Gertie does, too," Charlie piped up. "At least, she used to before she got stroked."

"Before she had a stroke," Zeke gently corrected. He may not be a competent reader, but his parents had insisted he speak well. Or at least, his dad had.

"Can we ride her?" Andy tugged Zeke's hand.

"Sure." Zeke lifted Andy onto Pandora's bare back. She'd had a soft winter and was plenty wide. "Hold on to her mane."

"I've been brushing her every day." Davey was a mature nine-year-old, a true help around the ranch with the stock that wasn't destined for the rodeo. "Charlie's been sneaking her oats."

Zeke smiled. That explained Pandora's girth.

"Horses like oats," protested Charlie with such vehemence he nearly fell backward off the stall door.

Davey righted him before Zeke could. "Oats make horses fat in winter."

Alex tugged on Zeke's hand and pointed at his brother. "Me, too?"

Zeke lifted him onto Pandora's back behind Andy. His mare swung her head around, rubbing it against Zeke's jacket. "Yeah, I missed you, too."

"Are you coming back soon?" Davey asked. "It's almost spring. Emily's bringing heifers down for calving soon."

"He's not coming back." Andy looked down his nose at Davey. "He's not a cowboy anymore."

"He's our nanny," Alex said, just as stubbornly.

"I told your mother I'd watch you for a month or until she found someone else." Or she fired him. "And I always keep my word. But I also promised Franny I'd be back this spring."

The twins pouted.

Pandora swished her tail. She swished and swished, finally hitting Alex in the face.

He jolted, feet flying out and then back to her sides in a swift kick.

The mare stomped her rear foot and shifted quickly, still wielding her tail. Alex lost his balance, grabbed his brother's jacket and then they began to fall off the far side of the horse.

Zeke managed to grab each boy by the ankle, but Pandora was no help. She pranced out from under them. Luckily, Zeke was able to let them down easy in the straw.

"Are you okay?" he asked his wide-eyed

charges. "Fingers and toes intact?" It seemed appropriate to use Sophie's safety check.

The twins nodded.

Davey laughed. "They landed in manure."

His brothers joined in on the fun, chortling.

Alex and Andy turned to look at each other, noticed their heads were in muck, screamed and scrambled to their feet.

"Hang on." Zeke grabbed on to their shoulders, much the way he had when they'd wanted to pretend fight yesterday as Old Jeb and Merciless Mike Moody. "It washes off."

Andy tugged, trying to free himself. He glared at Davey. "You did that on purpose."

"Davey's not to blame. It was my fault." Zeke shouldn't have put them up on Pandora's back without there being a saddle to hold on to. "Davey, open the stall door."

"Mom is going to be mad," Andy promised. "Real mad. At you, Zeke."

"I bet." The worst part about telling Sophie wasn't going to be her angels having fallen into manure. It was going to be their falling. Period. Zeke bet nannies trained at Young's Academy didn't let their charges sink in manure.

"I'm mad at you," Andy huffed, glaring at Zeke.

"Get it off me," Alex pleaded, shivering. Manure fell in clumps off the back of his head.

"Give me a minute," Zeke said.

Once they were outside the stall, Zeke removed their jackets. Manure was caked on their hair, their necks and their shirt collars. Zeke took off their shirts next, shaking the fabric free of dung and then turning the shirts inside out to brush down their hair and necks.

Davey hadn't stopped laughing. "This is better than the time Charlie fell in the lake."

His laughter drove Andy to wail, and then the little boy's wails turned into tears.

"Davey," Zeke said sternly. "Laughing at people isn't nice. Go find these boys some clean shirts and a sweatshirt or old jacket to keep them warm."

"Yes, sir." Davey sobered and hightailed it back to the house. He knew when to call it quits.

Charlie and Adam followed him.

"Hey." Zeke leaned over until his nose nearly touched Andy's. "Cowboys don't cry, especially when they aren't hurt."

Andy pressed his lips together and tried to stop crying.

"But we're not cowboys." Alex snuffled.

That sent Andy back over the edge of tears. So much for reasoning with them.

Zeke led the boys to the back of the barn

where there was a hose. He turned it on and took a squirt of liquid soap that was on the shelf. The water was icy, but there was no way he was taking Sophie's kids home in Shane's fancy SUV covered in horse manure.

"Lean over so I can wash it out of your hair," Zeke instructed.

Alex did as he was told, whimpering.

"I remember the first time I fell off a horse." Zeke gave the boy's hair and neck a quick rinse, soaped him up and then rinsed him off again. "I was riding my mom's bony old mare bareback. Misty jumped over a fallen tree in the pasture and left me behind." Sprawled on a log.

"You fell off a horse?" Andy couldn't believe it. "But you're a cowboy."

"You know what they say about cowboys?" Zeke removed his jacket and button-down, using the checked outer shirt to dry Alex off. He put the boy into his jacket and had him stand away from the water. "If you haven't fallen off a horse and got back on, you aren't one."

Andy sidled toward the water. "You fell off more than once?"

Get back on that horse, boy. His father scowled at a young Zeke, who was sprawled on the ground, elbow scraped and stinging.

Shaking off the memory, Zeke set about getting Andy clean. "I can't count the number of times I've fallen off." Or the number of times he'd been on the receiving end of his father's brand of tough love. "I bet when you were little and learning how to walk you fell down a lot. Didn't stop you from walking, did it?"

Andy processed his words in silence. Or perhaps he was just gritting his teeth against the cold water. He waited until Zeke was drying him off to ask, "Did your T-shirt get a hole from falling off a horse?"

Zeke glanced down at his faded blue T-shirt. He'd forgotten it had a hole near the hem. "No. That tore when I was fixing a barbed wire fence in the high country last spring." Zeke made clothes last as long as he could.

Davey returned, carrying dry clothes. Shane and Franny were right behind him.

"Do we have to get back on?" Alex looked small and scared in Zeke's oversize jacket.

Zeke's father would have said yes. But these were city kids, used to comfy temperature-controlled playrooms and tidy, tucked-in clothes.

"Do you want to get back on?" Zeke asked instead.

Both boys shook their head.

"ZEKE IS REALLY good with the boys." Laurel swept dust out the trading post doorway, pausing to lean on the broom. They'd cleaned a good deal of what was going to be the retail space.

Roy had lit a fire in the fireplace. The trading post was warm for the first time since Sophie had been poking around inside.

"Just look at Zeke." Laurel pointed across the road. "He's having as much fun as the twins are."

Sophie was disinfecting the counter. She glanced up. She'd heard Shane's SUV return a few minutes earlier. Now she heard laughter.

Zeke threw snowballs at the twins, who were hiding out of Sophie's sight on the other side of Shane's SUV. Zeke tossed gentle lobs that had the boys squealing gleefully, a sound that punctuated his deep laughter and made something inside Sophie sigh with longing.

Not for Zeke specifically… Although she'd been sure he'd been about to kiss her in the inn's alcove earlier. Although she'd been disappointed he hadn't.

"A guy like Zeke would make a great husband and father." Laurel passed a hand over her baby bump.

"Don't." Sophie went back to scrubbing years of grime off the counter.

"I'm sorry if…" Laurel grinned. "It would just be great if you'd stay here in town with me."

"I thought that's what I was doing. Opening up the trading post." Leaving her past behind. "Why do I need a man?"

She resisted the temptation to glance up at Zeke once more.

We're different.

It felt like a lie.

"You can leave anytime." Laurel came over to lean her elbows on the counter. "You could hire someone to run this place. I know you. Art is your thing. City life is your thing."

Sophie didn't deny it. Instead, she turned her cousin's words around. "A month ago, I would have said Hollywood was your thing."

Her cousin had successfully designed costumes for movies and sewn evening gowns for the red carpet.

Laurel's gaze turned rueful and her chin dipped. "I won't be wearing red carpet dresses anymore. Although I won't rule out sewing another premiere-worthy gown." She lifted her head and her smile. "You can find it in your heart to love more than one thing, I hope. I'm selfish. I want you to be happy, but I want you to be happy here with me."

"I'm trying." Sophie was happy. She'd been spending more time with the boys than she had since her maternity leave. She loved that. It made her feel like a good mom.

And then there was a tall, ginger-haired cowboy...

"That's all I can ask." Laurel came around the counter to stand next to Sophie, which was an invitation to hug, at least in Sophie's book.

Laughter from across the street drifted up to them.

"Pretty soon, there won't be any more Sled Hill." Sophie shook her head. She hadn't imagined being in Second Chance this long or even long term.

"Won't that be weird? Second Chance without any snow." Laurel rubbed her tummy. "I just had the strongest craving for pepperoni pizza."

"Don't say that in front of the boys." There was no pizza parlor in Second Chance, other than the kind that came in boxes in the frozen foods section. And they'd discovered those didn't taste so great when cooked in the microwave. Just one more reason to move out of the inn and into a place of their own. But moving meant staying. And staying meant no more Monets, Cartier diamonds, Wedgwood china...

Laurel's gaze turned distant. "I'd top my

pizza with fresh tomatoes and cooked broccoli. And kale. Lots and lots of kale."

"I suppose if you're going to dream, dream big." Vegetables on pizza wasn't Sophie's thing, unless she counted olives. "When Cam gets here—" an arrival her brother kept delaying "—he'll make us all sorts of good food." He was a master chef.

"His risotto is like heaven." Laurel rubbed her baby bump again.

"I'm partial to his desserts." Sophie met Laurel's gaze.

"Tiramisu," they both said together.

Male laughter drew Sophie's attention again. Zeke had one boy tucked under each arm and was walking back to the inn, carrying them like sacks of potatoes. There was only a small hitch to his stride.

And a big hitch in her heart.

"I think it's time for a break," Sophie announced. She wanted to hear how the day was going for her boys.

Laurel followed the direction of Sophie's gaze. "Do you need time alone with your cowboy? I can watch a movie with your adorable little heathens."

"Don't start." Sophie tied the ends of a trash bag and carried it to the door.

"I can't start what's already begun." Her cousin tsked. "You can fool yourself some of the time, Sophie. But you can't fool me when it comes to love."

Sophie was afraid Laurel was right. Didn't mean she had to act on those feelings. There was too much in her life that was uncertain.

They closed up both buildings and made their way down the short slope and across the street to the inn. More laughter greeted them as they hung up their coats and stomped what little snow there was from their boots.

Zeke sat on the couch bookended by her sons, smiling indulgently. His arms were draped casually over their shoulders, but there was nothing casual about the way the image made her heart race and her mouth dry.

This is how fathers are supposed to be.

Sophie had the strongest urge to join them on the couch, to seek out Zeke's gaze, to be included in the warmth of his indulgent smile. And she wasn't even hormonal, like Laurel.

She stayed where she was near the door and adjusted her glasses.

"You did not land in a pile of manure," Gabby was saying.

Laurel hadn't noticed the preteen sat on the fireplace hearth.

"Uh-huh." Andrew popped off the couch and propped his hands on his hips. His fighting position.

"I'm not arguing with you, silly." Gabby patted the empty space next to her on the stone hearth. "I'm admiring you for not crying about it."

Andrew hesitated, and then sat down beside her, glancing tentatively at Zeke. "Cowboys don't cry about getting dirty or falling off horses."

Oh, there'd been tears, all right.

Sophie's breath caught in her throat.

Details began registering. Andrew and Alexander wore red hooded sweatshirts she'd never seen before. They were too large. The waistbands hung midthigh. Horses. Manure.

"You were on a horse?" The Mama Bear inside Sophie roused itself from hibernation and growled. "I don't recall giving anyone permission to ride a horse."

"No, ma'am. You did not." Zeke stood. He was tall and looked fit enough to ride a horse. "But there was no riding. It was more like *sitting on top of* a horse. And they looked mighty fine on Pandora's back, let me tell you." He took stock of her expression and paused. Cleared his throat. "Anyway… One thing led to another. Pandora flicked her tail and—"

"My babies fell off a horse!" Sophie hurried to the couch, pulled Alexander to his feet and gave him a thorough examination that had him squirming to get free, proclaiming he was fine at the top of his lungs. "Are you hurt? Holy mackerel. There's no doctor in town if you're hurt." She turned her attention to Andrew, cradling his face in her hands. There were no gashes or bruises and his eyes weren't dilated.

"I'm fine, Mom." Andrew sounded like he was Gabby's age—twelve, not four.

"They're both fine." Zeke laid a hand on her shoulder.

Sophie shrugged his touch away. "What were you thinking? Nowhere on that list I gave you this morning was there the words *horse* or *ride*. Did you even read the list?" And because she was scared and furious, she added, "Or is that giving you too much credit?"

His eyes narrowed and even though they still stood touching distance apart, he looked as if he'd moved to another state. "I was thinking that encouraging kids to explore and try new things would be approved by Young's Academy." His voice came out hard.

She'd wounded his pride.

She didn't care. Her babies had fallen off a horse! "Is this a joke to you?"

"No, ma'am."

"Mom." Alexander took her hand. "It's okay. Only my head fell in manure."

The world turned fuzzy around the edges. She tried not to gag.

Monroes didn't fall into piles of farm animal excrement.

Sophie swallowed. *"Manure?"*

Laurel began to chuckle, covering her mouth when Sophie glared at her.

"That was our vocabulary word today," Zeke said, straight-faced. *"Manure."*

"That's horse poo, Mom," Andrew explained with a note of pride.

Sophie pressed her glasses against her face with both palms and wished she had the nerve to press her hands over her ears. The germs... The filth... "Boys, get upstairs right now. You're taking a bath."

"Don't worry." Shane appeared at the bottom of the stairs, no doubt drawn by her fishwife shrieking. "Zeke cleaned them off with soap and a garden hose before they got in my Hummer. And then the Clarks loaned them some clean clothes."

"And that's it? Everything's okay now?"

Sophie's words rang in her ears. Every horrified note.

"Yes," Zeke said calmly. "Everything's okay."

It was on the tip of her tongue to fire Zeke.

But everyone was looking at her as if she was the one who'd done something wrong.

Or was about to.

"Outside," she hissed at Zeke. "Now."

"Yes, ma'am." Zeke ambled toward the door, ruffling each boy's hair as he passed. He picked up his cowboy hat off a hook, positioned it firmly on his head and stood with his hand on the door waiting to open it for her.

For two months, he'd sat in a wheelchair in this very room. For two months, she'd paid him little attention because he'd been more like a fixture in the inn than a person. This person. This man. A proud cowboy. A proud, now angry, cowboy. Who didn't look as if he was ready to take an employer's put-down sitting down.

What am I doing?

Everyone in the room stared at Sophie, waiting for her to explode. Horses. A fall. Manure. She had every right to let her feelings rip, let them shoot out toward Zeke like poison-tipped darts.

He could take it. His shoulders were back. His head high.

It was Sophie who couldn't stand to do it. She felt more like imploding, like returning Mama Bear to her hibernation cave, like taking a nice hot bath and then letting all her fear, frustration and worry dissolve and disappear down the drain.

"Sophie?" Zeke's voice. Almost tentative. Almost ready to extend an olive branch.

It was then she noticed the clown. The black velvet painting she'd given him hung on the wall by the door. On display. He'd sold it. Her gift.

Mama Bear refused to return to her cave.

Sophie jammed her arms into her jacket and marched out the door. She marched across the street and up the hill to the trading post, not pausing to make sure Zeke followed her.

He did. Of course he did. Zeke wouldn't shy away from confrontation.

In fact, when she had the door open, the lights on and the door slammed shut behind them, he was the one who started talking. "You have every right to be upset."

"You're darn right, I do." Mama Bear was ready to take a swipe at him, claws drawn.

He took his hat off and turned it around and

around, the picture of a ranch hand asking for forgiveness. "When it happened, the boys were upset, too."

Imagining their distress deflated raging Mama Bear. "They were?" And she hadn't been there to comfort them?

Good moms are always there when kids need comfort.

"Andy especially." Zeke cleared his throat as if he was distraught just thinking about it. "He likes to pretend he's invincible."

How did Zeke know her sons so well?

"And Davey Clark... He's older... And he laughed...a bit."

Sophie's heart constricted for Andrew's ego. Being the only girl with two brothers... She'd been the butt of jokes a time or twenty.

"I had a talk with Davey," Zeke continued. "And I had a talk with the twins. It's important they understand life is going to toss manure your way sometimes. And in the scheme of things, manure isn't worth crying over."

There's more to life than one tumble in manure.

Sophie nodded, even as she felt the anger ebb from her fingers to her toes, leaving her numb and in need of a good cry, because the danger was over, and Mama Bear could settle down.

"If you need to fire me, I'll understand."

Fire him?

How could she fire him when he'd done the right thing?

Other than letting her boys on a horse to begin with. "I'm sorry. I...I've been overreacting. Small-town life is new to me and..."

"I didn't go out to the Bucking Bull expecting to put Andy and Alex on Pandora." In typical Zeke fashion, he didn't make excuses. "They asked. It was a spur-of-the-moment decision."

"The worst decisions are made on the fly and I'm the fly's Exhibit A." Her shoulders sagged. "I came here when my dad disowned me because I thought I'd find peace with my grandfather. And since then, I've hired you and agreed to open this place." Sophie glanced around at the old store counter, the shell of a pedal car, the front end of a classic car.

What will I agree to next?

Zeke was silent for a moment or two. "In your defense, I was the only person available for the babysitting job."

"It's not you I regret." That came out wrong. Sophie hurried on. "I regret agreeing to open this place."

Zeke took a good look around. "I haven't been up here before."

How could he have been? He'd been injured and before that it'd been locked up tighter than the vault at Cartier.

He paced the length of the room, his limp more noticeable.

"I shouldn't have marched you up here. Your leg—"

"Is stiff." He cut her off, banging his hat against his leg. The silver on his hatband caught the light and flashed in Sophie's eyes. "No apologies needed. Getting out and about does me good. But this…" The slow half grin she liked returned. "This reminds me of the feed store back home."

"In a good way?"

"Yeah." His scrutinizing gaze landed on her. "I can see a display of silver baby cups behind the counter. And a display of trophies over there next to some of your antique skates. It'll be really nice. Really nice."

"It's just stuff." But she blushed.

He noticed, of course, because his gaze hadn't left her face. "You know, one year for Christmas, my grandmother gave me a teak statue of a dolphin. We didn't exchange more than a simple gift or two at the holidays, sometimes none at all." He closed the distance between them one step at a time. "My grandmother hadn't wanted me to go without. So she'd wrapped up something she'd kept on her shelves for years. But it was something I'd always admired. The dark color of teak. That dolphin's body arcing in and out of a wave like a bucking bronco. That was the most sophisticated item in our house, excluding my grandmother, who always demanded I wash up for dinner and put on a clean shirt." He stopped an arm's length away.

Sophie stared up at her handsome cowboy nanny, fascinated with him and his story. "And…"

"And—" he shrugged "—I still have that dolphin. It's nothing expensive or fancy, but it means a lot to me. And I think that's what you're doing here. You're giving people a chance to find something that was special to your grandfather and that'll be special to them. I mean—" he shrugged again "—you aren't gonna buy someone else's silver baby cup unless it speaks to you."

It made sense. *He* made sense.

"Unlike you," he went on, "I never had much use for expensive art and paintings. Heck, I've never even been inside a museum, if you don't count the Pro Rodeo Hall of Fame."

And she'd given him a painting. So different… "Did you sell Mitch the clown painting?" Did Mitch love it more than Zeke had?

"No, ma'am." His grin widened. "It's on loan. I thought it'd please more people hanging near the door than in my room."

"Oh. How thoughtful." It was something Grandpa Harlan would have done.

"Here's what I'm getting at." Zeke set his boots more firmly on the floor. "I bet there are more folks around who might be interested in buying affordable keepsakes, like my grandmother's dolphin, than there are folks who're in the market to buy a centuries-old painting that costs more than most people pay for a house."

Sophie blinked, processing his words.

"I mean…" Zeke sidled closer, still holding that hat in front of him, still rotating it around.

He was nervous?

Sophie's hands shook. She thrust them in her jacket pockets.

"What I mean is," he said, clearing his throat. The hand holding the hat dropped to his side and he closed the distance between them. "You stock this store with things people can take home and love at all different price ranges, giving them joy." His words faded but he didn't move away.

All she had to do to get that kiss she was curious about was lean forward and accept the fact that there were differences that pushed people apart and then there were differences that drew them together.

She waited too long because he started talking once more. "What folks buy here may make you feel better about the way things ended between you and your grandfather."

His words struck a chord inside her. "Who are you, Zeke Roosevelt?"

He shrugged, took a step away from her and put the hat back on his head, a signal her opportunity for a kiss had passed. "I'm your cowboy nanny, unless you still want to fire me."

How could she fire him? He was the Wild West version of Mary Poppins, fixing problems she didn't think could be fixed.

CHAPTER TWELVE

SOPHIE COULDN'T SLEEP.

The trading post would never be as posh and luxurious as a museum curator's office. The lack of cachet bothered her, although admittedly not as much since Zeke had shared the touching story about his grandmother's dolphin.

There were treasures to go through downstairs, just as Zeke had said. Items her grandfather had collected over the course of his long life. Grandpa Harlan wouldn't want them to be left in boxes. He'd been adamant his fine art collection was meant to be shared with museums so others could enjoy it. He'd wanted the things he'd collected to have life, to be loved.

And when she looked at Zeke, Sophie longed to venture from her protective shell and risk love and being loved in return. But doing so meant making a choice between being a city Monroe and being a country Monroe. She could open up the trading post and hire someone as a sales clerk, as Laurel had suggested.

Her family would support her no matter what. But if she left, she'd be leaving Zeke behind.

She stared at the ceiling and listened to Andrew's and Alexander's breathing. She listened to the wind push against the Lodgepole Inn's walls. Somewhere outside, an owl called.

Nothing answered.

Because everyone's asleep.

Inside and outside. The Lodgepole Inn was a creaky thing. If someone was up, she'd have heard them.

She hated being awake and unable to work.

If she was quiet, she could go through a box or two without being interrupted.

Sophie got out of bed and put a sweatshirt on over her pajamas and thick socks on her feet. She slipped into the hallway carrying her notebook. Her progress was marked in creaky floorboards. At the top of the stairs, she paused near Shane's door, listening.

The owl hooted outside.

No one upstairs called out to Sophie. Not the boys. Not Shane. The rest of the second floor was empty.

She hugged the stair rail, hoping it was the quieter way down. To her ears, she sounded like a big mouse—no threat, no need for anyone to wake. She flipped on a light and hugged the wall around the corner into the common room, creeping closer to her storage room. Emboldened that no one's sleep seemed disturbed, Sophie quickened her steps, still muffled by her socks.

Finally, she reached the spare room downstairs and turned on the light. Excitement filled her. This was like unpacking art for a special exhibit. She opened the closest box. Inside was a smaller box made of thin wood that held toy soldiers carved from wood and painted. They stood at attention and held swords to their shoulders. Their hats differed, as if they designated rank. And there was a small wooden ball. In modern times, it would be called a child's bowling set. Back when they'd been carved, the game had been called Skittles.

She held up a soldier in a red uniform, admiring the painter's skill in capturing a stern expression.

"The boys will love those." Zeke stood in the doorway to his room. He wore a soft blue T-shirt and a pair of blue jeans. His ginger hair was as rumpled as his smile.

She hadn't wanted to wake anyone, but of all the people in the inn, she welcomed Zeke's company.

What had Zeke said? *Oh, yeah.* "I can't let them play with these. They're antiques."

Zeke raised his brows.

"Maybe just once. Gently." She carefully returned them to their box in the way she'd found them. "This game was made popular by the British royal family over one hundred years ago." She pointed to her notebook and pen on the coffee table. "Can you write something down for me?"

Zeke hesitated, and then moved to do her bidding. But instead of opening the notebook, he handed it to her.

"Sorry." Her cheeks heated. "I didn't mean to treat you like my administrative assistant." He was her nanny and he needed sleep if he was going to work tomorrow. "Please, go back to bed. I didn't mean to wake you." She opened her notebook to a fresh page and scribbled notes about the game. She'd research prices on it later.

He gestured toward the wingback chair. "Why don't you sit, and I'll bring you boxes the way I did the other day. Your notes will be more detailed than mine."

"Are you sure your leg is up to it?"

He scowled at her, at his bare toes and at her again. "Yes."

She sat, much preferring his slow grin to that fierce frown.

"I'll take something else besides an apology." Zeke's frown faded.

A kiss. He wants a kiss.

Her heart pounded and she vowed this time if the opportunity presented itself that she wouldn't hesitate.

Zeke kept his distance. "How did you risk your fingers and toes?" The question was so innocuous but the look in his eyes held a deeper meaning. That look said: *I want to know everything about you and I want you to know everything about me.*

The bottom dropped out of Sophie's stomach. With a deep breath, she pulled herself together again, only to enter Flutterville when he smiled. She tucked her hands out of sight beneath opposite arms. "You know that question is off-limits."

He shrugged. "But I don't know why it should be. Maybe I'll ask Shane."

"Don't you dare." Shane would tell him.

"Rule of three, Sophie. If you don't tell me the third time I ask, I'll have to ask your brother." Zeke brought her a box that contained an assortment of carved zoo animals with ring bases. Some were made of wood, some of ivory. An elephant was carved in jade.

Sophie held one up. "These look like baby rattles or teething rings." They couldn't be. Not when some of them were made out of wood.

Zeke picked up the elephant. "My aunt used

to have fancy napkin ring holders like this. I only saw them once—I only saw her once—but her entire table was decorated like we were on safari."

"If they aren't napkin ring holders, I suppose they could've been used to hold the fabric of a dress." Sophie made note in her book and then wrote "ring holders" on the cardboard flap.

Zeke whisked the animals away and brought her another box. "This one's heavy." He set it on the coffee table, letting her open it.

"It's a strongbox." She set her pen and paper aside. "And it's still locked."

Zeke lifted it out. "It looks like something you'd see in the movies on a stagecoach." He shifted the box side to side. It was empty.

"Merciless Mike Moody," Sophie breathed.

Zeke shook his head. "You've swallowed too much of Egbert's eggnog."

"Come on. This is too big a coincidence. It has to be the bandit's box."

"His *empty* box."

"Mom?" Despite calling her name, Andrew shuffled over to Zeke and raised his arms to be picked up.

Zeke did as requested, wrapping his arms around her son as tenderly as if the boy were his own.

Sophie's heart melted.

Their eyes met.

It was there, she realized. The attraction she'd denied to Laurel days earlier. It was there in the heat of his eyes. He felt more than friendship for her. She imagined a similar passion might be mirrored in her own gaze.

"Is it morning?" Andrew yawned.

"Not yet." Sophie stood. "Let's go back to bed." She placed her notebook on the box and took Andrew into her arms. "Good night, Zeke."

Upstairs, she fell asleep easily, not worrying about how the trading post could be made into a more sophisticated place, but thinking of Zeke and wondering how those strong arms would feel around her.

She imagined it would feel like home.

DAYS AFTER HE and Sophie had explored boxes in the middle of the night, Zeke woke early.

He made coffee and sat in a chair in the common room, recalling the way Sophie's face blossomed with happiness as she sifted through the contents of box after box, the way she glowed when relating tidbits from her past. The more he got to know her, the more he wanted to know.

Shades of shamrocks, rainbows and pots of gold.

She was the last woman in the world he should develop feelings for.

The sound of murmured voices came from Mitch's apartment. Upstairs, one of the twins giggled.

Everyone had someone. Except Zeke.

That wasn't quite true. Zeke had friends in Second Chance. He had a job, today at least. His father was still alive, living in a one-room shack on the land they'd once owned, too stubborn to let Zeke care for him. What Zeke didn't have—what he didn't dare wish for—was a family. He wasn't going to find one with the wealthy, well-educated Monroes. Families like the Monroes expected incoming members to certify their intelligence with college degrees from prestigious universities. He shouldn't dream.

A cowboy's life was mud, blood, guts and unsung glory. Standard stuff. Put in your hours and collect your paycheck.

He'd received his first paycheck from Sophie. He'd signed it over to Mack so she could order the last of his truck parts. What he had to do next was stop smiling at Sophie every time she got excited about something in one of those boxes. He had to stop letting his gaze linger on hers or drop to her lips. And he definitely had to stop all thoughts about kissing said lips.

The pragmatic side of him couldn't wait for Sophie to hire a more appropriate nanny. The romantic side of him hoped Shane was right and she'd never convince someone from Young's Academy to work in Idaho.

Sophie's notebook sat on the coffee table.

Zeke reached for it. He flipped through the pages, admiring Sophie's loopy letters and the jumble of words. So many words.

"Did Sophie give you permission to read that?" Shane appeared at the corner of the common room, having descended the stairs on silent feet.

"No." Zeke closed the notebook and tossed it back on the coffee table.

"What does it matter if he reads it or not?" Mitch opened the doorway to his apartment. He held an empty coffee mug. "Are there secrets to the Monroe fortune in there?"

"Kincaid…" Shane shook his head. "If I wasn't coffeeless this morning… If you weren't going to marry my cousin… I'd have a great comeback for you. One that really stung."

"Instead, in the comeback department, you stink." Mitch gave Shane an expression that was almost a smile. "Get yourself a cup of brew and try again later."

"Thank you." Shane smirked.

"Besides, you seem to need it more than I do." Mitch got in the last word.

Shane disappeared into the kitchenette as the familiar sound of four-year-old bunnies hopping down the stairs filled the inn.

"Zeke!" Alex ran across the common room and leaned against Zeke's leg, digging his elbows into Zeke's thigh. "I brought my favorite book for you to read." He turned the cover toward Zeke.

Who didn't have to read to recognize the book.

Mama Duck, Papa Duck.

Zeke smiled to cover a sigh and lifted the boy into his lap.

"You promised to read it for real," Alex said.

Zeke had been evading that promise for days.

"Zeke!" Andy ran to join them, wriggling into his lap.

The boys smelled of soap. Their hair was slicked back. Zeke knew the clean look wouldn't last. There'd be oaty-meal stains on their shirts and twigs in their hair by noon. They may have been born in Philadelphia, but they were turning into rough-and-tumble mountain kids.

Sophie poked her head around the corner with an expression that was too serious for this early in the morning. Had she heard Shane asking Zeke if he'd read her notebook?

"Read," Alex demanded.

"Read," Andy echoed.

Zeke lowered his voice to Roy's gravelly octave. "There was once a big, bad wolf."

Both boys did a double take, looking at each other, openmouthed. Jerking their awestruck stares at Zeke, and then returning to look at each other.

"This is *Mama Duck, Papa Duck*," Alex said.

"I know," Zeke said in his regular voice. "Let's use our imaginations to tell this story." *Tell*, not read. He opened the book. "It was known far and wide that the big, bad wolf ate eggs for breakfast. He was particularly fond of *duck* eggs." Zeke turned a page and pointed to the female mallard. "Now, Mama Duck… She knew she was going to lay some eggs and she wanted them to be safe. Because that's what mamas do. They protect their young. So, she and her husband went out looking for a safe place to raise their babies."

Andy turned the page and pointed. "They flew to a farm, but a big dog scared them away."

He pitched his voice low, like Papa Duck. "This place is no good. It's too scary."

Alex turned the next page and pointed at a picture of a city, pitching his voice high, like Mama Duck. "This place is no good. It's too busy."

The twins turned the next page together and perused the drawing of an island in the middle of a city park.

"Here?" Andy asked in Papa Duck's voice.

"Here," Alex said in Mama Duck's voice.

"That's right," Zeke said. "The island in the park was the perfect place to raise babies. Pink swans and all."

"I love this story," Andy said contentedly. "It's always different but always the same."

"Kind of like life." Shane came to sit on the hearth, cradling a mug of coffee with both hands.

"That was fun, but…" Alex sighed, closing the book and hugging it to his chest. "Next time we read this, can we read the words? *The real words?*"

"Your mom is better at reading than I am." Zeke patted the boy's shoulder.

"I'm sure that's not true." Sophie set bowls of oatmeal on the coffee table.

"I want Zeke to read the book." Alex picked up a spoon. "After we eat oaty-meal."

Zeke's gut clenched.

He didn't like breaking his promise to a young boy, but he wasn't going to read that book.

Ever.

CHAPTER THIRTEEN

"I WANT TO read books." Alex stood in front of the fireplace, pouting at Zeke.

Sophie and Shane had left. Mitch was walking Gabby to the diner, where independent study was going to be in session. If Zeke attempted to read the book now, no one but the twins would witness his weakness.

Zeke glanced at Alex's book, swallowed hard, made up his mind and chose pride over his promise.

"We need to go check on my truck before we read any more." Zeke put on his jacket and then held out a coat for Alex.

Who held his ground.

Jacket on, Andy peered out the front window. "You don't have a truck."

"I do. It's next door being fixed." Or it would be fixed in another week or so.

"Why do we need to see it?" Andy hopped toward his twin.

"Because it's broken." Because Zeke needed

a diversion. "Don't you want to see what a truck engine looks like?"

"No." Alex thrust out his lip and hugged his beloved book.

"Hey." Andy reached his brother and gave him a hug. "We promise to read later. I want to see that truck. It's the one that crashed, remember? We saw the tree. And the tree is what broke Zeke's leg."

That wasn't precisely true, but before Zeke could clarify what had happened in terms four-year-olds might understand, Alex relented.

"Okay." Alex put *Mama Duck, Papa Duck* on the coffee table. "But only because you promised books later."

That didn't make Zeke feel any better.

A few minutes later, they'd traipsed through the melting snow puddles, beneath dripping eaves, invaded the general store, walked through the side door into the garage and stopped next to Zeke's truck.

"I expect your radiator any day." Mack had followed them out to the repair shop. "I hope to get it put back together and running in another two weeks. I get some overheated cars up here come spring and summer. Gotta have the space to work on them."

Zeke understood and hastened to reassure

her. "In two weeks, I've got to be back at the ranch."

"You can't leave us." Andy's head came up. "You're our nanny. *Our* nanny."

"He doesn't know French," Alex huffed. "He doesn't read books. He's no nanny."

Zeke nodded. They deserved so much better.

A bell rang in the general store. "That's the front door. Turn off the lights when you're done visiting." Mack hurried off.

"Promise you won't leave us." Andy tugged on Zeke's hand. "Not ever."

"I can't." Zeke's throat threatened to close. The boys had stolen his heart. "You're missing your chance to climb on my truck."

"Come on, Andy." Alex pulled his twin toward the truck. "He's just like Dad."

And that didn't sound as if it was saying much. Zeke frowned.

Andy went to stand at the front bumper, staring at the bent metal in awe. He pointed at the damage while staring back at Zeke. "Did you do this?"

"Yep."

Alex joined him, gaping. "Did you get in trouble?"

"I broke my leg." Thankfully, Mack had cleaned the blood from the cab, removing the plastic floor mats.

"And you didn't get in trouble?" Andy's brow furrowed.

"Nope."

Alex's brow made near identical furrows. "Your mom wasn't mad?"

"My mom..." Zeke hadn't seen his mom since he was their age. "This is my truck. If anyone was to get mad about all the damage, it'd be me. But what's the point of getting mad? It won't change anything."

"So..." Andy looked Zeke up and down. "If you weren't mad, did you cry?"

Alex elbowed him in the ribs. "Cowboys don't cry, remember?"

"I didn't cry," Zeke said absently. He'd been in shock from the sight of blood and bone—his, not some nameless heifer's. "You can climb in the back if you want. Just be careful."

Wide-eyed, the boys ran to the rear of the truck. The tailgate was crunched where Franny had rear-ended him. They scrambled up and into the bed, exploring every inch. They hopped up and down to test his shocks, not that he'd asked them to, but because they hopped on everything.

"What's in there?" Andy peered into the back window of the cab.

Zeke lifted the boys down and opened the passenger door to let them climb inside.

Alex opened the glove box. "Look! It's Zeke's favorite book, *Under the Big Bright Moon*." He handed the book to Zeke. "Can we read it later?"

"Sure." He'd forgotten it was in there. Cowboys didn't keep baby books around where anyone could see them. Zeke stuck it in his inner jacket pocket.

"Look at this rope!" Andy had tumbled behind the front seat and picked up Zeke's coiled lariat, the one he used to rope cattle. "We can tie up bad guys, like Merciless Mike Moody."

That made Zeke think about the strongbox Sophie had found.

Andy dug around to see what else he could find, which wasn't much.

Alex moved into the driver's seat. "Where's the wheel?" He held out his hands where the steering wheel should have been.

"I need a new one." Zeke opened the door wider. "Come on. Bring the rope. I'll teach you both how to be a cowboy."

"But we don't have horses." Alex scooted across the bench seat.

"And we don't have cows." Andy tumbled over the seat back, clutching the rope.

Zeke took the lasso from him and threaded his arm through the coils, bringing it to rest on his shoulder. "I'm going to teach you how to rope and then someday, if you're good, I'll take you out to the Bucking Bull and let you ride Pandora and try roping a calf."

"We're too little." Andy grabbed Zeke's hand and skipped toward the door, tugging him along.

"You're not too little. Last year, Charlie started throwing a lasso from his pony." Zeke opened the door and held it for the boys to get through, turning off the light before closing the door. "And Davey is only nine, but he can rope a calf." As long as the calf was standing still.

The boys captured his hands and tugged him toward the exit.

"We'll ride with a saddle next time?" Alex asked suspiciously.

"Will you tie us on the saddle so we don't fall in horse manure?" Andy giggled.

"Yes to the saddle. No to being tied up." Zeke thanked Mack on their way out, promising to make another payment at week's end.

Zeke borrowed one of Mitch's two kitchen chairs and showed the boys how to rope. It was sunny outside and relatively warm compared with winter temperatures. Zeke didn't even mind the wind gusts.

He was reminded of his father teaching him to rope, showing him the sweep of the arm, the curl of the fingers, the flick of the wrist, much as he imagined suburban dads teaching their kids how to throw a baseball. He encouraged the boys to repeat the motions over and over without the lariat until they were ready to hold the rope and give it a go.

Alex went first. He swung the lasso around too quickly, released it too late and nearly castrated Zeke, who'd been standing to his left.

Andy wasn't much better. He didn't wait for Zeke to step back before he swung the stiff noose and whacked Zeke upside the head.

Ears ringing, discouraged but not ready to quit, Zeke let them try several more times, although he stayed a safe distance away.

Aided by a gust of wind, Andy threw the lasso straight into Zeke's face. "I suck at cowboying." Slumping, he dropped down to his knees.

Zeke covered his nose with one hand and tried to reassure the kid that wasn't true.

"I suck, too." Alex sat on the chair they'd been trying to rope.

"Nothing worth having is worth giving up on." Zeke's father's words.

Although, Zeke couldn't remember bruising his daddy in the course of learning to rope. His nose stung and had started running.

"I'm bored." Andy got to his feet, not bothering to brush the dirt off his knees.

"Me, too." Alex stood, just as ready to find a new adventure.

Zeke sniffed, formulating a plan for the rest of the day's activities. Maybe the boys needed to practice a different skill. The snow had finally melted on Sled Hill, which left Zeke fewer options for entertainment. Not fishing. Not riding or roping. Not hide-and-seek. Which left... Baseball. Mack had just received a shipment of sporting equipment. He wouldn't attempt teaching them to bat—therein lay certain danger—but throwing and catching? That would be safe enough, wouldn't it?

"If you're ready for a study break—" Roy stood outside the Bent Nickel, holding a coffee mug; he used it to gesture toward Zeke "—and it looks like someone could use one—Ivy'll make you some hot chocolate."

With gleeful gasps, the boys sprinted toward the diner.

Zeke didn't immediately follow. Partly because he wanted to coil the rope, but partly because his nose seemed to be bleeding. *Shoot.* He bent forward as he walked so most of the blood dropped on the snow-dotted ground.

When he passed the general store, Mack stepped outside and handed him a tissue. "Squeeze until it stops bleeding."

A brief thanks and a few more steps, and Roy

held the door to the Bent Nickel for Zeke. "Sit in one of them booths and tilt your head back."

"I've had a bloody nose before." *Jeez*. You'd think he was from the city like the Monroes, the way folks babied him.

"Can't a body be civil to a wounded man?" Roy hurried ahead. "I'll get you a cup of coffee."

"I put two hot cocoas on Sophie's tab," Ivy said from behind the counter, where she mixed powdered chocolate with hot water.

"I can pay for two hot chocolates," Zeke grumbled, suddenly annoyed that he was being treated like a penniless invalid and stared at by the kids studying in the back corner. He sat heavily in Sophie's regular booth and tilted his head back, squeezing his nose.

"There's blood out on the walkway." Shane entered the diner and went straight to his nephews. He looked them up and down. "No blood here."

"It's not us, Uncle Shane." Alex pointed at Zeke.

"I hit him with the rope," Andy admitted, grinning. "We both did."

"No hard feelings." Zeke supposed he'd be grinning, too, if he was nearly five and had gotten the best of an adult.

"You shouldn't beat up on your nanny." Despite his words, Shane grinned just as broadly as his nephew. Shane approached Zeke. "Can I get you to sign an agreement saying you won't sue?"

"Sue for what?" Zeke pinched his nose harder.

Shane settled across from him in the booth. "For damages."

Right. Zeke chuckled. "A bloody nose makes you more nervous than a fishhook ripping through my toe?"

"What?" Shane clearly wasn't up to date on his nephews' nanny's injuries. "Boys!"

The twins quickly filled their uncle in on their fishing expedition.

Shane shook his head. "I'm beginning to question my sister's choice in hiring you without providing health-care coverage."

"Lucky for Sophie, it's only temporary." Zeke took a clean napkin from the holder and dabbed at his nose. Still bleeding. He pinched some more.

"Good thing they're too young to take hunting." Roy was laughing it up from a safe distance away.

Sophie entered, looking worried. "I saw blood in the snow from the trading post." She hurried to her boys. "Is everything okay?"

Everyone pointed to Zeke.

"Bloody nose." He raised a hand. "Nothing to call the doctor about."

"We don't have a doctor anymore," Shane murmured, glancing across the street toward the doctor's empty cabin.

"Mitch couldn't convince the doctor he interviewed the other day to visit?" Sophie patted her brother on the shoulder. "Let's not go kidnapping another MD."

"I'd caution you to refer to past events without the K-word." Shane got out of the booth to get some coffee.

Zeke wasn't proud of the fact that he'd been along when Roy and Shane asked a doctor out to dinner and hadn't told her they were driving her up to Second Chance for said meal. Quicker than you could say, *"Whoa,"* they'd been snowed in. A few days later, they'd been lucky the doctor hadn't pressed charges.

The twins took their hot cocoa to the back corner, where Eli Garland, the home study teacher, gave them paper and crayons. They told him they were making a special note for their mother, which would please Sophie to no end.

Sophie cradled Zeke's chin in her palm, peering at his face.

Zeke froze, holding his breath.

Kiss her, Roosevelt.

There were too many reasons not to, starting with his economic and educational void and ending with their rather large audience.

From the community coffeepot a few feet away, Shane cleared his throat.

"Don't say a word, brother dear." Sophie turned Zeke's head from side to side. "Thank heavens they didn't hit you in the eye."

Zeke's manhood required defending. "I've been trampled, gored and bit by larger stock than Alex and Andy."

"Hopefully, that means you won't sue." Shane's phone rang. He went outside to take the call.

Sophie sat down across from Zeke, righting her glasses. "I'm sorry."

"Don't apologize." Zeke pressed a fresh napkin to his nose. "I have all my fingers and toes. Besides, I'd rather you tell me—"

"I'm not sharing that secret." But he earned a smile for his efforts.

Egbert entered the diner, leaning on a cane. "There's blood outside on what little snow is left on the sidewalk."

"Bloody nose. No worries." Zeke raised his hand again.

Egbert lumbered over, tossing half his white locks over his shoulder. "Do you know, I didn't get to finish the story about Merciless Mike Moody and Old Jeb the other day." He studied

Zeke's face before pulling a chair over to sit at the end of the booth.

"I hadn't realized there was more to the story," Zeke murmured.

"There was more?" Sophie wasn't as quiet in expressing her doubt. "Was he arrested? Did the posse or the townsfolk find his stolen loot?" Her glance collided with Zeke's.

She hasn't told Egbert yet about the strong-box.

"No, no, no. It's better than that." Egbert got to his feet and hobbled with his cane to the coffee table. He filled a mug with coffee and then returned, stroking his white Santa beard as he contemplated his small audience. "Where did we leave off?"

"Um?" Sophie scrunched her nose.

Zeke remembered. "Old Jeb was stabbed, and his wound cauterized."

"And the posse was hot on his tail!" Holding his beard close to his chin, Egbert took a generous sip of coffee. "Old Jeb had left his mark on the fleeing desperado. Merciless Mike Moody left a trail of blood that was easy to follow through the mountains."

"Was this a hanging state back then?" Zeke wondered aloud, making sure the twins weren't making problems with the students in the corner. They were coloring quietly.

That's where they belong.

Not in Zeke's care.

"We hung cutthroats and horse thieves back then," Egbert confirmed. "But that wasn't to be Merciless Mike Moody's fate. They tracked him through the afternoon. He was wanted for murdering the stage driver, robbing the stage and stabbing Old Jeb. They were determined to get their man. They caught his horse at one point, but Merciless Mike Moody wasn't to be found."

"What about the gold he'd stolen?" Zeke dabbed his nose with a clean napkin. There was very little blood.

Sophie gave him a look that said: *Be quiet.*

He'd much rather she gave him a look that said: *Are you okay?*

But nannies couldn't be choosers.

"I'll get to the gold in due time." Egbert took another beard-pressing sip of coffee. "Meanwhile, the posse began to wonder if he'd evaded them again. And then there was a mighty rumble, as if the mountain itself was frustrated with their pursuit."

"What was it?" Sophie asked, on the edge of her seat. "Gunfire?"

"A herd of stampeding buffalo?" Zeke guessed.

Egbert turned to his captive audience, meaning Sophie and Zeke. "An earthquake. Short, but severe enough to dislodge boulders from the mountaintop."

"Here it comes," Zeke murmured, anticipating the gruesome end to the evil Merciless Mike Moody.

Sophie gave him another one of the *be quiet* looks.

"And then they caught him." Egbert stared into his coffee mug morosely, before setting it on the table. "Kind of. One of those boulders landed on him." He clapped his hands together, making Sophie jump. "Flattened him like a bug."

"What about the loot?" Sophie asked. "The gold? The strongbox?"

Egbert's eyes sparkled. "They never found the stolen gold or the box it was in. Folks around here used to say Merciless Mike Moody managed to squirrel it away in his secret hideout before the earthquake hit." He drained his coffee. "Before the earthquake hit *him*, I should say." He chuckled some more and then got up to refill his mug and leave money in the coffee jar.

"No one found the gold?" Sophie smirked at Zeke.

"No one." Egbert shook his head before drifting to the back corner to say hello to the students. "Maybe you'll find it someday, hidden in one of those boxes your grandfather filled."

"Don't get your hopes up," Zeke cautioned his boss, not believing there'd been anything of value in the strongbox to begin with. "From what I've heard, every teenager in town for decades has gone searching for Merciless Mike Moody's treasure."

"I found a pickax and a shovel in the trading post," Sophie whispered.

"All that proves is Harlan—or someone else—went looking for buried treasure."

"He found it," she insisted. "How else do you explain how my grandfather could leave here, go to Texas and have seed money to dig an oil well?"

"There was Irene," Zeke reminded her. The mystery first wife of Harlan. "She could have been wealthy."

Sophie didn't look convinced.

Alex ran over to Zeke, climbing up next to him in the booth. "I'm ready for quiet time."

Reading books, he meant.

Zeke went cold. "I think we should look for Merciless Mike Moody's treasure first."

Sophie stared at him as if he'd gone mad.

CHAPTER FOURTEEN

"MOM!"

Sophie stopped cleaning the green porcelain bathroom sink and came into the trading post's main room. "Andrew?"

"We found nothing." Her son dropped to his knees inside the trading post doors. "I'm so tired." Ever the drama king, he collapsed onto his side.

Sophie wiped her wet hands on a rag.

"Is he dead?" Roy stepped inside. He was installing the Edsel's front end on the outer wall.

"Worse," Sophie said. "He ran out of gas."

"Chocolate. I need chocolate." Andrew scrunched his eyes closed.

"Mom!" Alexander ran into the room. "We went hunting for buried treasure." He grinned from ear to ear. "And do you know what?"

"You didn't find none," Roy said, getting back to work.

"I found a penny!" Alexander held it up, as excited as if he'd found Merciless Mike Moody's fortune.

"What?" Andrew sat up. "Lemme see!"

"No. You gave up. No penny for you." Alexander waved his hands in the air and danced about.

Zeke, otherwise known as the man who'd probably planted a penny for Alex to find, set two shovels against the log wall, missing Sophie's sigh of longing. He tsked at Andrew. "You missed out, bud."

Andrew protested.

"Here." Sophie hurried over to the sales counter. "I found my own treasure. A buffalo nickel." She gave it to Andrew.

"My treasure is better than your treasure." Andrew tried to rub in his find to Alexander, who said, "My penny is prettier."

"I'd say you boys are even." Zeke picked up the shovels. "Let's return our tools to Mitch and get some lunch."

"Oh, wait." Sophie reached under the counter. "Eli brought some books by for the boys to read."

"Books!" Alexander handed Andrew his penny. "You can have my Merciless Mike Moody treasure. I'll take the books. Let's read one now!"

"We'll get to those books after lunch." Zeke disappeared out the door. "Come along."

And as if he was the Pied Piper, her sons followed him.

Without so much as a kiss or a call of goodbye!

"Digging for buried treasure in the middle of winter," Roy huffed.

"It's March." Sophie went to stand in the doorway, watching the twins reach the road, take hold of Zeke's hands and cross safely.

"And the ground's still frozen."

"It was imaginary play. It's good to use a child's imagination." Since Zeke had begun watching them, they'd been playing outdoors more than they would have in Philadelphia.

"And it's good to have a dose of reality, too." The old man set a screw on the tip of his drill. "There's no treasure to find."

"He found it, didn't he?" Sophie turned to look at Roy. "My grandfather found Merciless Mike Moody's treasure."

Roy didn't say anything.

He didn't have to. She could tell by the stiffening of his thin shoulders that it was true.

"THIS IS BETTER than lunch at the diner." Alex sat on a pillow beneath a sheet stretched across the two beds in his room at the Lodgepole Inn.

"Camping out indoors rocks." Andy lay on two pillows next to his twin. "I have so many books." He patted his stack from Eli. "Many, many books."

"I brought a book, too." Zeke opened *Under the Big Bright Moon*. His mother had read it to him over and over as a child. He knew it by heart. "I'm reading this one first." And he did, reciting it word-for-remembered-word.

When he was through, he glanced at the boys. Their eyes were nearly closed.

"It's been so long since I read this book, I'm going to read it again." And Zeke did.

This time when he finished, the boys were dozing, breathing deeply.

Lowering his voice, Zeke recited the book a third time. That was the charm. The boys were now asleep.

Zeke got up and left them to nap.

"Zeke. Thank heavens." Gabby handed him a stapled set of pages. "I have to memorize this speech. Tell me if I mess up."

How am I supposed to do that?

"Not now, Gabby." Zeke set her speech on the check-in desk and glanced through the window toward the trading post. The door of the trading post was closed. "Wouldn't your dad be a better choice for this?"

Wouldn't anyone who could read be a better choice for this?

"Dad would, but he's out chopping wood

with the chain saw." She picked up the pages and studied the words. "He says he might cut off a foot if he doesn't pay attention."

That sounded sensible, if inconvenient for Zeke. "And Laurel?" Mitch's fiancée?

"She's watching him for safety reasons." From the way Gabby rolled her eyes, Zeke got the impression she'd also tried to recruit Laurel.

"Can't Laurel watch your dad *and* follow your speech?"

"Too late." A shake of her strawberry blonde head. "They went woodcutting on the Bucking Bull's property."

"What about Ivy?"

"Nick—" the diner owner's young son "—tried to fry bacon and burned his hand. She's banned all *distractions*—" this was said with air quotes "—from the Bent Nickel. She didn't even make us french fries today."

Ivy was known for her big heart, her lack of skill in the kitchen and her tendency to feed every child who entered the diner whether they ordered food or not.

"And Shane?" Zeke was grasping at straws now.

I need to get back to the open range.

"Gone somewhere." Gabby gestured toward the front of the inn, which was missing a big black SUV.

Zeke had no more valid excuses. "What is the poem?" Maybe he knew it. He could recite *'Twas the Night Before Christmas* and *The Raven*.

"It's a *speech*." She rolled her eyes.

"Oh."

Oh, no.

Zeke didn't know this one. He took her speech and went to sit down on the couch, staring at the words that might just as well have been Morse code. Gabby was an excellent student and an overachiever. But maybe it'd be okay. She'd probably already memorized the speech and catch herself if she faltered.

Gabby paced and did some panicked heavy breathing.

He stared at the page and then up at Gabby. Why was she moving? "Is this one of those assignments you have to act out?"

"No. I'm nervous." She shook out her hands, and then bounced on her toes some. She tilted her head from side to side. Warming up like a boxer about to begin the first round. "Don't look at me."

Zeke dutifully turned away. At this rate, she'd never get to the recital part.

"Uh, hello, everyone…" She cleared her throat. "Oh, shoot. Let me start again." More pacing. More huffed breathing.

"Okay." Zeke settled back in the cushions and closed his eyes. "Tell me when you're ready."

If Gabby discovered his secret, would she keep it? Would she make fun of him in front of her father and Shane? Would she think she could teach him to read? His gut churned at the thought.

Everyone who learned of his weakness thought they'd be the one to teach him to read. He'd given up on that miracle a long time ago.

"Ladies and gents of mirth…" Teen footsteps drew closer to Zeke, a pounding of upset heels on wood.

Gabby continued speaking. Her words… they sounded familiar.

The footsteps halted near Zeke's feet. "You're not looking at the notes." Gabby's voice. Brimming with disbelief.

Brimming with irony. With satire. Familiar satire. "Zeke?"

"Sorry, I…" Zeke opened his eyes and stared at the preteen. "Wait. Wasn't this a video on social media? A song?"

"Yes." Gabby waved irritably. "But it was a speech. I think. Maybe." She frowned. "I'll have to check my research."

"It doesn't matter to me where it came from." He'd seen the video enough times to remember it. Zeke breathed easier, holding the paper in front of him, though he didn't need to be able to read it. "Proceed."

As Gabby recited the words, Zeke hummed the tune in his head.

SOPHIE LISTENED TO Gabby recite her speech from the room filled with boxes. She'd burrowed into the stacks, backfilling her path with boxes piled one on top of the other until she'd reached the far wall. She had enough merchandise in the trading post to open, but since she wasn't open, she was using the time to go through more boxes.

"You can't just blurt out the words," Zeke told Gabby. "There's a cadence. You know what a rapper is, right?"

"*I* know what a rapper is." Gabby's words were stiff with indignation. "Why does an old cowboy know what a rapper is?"

"I don't watch much television, but I listen to a lot of music." Zeke didn't sound upset at the young girl's assumption.

Sophie had made assumptions about Zeke, too. That as a cowboy he'd be uneducated. Not as smart as a professionally trained nanny. Not as adept at keeping her rambunctious boys occupied and challenged.

"Do you want me to lay a beatbox soundtrack?" Zeke asked.

There was a pause. "You know how to do that?"

Sophie paused, too. If truth be told, she'd been standing more than working since Zeke had come downstairs, listening to him. Because yes, truth, she was enamored. Attracted. Mesmerized by a man who was so completely different from her it scared her down to her very bones. Different didn't work long term.

Something upstairs thudded.

One of my babies fell on the floor?

Sophie whirled, bumping into boxes.

"Sophie?" Zeke appeared in the doorway.

She righted her glasses and tried not to look at him as if he were a work of fine art. She was afraid she failed.

"Hey." She pointed to the ceiling. "I thought I heard the boys upstairs. Can you check on them? It sounded like they fell off the bed."

"They're napping on the floor." He shouldn't look at her like that, like he considered her a classic, too. "Andy has a habit of throwing his leg out in his sleep."

True.

She combed her fingers through her hair, unable to look away. This was worse than when she'd been in high school and Thornton Woodley had let her cut in front of him in line. She'd thought he'd done it so he could talk to her. In reality, he'd wanted to talk to Clarissa Finkelstein, who'd been standing behind Sophie.

What did Zeke want?

She knew the answer to that question. He wanted to get his truck fixed and return to that fly-swatting horse of his.

"Do you need help getting out?" Zeke, always the helper.

"Weren't you helping Gabby?"

He glanced over his shoulder toward the sound of Gabby blowing raspberries in a pattern. She had a long way to go before she was rap-ready. His gaze returned to Sophie.

"Ugh," Gabby said. "Don't listen. I'm going to my room and downloading that song."

"She's practicing." Without being asked, Zeke began hefting boxes to free Sophie.

"Thank you." Now that he wasn't looking at her, she could breathe easier, adjust her glasses, tug down her sweater, prepare herself for Zeke in close proximity. "I owe you an apology. You proved me wrong."

"About Merciless Mike Moody's gold?" His brief smile touched the bruised corners in Sophie's heart. "Did you find an old bank book of Harlan's?"

"No." They were on different wavelengths.

Such a good thing. Except… "I tossed Young's Academy in your face the day I hired you. You're good with kids. With my kids." *With me*.

He chuckled softly. "You mean when I drop them in manure?"

"No."

"Or when they beat me up with fishhooks and lassos?"

"No." It was important to give him this compliment. "You've done more diverse activities with them in a few days than I've done with them in a few months." And here she'd thought she was being a great mom. At best, she was middling, spending time away from them while she set up a business she didn't wholly believe in. She wasn't even sure it would support her.

"To make money, you have to be passionate about what you do." Grandpa Harlan had sat next to Sophie on a bench in the National Portrait Gallery. "Because a passion for a business is like a rich cake with a cherry on top."

"Grandpa, I love art." It was the summer she'd turned sixteen. Grandpa had taken the siblings and cousins to Washington, DC. "Even though I know nobody makes money who loves art, not even artists."

He'd wrapped his arm around Sophie. It was a faded-flannel-covered arm. He wore flannel year-round. He smelled like coffee and fabric softener. Familiar, comforting smells. "Who said you have to make money to be successful?"

"Dad. Holden. Shane. Uncle Ian. They all say I need to pick a Monroe business to work in." Sophie wasn't interested in business. She was fascinated by art, the people who created it, and the lengths they went to for it. "They all say I need to look ahead to college. They all say—"

"Stop right there." Grandpa Harlan had a way of frowning that could intimidate a Secret Service agent. "If it's art you love, that's what you'll study. And if you decide to change course, who's to judge? Look at me. I've reinvented myself a half dozen times. Trust your feelings." He'd stood, drawing her to her feet. "Come on. The museum I loaned my Andy Warhol painting to also has a treasure chest full of gold doubloons on display. There's a story behind that, I bet." He liked to tell stories. "Sometimes stories lead to interests that lead to passions that lead to making money."

Thinking back on his words, Sophie didn't feel so bad about her lack of passion. According to Grandpa Harlan, it would come. Thinking back on that day, she suddenly remembered Grandpa Harlan's fascination with Western bandits and pirates. Oh, he'd found Merciless Mike Moody's money, all right.

"Don't be so hard on yourself," Zeke said gruffly. "They're good kids. You're lucky." Kind words considering she'd trapped herself in a storage room again. "And you're a good mom. They see it, too."

His kindness combined with memories of her grandfather drew more admissions. "I was almost trampled by a moose."

"Today?" Zeke straightened. "I've never heard of anyone seeing a moose in these parts."

Sophie waggled her fingers to clue him in that this was her daring, almost disastrous secret. "Back in the day."

"Fingers and toes." His grin grew slowly.

Sophie waited for it to reach its full potential. "During a family vacation in Canada, Shane enticed me into the woods. I agreed because I wanted to get a sample of lichen that glows in the dark." He'd been right about intellectual curiosity getting her into trouble. "I guess we wandered into a bull moose's territory."

Zeke's smile faded. "What happened?"

"He charged me." She'd never imagined such a slow-moving, furry creature could look so ferocious. She could have sworn his eyes blazed red. "I fell." Her gaze caught on the scar on her left hand. "And then Shane did the stupidest thing. He shouted and jumped around to draw the moose toward him. And then he threw himself on the ground and played dead."

"Why?" Zeke looked dumbstruck. "Did it work?"

"Yes. Because it's Shane and everything he does is the right thing to do." Shane was the family's golden child. He'd never faced a problem he couldn't eventually fix.

"But…how on earth did he know what to do?"

"That's the worst part." Truly. "He learned it by playing some stupid video game, defeating ogres or something with his horde."

Zeke was speechless. But the way he stared at her spoke volumes. Heart-fluttering volumes. She was lucky several stacks of boxes separated them.

"Anyway, Shane may be brash and sarcastic—"

"And a really bad driver."

"—but he knows what he's doing." All fluttering stopped. "I can't always say that of myself."

"You do fine." Zeke's smile was supportive, at least before his expression deepened into a mischievous grin. "But now that you've told me this, I have to recategorize one of the most annoying Monroes as one of the most respected."

His green eyes sparkled with humor. "Which—as I'm sure you understand—is a big leap."

Sophie chuckled. "You know, the danger of being a Monroe is being overeducated and pompous."

"Like Shane?" Zeke spared her a sparkly-eyed glance.

Sophie shook her head, trying not to encourage him. "More like my cousin Holden." Who'd come to town unexpectedly a few weeks ago and left just as quickly.

"Hands down. Holden is my least favorite Monroe."

Sophie righted her glasses, not willing to argue the point. Holden was the most pompous, if not the most educated. "I want Alexander and Andrew to be grounded and learned." Not educated via video game.

"They will be."

In Philadelphia, she hadn't been certain they'd be grounded. But she was certain of it here. In Second Chance. There was one reason to stay. And staying was a reason to kiss Zeke.

Sophie's phone chimed with a reminder. She glanced at the screen.

Sign boys up for kindergarten.

"Oh, no." Her boys may have been grounded, but the rest of their education was at risk.

"What's wrong?" Zeke paused.

"I'm supposed to register the twins for private kindergarten tomorrow. In person or my position on the consideration list will be lost." Mama Bear roused and growled. She'd make any sacrifice to prepare her children to excel. Her old life was slipping away. And as much as she wanted to kiss Zeke, she wasn't quite ready to fully commit.

"The boys will get a different education here."

She gave him a look, unable to hold back Mama Bear's sarcasm. "Roping and fishing?"

"Good men—*successful men*—have been raised in this town," Zeke countered. "Your grandfather for one. And look at Gabby. She loves to learn, and Eli Garland pushes her, perhaps more than she'd be pushed in a traditional school."

"With rap songs and history assignments about this small town?" Mama Bear grumbled about the differences between Second Chance and Philadelphia. "I planned on the boys being bilingual, on them learning global history and being challenged with new technologies."

"Is it the quality of education they'd miss out on that bothers you?" Zeke's voice lowered. "Or what other people think about the education they'd get here?"

Sophie stomped her foot. "Are you judging me?"

He was.

He was. He was.

Zeke held up his hands in surrender. "I'm the last person in the world to judge anyone on the education they want or receive."

Before she said something she'd regret, Sophie edged past boxes, past Zeke. "I need some fresh air."

She grabbed her coat and headed outside.

CHAPTER FIFTEEN

ZEKE SHOULD LET her go.

He was a poorly educated cowboy and she had two degrees. He had no right arguing with her about her choices in education for Alex and Andrew.

He put on his jacket and hat anyway, and stepped out onto the porch, spotting Sophie almost immediately. She stood at the top of Sled Hill, arms wrapped around her tighter than a cinched saddle.

He walked over to join her, taking his time, needing to figure out what to say. In the end, he reached her and said nothing, shoving his hands in his jacket pockets.

The sun bathed the valley in light, revealing green buds and small white blossoms about to open. The Salmon River gurgled past. And still they said nothing.

Sophie's hair lifted in the breeze, batted this way and that. She brushed the hair from her eyes and looked at him. "I only want the best for my kids."

Zeke nodded. "That's natural."

"Children are supposed to do better than their parents. That's how society judges them."

Zeke opened his mouth to disagree, thought better of it and closed it again.

"That's how *my family* judges them." She spoke heavily, as if she'd already failed Alex and Andy.

"Why is it important to meet other people's standards? If I judged myself by what other people thought of me or my father, or how we stack up to what my grandfather did, I'd label myself a big failure." Which he often did anyway, considering his reading skill.

"You're not a failure."

She had no idea.

She took his hand anyway, burrowing hers into his jacket pocket to do so. "Things are different here."

He nodded, because her touch held him immobile.

"It's like a pocket where time slows down, where the same rules don't apply as elsewhere." Her fingers wove between his. "Where I could kiss you and forget about Philadelphia and my family."

Kiss me?

Zeke did a double take. Had she just said...

"You want to kiss me, don't you?" Her glasses had slid down.

He should fix those glasses for her. He should get back and check on the boys. He should distance himself from her touch and her tantalizing question about lips touching. Because she wanted an education for her sons beyond the one he'd received. Because if she found out he couldn't read *Mama Duck, Papa Duck* that look of liquid interest on her sweet face would turn into concrete disgust.

He turned to face her anyway. "There's something you need to know about me."

"Are you a convicted felon?"

Zeke shook his head.

Her gaze dropped to his lips. "Are you married?"

"No." Thankfully, blessedly, no.

"Then I don't care." Sophie rose up on her toes, pushed the brim of his hat back and kissed him.

She kissed him gently, but not tentatively. She kissed him the way she went through life—taking care of those around her, holding on tight to show she cared, but holding on loosely enough they could have some independence. It was a kiss of welcome. A kiss of want.

A kiss he had no right receiving.

But receive he did, wrapping his arms around

her, drawing her close, breathing her in and wanting to never let her go.

He let her go anyway. At the first sound of an engine pushing a car over the summit a mile or so to the east.

He righted her glasses, righted her jacket, but he couldn't do right by her. He couldn't undo that kiss.

They stared at each other, standing close enough to kiss again. Standing carefully apart so as not to touch.

"Sophie, I…" he began at the same time she said, "Zeke, I…"

Silence descended once more. Or it would have if not for Shane's monstrous SUV drawing closer. The motor had a deep, throaty rumble that was loud enough to shake snow loose from a mountainside, had snow been on the mountainside.

"You shouldn't kiss me, Sophie."

"Why not?" She stared at him, one of those looks that didn't allow a man to escape.

"Because…" *I can't read.* "I'm not good enough for you."

"Why would you say that?" The disappointment in her eyes dug under his skin like a sharp sliver.

"Because…" *I can't read.* "Because…a man like me doesn't set down roots. Ranching isn't a lucrative business for most folks. I have to be ready to pick up and move on. Franny over at the Bucking Bull could decide she can't afford me at any time and I wouldn't hold it against her. My dad went bankrupt trying to keep our ranch afloat. I hardly make enough to fix my own truck."

Sophie was a Monroe. Surely, this was an argument she'd understand.

She stared at Zeke in silence before blinking her gaze away and adjusting those glasses of hers that never stayed in place. "That's not a good enough reason." She crossed her arms. "What's the real reason?"

Tell her.

He swallowed and…told her something else. "You don't have an endless supply of inventory. At some point, the trading post will be empty, and you'll have made peace with your grandfather."

"You're afraid I'll leave." The way she said it… The notion hadn't occurred to her.

"Those boxes won't stay full forever."

"I can buy new treasures." She smiled, and it was as if they'd never started this argument. "How wise of you to point out a fallacy in my business plan. Where did you go to school?"

Zeke blew out a breath. "No place special."

The words snapped out of him. He was touchy when it came to discussions about learning.

"College?"

"No, ma'am."

She bristled at the term.

"My father judged smarts by how productive you were on the ranch." Was he really considering telling her the truth? He pushed the conversation sideways. "What will you say if Andy... if *Andrew* doesn't want to go to college?"

Her brown eyes widened in horror. "Everybody in our family goes to college. I don't care if Andrew studies liberal arts. He's going to get a college degree."

"What if he wants to be a car mechanic? Or sell real estate?" Or be a cowboy?

She frowned, as he'd known she would. The wind ruffled her hair, but he ruffled her more.

"All I'm saying is you need to support Andy no matter what." The way Zeke hoped she'd support him if she knew his secret.

Shamrocks and rainbows...

Pipe dreams, more like.

"I'll support the boys regardless." And then she contradicted herself. "But they're both going to college." Sophie tried to slip her hand in his jacket pocket once more, frowning when he angled out of reach. "I'm sure your father loves and supports you in everything you do."

Zeke couldn't speak for his old man, although he supposed there was love of a sort there. Tough love qualified, right? "My father came from a long line of men who don't express their feelings."

"He supported you being a cowboy," Sophie said with certainty.

"That's because he's a rancher. My dad didn't think school was important enough for me to attend, not if it meant he was shorthanded on the ranch."

She frowned. "But you're not helping him now."

"No, ma'am."

"Please stop calling me that." Sophie laughed uncomfortably. "You make me feel old."

"Yes, ma—"

They grinned at each other.

If he stood there much longer, Zeke was going to kiss her again. Plain and simple. She was kissable.

Shane reached the intersection nearby, rolling through the stop because no one was there. That was Shane. Always making his own rules.

The Monroes. The rules were different for them. The consequences were different for them, too. Sophie deserved a man better than Zeke.

"I'll leave you to your thoughts." He turned.

"Zeke." Sophie stopped him with a hand on his arm. "Should I apologize for kissing you?"

"Hellfire! No!" That kiss was going to keep him warm at night for decades to come. It was going to fuel his dreams of a family filled with smart kids, ones who took to reading easily, attended college and went out in the world intent upon changing it for the better.

"Good." She removed her hand, leaving him feeling cold.

Old.

And lonely.

ZEKE HAD A SECRET.

Something he didn't want to tell Sophie.

Something that kept him from looking deep into her eyes and telling her he wanted a kiss or a date or a relationship.

Her heart said it didn't matter. She was falling in love with him a little more each day. He was the type of man her grandfather would approve of. More important, he was the type of man she should have waited for the first time around. Honest. Upstanding. Kind.

Sexy. Scintillating. Scrumptious.

Sophie carried a box to the trading post. It was finally warm in Second Chance. The snow had melted and revealed steps from the road to the trading post. A railing would be nice. She made a mental note to ask Roy about building one. And maybe a retaining wall. Some of the dirt below the trading post's porch had eroded onto the road.

Across the street, a truck pulled up in front of the diner and the three Clark boys tumbled out.

Sophie waved at the woman driver and carried her load inside the trading post. It was beginning to look marvelous. The new window let in lots of warm light. The display case was filled with merchandise. Sophie had enough inventory to keep her store stocked until Christmas. What she needed was more furniture to show her wares.

She unpacked the box, displaying three arrangements of miniature tea sets on one end of the sales counter.

A woman entered the trading post wearing blue jeans, cowboy boots and an assessing glance. "Are you Sophie Monroe? Shane Monroe's sister?"

Sophie nodded, tucking the empty box behind the counter.

"I'm Francis Clark from the Bucking Bull." The slender brunette held an envelope in one hand. "I have Zeke's mail."

"He's across the street with my boys." Sophie shouldn't accept his mail, but she was curious.

"I know where he is." Francis tapped the envelope on the tips of her fingers. "Zeke's coming back to work for me in a few weeks. He told me so."

Was she jealous of Sophie being Zeke's employer? Were they romantically involved?

Sophie righted her glasses and stared more closely at the woman. "He's just helping me out until his doctor clears him to ride."

Francis nodded. "I gave him his mail several days ago when he came out to the ranch, but…"

"You have more," Sophie finished helpfully.

Francis nodded. "And I don't believe he'll have read the mail I gave him."

"Oh, I'm sure he has." Being a nanny didn't keep him so busy he didn't have time to open his mail.

"And I'm equally certain he hasn't." Francis shifted her weight from side to side as if she held a baby who needed comforting. But her arms were empty of everything, save the envelope. Zeke's envelope. "I'm not sure how to say this. I care about Zeke but…"

Sophie stiffened.

"And he'd likely want to ream me out for telling you, but someone has to watch out for him in case he doesn't return to the Bucking Bull."

"Zeke is perfectly capable of—"

"He can't read," Francis blurted through thin lips.

Cold found its way beneath Sophie's jacket, burrowing to the marrow of her bones.

If this was true...

It was a big difference between them. An insurmountable difference no kiss could bridge.

Shane. Her parents. Her friends in the art world. They'd all look down on Zeke. And Sophie...

I always judge a man by what he does, not where he's come from. Grandpa Harlan's testy words, directed at Holden when he made fun of the gardener's dirt-smeared coveralls.

What kind of person would Sophie be if this made a difference in how she felt about him?

Besides, there was no way it could be true. Zeke was too intelligent. So what if he had dyslexia or some other reading disability? It didn't change the way she felt about him.

There was love in her heart for the man, raw and tender. There was hurt that he hadn't told her, understanding about why he hadn't told her, longing to make it right. But there was love.

And yet...

"I can't believe it." But Sophie couldn't shake the cold feeling that she was wrong.

"Zeke's very good at hiding it, but he needs help with some things." Francis held up the envelope. "Bills, for one. Although I taught him how to pay those online. In my experience he'd rather open a cold beer than an envelope, even if he recognizes the company logo and can find the amount due."

Sophie didn't know what to say.

Francis tried to smile. When that didn't work, she set the envelope on the sales counter.

It was proof.

This was Zeke's secret. And she'd had to hear it from a stranger, a woman who had no right to tell her. Who probably had an agenda, because she hadn't left.

Mama Bear sat up and growled. "You did this on purpose."

"What?"

"You shattered my image of Zeke." Mama Bear clenched her claws. "You think I'll fire him, which would mean he'd return to work for you that much sooner."

"I didn't mean to upset you." Sorrow lined the woman's eyes like a much-trusted friend. "Word around town is you care about Zeke. As for me... The Bucking Bull can get by without him. It'll be hard, but the less I pay employees, the more food I can put on my table." Her eyes welled with regret. "My grandmother says I can't solve the world's problems. I shouldn't have said anything to you. I'm sorry." And with that, she left.

Leaving Sophie with a jumble of emotions—anger at being deceived, empathy for Zeke's struggles, pride at the lengths he went to fit in, guilt that she didn't want anyone to know.

Who cares if you're no good at sports? Grandpa Harlan had told Sophie after a soccer game where she'd sat the bench the entire time. *Look at all the other things you're good at.*

Zeke was good at many things.

What was she going to do? March across the street and challenge Zeke to read a book or the list of activities she'd given him? Pretend she didn't know? Neither would stop her heart from breaking if she let this come between them.

You think I care what that painting is worth? Grandpa Harlan's thin, weathered face came to mind, his oxygen cannula askew on his upper lip like a pasted-on clear mustache. *I love it. And when you love something, you want to hold on to it.* His eyes had filled with tears. *And when you can't...*

Sophie locked the door and went to find Zeke.

CHAPTER SIXTEEN

"Mom!"

Sophie entered the inn and was immediately greeted by the boys, who left their game of checkers to give her a hug.

Zeke wanted to greet her with the same enthusiasm, perhaps embellishing a greeting with a kiss. He made do with a smile. He had no right to kiss-laden greetings when she didn't know the truth about him.

"What have you been up to?" Sophie asked them, which was odd considering she'd left only a half hour ago. "Have you been reading?"

Call Zeke paranoid, but Sophie might have looked at him too intently when she asked that.

"We're going to read as soon as we finish playing checkers." Andy ran back to the board.

Alex followed, scratching his cowlick. He was about to lose the game and was in no hurry to return to the board. "Zeke wants to start with *Under the Big Bright Moon*. It's his favorite book."

Andy finished the checkers match by jumping over Alex's remaining pieces, wiping the board of all black checkers.

"Is the game over?" Sophie sat down on the far corner of the couch and adjusted her glasses, lenses aimed Zeke's way. "I might take a break and listen to Zeke read."

She knows.

A twinge of unease shuddered down Zeke's spine. He immediately rejected the notion, but that didn't keep him from attempting another diversion. "You should keep on working. We might play another game before our next book. Or the boys might make you a card." They enjoyed coloring.

Sophie's gaze hardened.

She knows.

His gut twisted. *How?* How had she found him out?

"What game, Zeke?" Andy was always up for action.

What game indeed.

"I Spy," Zeke blurted.

Alex picked up a book, but looked interested, as if a game wasn't out of the question. "How do you play that?"

"You choose something in the room but don't tell anyone what it is." Zeke tried hard not to look at Sophie, but that was like not looking at the brightest spot in the room. "And then the rest of us ask you questions trying to figure out what you chose."

"I choose this book." Alex held it up.

"What you choose has to be secret," Zeke said patiently, despite an inner voice telling him it was time to retreat, to quit, to run.

"Oh! Oh!" Andy's hand shot in the air. "I have something. Ask me! Ask me!"

"What is it?" Alex asked, half pouting. He wanted someone to read him books.

And he'd get that someone, just as soon as Sophie fired him.

"My something is my jacket." Andy ran over to the door and held up his jacket.

Zeke was beginning to think it would have been easier to try to read Alex's book than to teach them the game.

"Grandpa Harlan used to play I Spy with us." Sophie still stared at Zeke in a way that boded public shame and severance pay. "Let me try. I spy something…"

"Is it red?" Zeke asked, wanting to end things quickly and thinking of Sophie's glasses.

"No." Sophie reached out her arms, beckoning the boys to come closer. "You have nineteen questions left to figure out what I spied. And I can only answer your questions with yes or no." She glanced back to Zeke.

Can you read? That was a yes-or-no question.

"Is it bigger than a breadbox?" Zeke asked.

Sophie nodded.

"Is it Zeke?" Andy asked.

"No," Sophie said.

"What's a breadbox?" Alex asked.

Zeke framed the size of his grandmother's breadbox in the air. "It's where you store bread when you don't store it in a cupboard. It's something you find in a kitchen."

Andy ran into Mitch's apartment, easy to do since the door was open. "Is there a breadbox in here?"

"No." Gabby poked her head through the doorway. "What's a breadbox?"

"I feel old," Zeke said.

"It's bigger than a breadbox," Sophie answered, her gaze drifting toward Zeke's side of the room. "That's three questions."

As inconspicuously as possible, Zeke took stock of what was around him. "Gabby, pull up a picture of a breadbox on your laptop and show it to the boys. Is it blue?"

The twins turned to their mother, waiting for her answer.

"No. Four questions."

Not being blue eliminated the nearby chair and the blue-and-brown quilt on the couch.

There wasn't a lot in the common room to begin with. "Is it brown?"

Sophie's cheeks turned a light shade of pink and her gaze dropped to his feet. "Yes. Five questions."

His feet? "Is it my cowboy boot?"

"I suck at this game." Sophie tossed her hands dramatically. "He's right."

"Oh! Oh! I want to play." Andy crouched on his knees on the floor in front of his mother. "Ask me."

"Is it brown?" Zeke asked before Sophie could ask anything.

"Yes." Andy grinned.

"Is it my boot?"

"Yes." Andy fell back on the floor laughing.

"How did you know what he picked?" Sophie asked Zeke.

"I know how these boys think." Zeke tried to smile, tried to ignore the heavy feeling of impending doom.

Sophie's expression sobered.

She knows.

No more kisses for you, Roosevelt.

No more paychecks either.

"Under the Big Bright Moon," Alex grumbled. "Then I'd like to read *Mama Duck, Papa Duck* for real."

"We can start with your book." Why not?

Zeke could tell by the expression on Sophie's face his days as a nanny were numbered. He cleared his throat. "So in this entire family of ducks... How many ducks are there again?"

Alex opened the book and the boys pointed to the ducks on the page and counted.

"Two ducks?" Zeke waited for the boys to nod. "Do you know the sound ducks make when they walk in shallow water?" When they shook their heads, he said, "Splish, splash, splosh."

"Can we read it this time?" Alex wanted his story done the *right* way.

"I like the way Zeke reads it," Andy said. "It's fun."

"It's not fun. It's not even the same story!" Alex stomped across the floor. "I like *Mama Duck, Papa Duck* because that's how *real* families are. Babies come and daddies stay."

"Alexander," Sophie whispered in a strangled voice.

"Daddies don't stay." Andy got to his feet and did some stomping of his own. "Our dad doesn't love us. Not like in the book."

"Andrew." Sophie stood and with some effort captured their hands, drawing them into her arms. "Alexander. Your father loves you."

Alex stuck out his lower lip. Andy glowered. They may have been four, but they were victims of divorce, just like Zeke. Except in reverse. "There are all kinds of love in this world," Zeke said, remembering how hurt he'd felt when his mother left.

"I don't need the cowboy prophet now." Sophie glowered almost as well as Andy did.

"There's the casual I-love-you-man love between friends," Zeke continued, ignoring his almost former boss's request. "There's the I-enjoy-your-company-at-Christmas love you have for family. And there's the I-can't-live-without-you kind of love you have for your spouse."

He couldn't pull his gaze from Sophie. He should have. He should have been ashamed that she knew his weakness. Instead, he felt a pang in his chest near his heart. He'd let himself believe in shamrocks and rainbows, just a little. Just enough to fall for Sophie. To imagine she could be his. Maybe not forever, because that would be wishing for too much. But for a few weeks until he returned to ranching.

Hell. He'd settle for a day.

Not that rainbows were going to end at his feet. Sophie wasn't looking at him.

Alex's brow wrinkled. "What about dad love?"

"Zeke's oversimplifying things." Sophie gave Zeke a look that said: *Butt out*. It was a relatively gentle request to back off, but a request nonetheless. "Moms and dads love their kids no matter what."

"Not dads." Alex crossed his arms over his little chest.

"Not dads who don't visit." Andy mirrored his twin.

"Some dads can't say I love you." Zeke stood, his voice husky. "Some dads can't visit all the time. And love shouldn't be judged by how often you see someone or how often you say the words out loud or even by how many cards you write. Love should be judged by how often you keep someone in your mind and in your heart." Which was where he was going to keep his feelings for Sophie. Locked up.

He escaped to his room and hoped Sophie wouldn't follow.

"You can't read." Heart stitched together with a thin thread, Sophie closed Zeke's bedroom door behind her.

"I can read some." Zeke sat on the corner of his bed holding a stack of envelopes. "Let's not draw this out. You're firing me, and I've got no beef with that." He stared at his bills. His unopened bills.

Sophie wanted Zeke to look at her. Deep down, she wanted them to be on the same level, to face this together. Selfishly, she knew firing him wouldn't solve her problems. Or his. "Why do I get the feeling you believe you're not as smart as other people?"

His chin thrust out. "Most people learn how to read in school."

"Didn't you tell me your dad pulled you out of school sometimes?"

His expression turned grim. "That shouldn't be an excuse."

"It's not an excuse. It's a *reason*."

Zeke's shoulders were up around his ears. "I'm not as educated as someone who went to college. That's not a reason or an excuse. That's a fact."

"You hold your own with Mitch and Shane. And me," she added, because he did. "You've got to be clever to function in today's world."

"Can we get to the firing part?" He tossed his mail on the bed.

"No." She added the envelope Francis had given her to his stack.

Zeke raised his head and met her gaze, his green eyes brimming with regret. He hadn't meant any harm by taking the job and not telling her about his reading level.

"I'm not firing you."

"Is this because we kissed?" His words

couldn't disguise his hurt. "Because of some legal liability between employer and employee?"

"No." Sophie tried to form the words: *It's because I love you.*

Not believing her, Zeke smirked before she could make a sound.

Mama Bear rumbled to life, angry at Zeke's betrayal, angry to have fallen for a man who was less than perfect, just flat out angry. "I'm not firing you because you're good with the boys. You teach them things. You make them think."

"But I can't read to them." His gaze fell away. He wasn't proud of that fact.

"I should be doing that. I should have noticed my boys needed reassurance about their father. I should have tried harder to keep him in their lives."

Good moms encouraged positive interaction with their divorced husbands.

"You've been distracted." Zeke shrugged. "Busy."

"Don't do that." Sophie's voice welled with Mama Bear's anger. "Don't give me an out when you won't give yourself one."

He stared at his clasped hands. Zeke was hurting. How she wanted to wrap her arms around him and reassure him everything would be all right, not just today, but forevermore.

She stayed put.

"Mom?" Alexander entered the room, his brother on his heels. "Is Zeke in trouble?"

Sophie considered Zeke closely, the proud lines of his face, the firm chin, the regret-tinged eyes. He didn't want to face facts. But sometimes you needed to face the truth to move on. She'd never get closure with her grandfather, not for certain. As Zeke had told her, she'd only be able to try to fulfill his wishes given what she knew of him and what she felt was right.

Firing Zeke wasn't right. Trying not to love him wasn't right.

"Mom?" Andrew asked.

"Yes." Sophie sat next to Zeke and put her arm around him. He stiffened. "Zeke's in trouble, but not the way you think. He can't read the way he should. And do you know what that means?"

Zeke turned his head to look at her but said nothing.

"Time-out?" Andrew asked, somewhat hopefully.

"We have to help him get better."

Zeke shook his head. "Everybody wants to teach me something. It never works. Don't do this."

"*I'm* not going to teach you anything," Sophie said. "Didn't you know? Alexander and

Andrew helped each other become better readers. I don't know why they can't help you."

Zeke white-knuckled his hands.

"Unless you're afraid," she whispered. Not that it mattered how loud she spoke. The twins heard anyway.

Zeke's gaze lasered onto hers.

"Unless you're afraid of hard work and being vulnerable." It was a challenge, one she hoped he'd accept. "If you want something, you have to work for it—jobs...skills...*relationships*."

Zeke's green eyes widened. He gave an almost imperceptible shake of his head.

"I'm not afraid to try reading with Zeke." Alexander came to stand between Zeke's legs. He placed his little hands on the man's broad shoulders. "If you get scared, tell us. We'll hold your hand."

Andrew wormed his way next to his brother. "Chocolate helps, too."

"So?" Sophie's hand drifted to Zeke's waist. "Are you man enough to be our nanny?"

"Nanny work is hard work," Andrew said sagely. "Like being a cowboy."

"But we love you." Alexander nodded. "You can do it."

Zeke nodded. She'd given him no choice by bringing in the big guns—her two adorable little heathens.

"Yay!" Andrew ran out of the room. "We're going to teach our nanny how to read!"

"Yay!" Alexander followed. "We're going to read every book in the house!"

"Do they have to tell everyone?" Zeke muttered.

"Yes." Sophie laid her head on his shoulder. "You have nothing to be ashamed of. Not of your skill level and not of being with me."

But deep inside Sophie, where doubts about the trading post lingered, a small voice that sounded an awful lot like her snooty cousin Holden whispered, *Really?*

CHAPTER SEVENTEEN

"YOU SHOULD RETHINK THIS." Anger. It coursed through Zeke's veins. He got to his feet. "Not only am I not worth the effort, but I don't want my failings put on display for the town's amusement."

Sophie's glasses had slipped. She tilted her head back to look at him properly. Her eyes flashed with that spunk he'd admired for months. But there was compassion there, too. And determination.

Zeke bit back a curse. "You know…I'm trying to do you a favor."

"By quitting and not letting yourself fall for me?"

"Yes!" How could she understand and still not fire him?

Sophie captured his hand and used it to draw herself to her feet.

The air between them was charged. A few hairs on top of her head floated. Like she was floating. Above him. Above her Monroe-ness.

"How many times have you assured me I was

a good person?" Her eyes were luminous magnets he couldn't pull away from. "What kind of person would I be if I judged you for—"

"Being illiterate."

"Being a bad driver." She shrugged. "Everyone has their bailing point in a relationship. I just realized reading proficiency wasn't mine."

"You don't know what you're saying. You haven't thought this through. I can barely read. Do you want to know what that means? I can't read a prescription bottle. Or a job application. Or a form for credit." He sucked in air, but it wasn't enough. He still felt light-headed. "If I can't fix my truck, how am I going to buy a replacement?"

"But you've got me now. And Shane. And Laurel. And the boys." Sophie released him from her gaze long enough to pick up a bill. "And Francis. You have people who'll look out for you."

He shook his head. "It makes me a burden. Nobody wants that. Even you. *Especially you.* You'll get tired of me. I'll embarrass you and you'll wish you'd done the right thing today."

Sophie poked his chest, much the way Alex had done when he hadn't read *Mama Duck, Papa Duck* properly days ago. "Don't you say that. Don't you ever say that. You could never embarrass me."

He laughed. A dark, god-awful sound. "I may not be able to read, but you can't see."

She poked him again, glaring.

When was the last time anyone had fought for him? He couldn't remember. And yet, he couldn't let Sophie do this. To herself or to him.

"Why are you putting yourself through this, Sophie?" His voice had dropped to a gruff whisper. "You don't love me. And I..." He couldn't say it.

"You know nothing." She poked his chest a third time. "The way I feel about you has nothing to do with how well you can read."

"It should!" He tossed his hands. "I quit." She'd given him no choice.

"You will not!" Instead of poking him, she grabbed on to his arms, on to his heart.

"I'm saving us both...*everything*!" Crushed dreams of shamrocks and rainbows and pots of gold. "Let me go," he choked out in a whisper.

There were tears in her eyes. It was almost his undoing.

The twins burst back in the room and climbed on his bed.

"We brought books!" Alex held two in the air.

"You could save us both from everything that hurts when things go wrong." Sophie blinked and righted her glasses. "Or you could fight for everything. For all of us. And a future to-gether."

She was fighting for him? For *them*?

For a moment, Zeke couldn't breathe.

The smart thing to do would be to walk out and never look back. He could get a ride to the Bucking Bull.

The twins would get over him, latching on to their next nanny with equal enthusiasm.

Sophie would get over him if given time to think this through.

And Zeke…

Zeke would never get over her. Never get over *them*. Sophie's family would stay safely in his heart.

So it made no sense when he climbed up onto the bed and let the twins bookend him with their warm little bodies, hopeful smiles and stacks of books.

It made no sense when he stared at Sophie as if she was his newfound pot of gold, the love of his life, the woman his grandmother had told him would come along.

It made no sense…

"Roy, I NEED shelves and tables for the trad-ing post." Sophie sought the old man out at the diner. She was drained from her confron-tation with Zeke, but it was more important than ever that the trading post succeed, that she fully commit to stay. "Do you know where I can get some?"

"There's wood and antique furniture in the schoolhouse. All you have to do is pull stuff out." Roy continued to sip his coffee.

"I'm ready whenever you are." Sophie was too wired to have coffee and wait for the old man to feel like helping her.

Roy squinted at her. "Can I finish my coffee?"

"Sure." Sophie sat at the counter and waited. She waited while Roy made a circuit through the diner, while he topped off his coffee cup, while he went to the bathroom.

"Ye-up. I'm ready now. The sun should be up high enough for the ground around the schoolhouse to be dry."

They stopped at the inn to pick up the keys. Roy made small talk with Mitch, rubbing his breastbone and holding back belches. It was clear the old man needed a better diet. All that fat-laden food and multiple cups of coffee seemed to be wearing on the old guy.

"Mom!" Andrew hopped down the stairs. "Can we come to school with you? We'll sit and color."

"It's no longer a schoolhouse, kiddo." Roy

pushed up the sleeves of his faded blue coveralls. "Used mostly for storage now."

"Zeke read *Mama Duck, Papa Duck*," Alexander reported, hopping down after his twin. "He was a cranky pants."

"I'm not sure we want him along, then." Roy ruffled Andrew's hair.

"He'll be fine as long as he doesn't have to read." Andrew hopped toward the door and his jacket.

"He doesn't read much better than us." Alexander ran to catch up with his brother.

"Really?" Roy looked intrigued.

"Really." Zeke climbed down the stairs on heavy feet. "I don't see why everyone has to know."

"But now everyone will," Mitch murmured apologetically. "Small town and all."

"Can you read—" Roy glanced around "—that plaque on the wall?"

"The one that says welcome?" Zeke groused.

"Yep, that's the one." Roy nodded. "Just wait. I'll find something you can't read."

"Won't be all that hard," Zeke grumbled, putting on his jacket.

Oh, her nanny was a cranky pants, all right. Sophie went over to him and kissed his cheek, a reward for standing tall.

"You shouldn't do that," Zeke growled, but his words lacked bite.

They traipsed down the highway, through the intersection and up the small hill to the white steepled schoolhouse.

Roy opened the door and stepped back. "Be careful poking around in there. Things are stacked like dominoes."

"I'm familiar with the Second Chance storage technique." Since that's what she'd dealt with at the trading post. "Do you know where tables and bookshelves are?"

"Sure, I do." He'd retreated to a path beneath the schoolhouse. "On the far side. And at the front."

"Basically, far away from the door," Zeke deadpanned, still in crank mode.

"Basically," Roy said cheerfully. "If it was easy, someone would've cleaned that place out long ago."

"How about we help the lady by passing back boxes until we can get what she needs?" Zeke stepped in Roy's path.

"Sure, sure. We can do that." Roy glanced at Zeke's boots. "Sophie can pass things out to you and you can pass it to me. I'll do most of the walking, seein' as how you're still limping."

"Seein' as how..." Zeke climbed the steps

without so much as a half limp. "Boys, stand back and stay out of trouble."

Sophie kissed the crankster's cheek again.

"What was that for?" Zeke touched his cheek.

"You fought for us. For me." Twice. "And look. There's enough inventory here to last a long time."

Zeke sighed heavily. "If you go on about me being your hero, I just might have to quit."

"No-no-no." The boys surrounded him and told him in no uncertain terms that wasn't going to fly.

Zeke gave Sophie a long-suffering look, but then he smiled at the twins and ruffled their hair.

Sophie knew she could make this work, but she turned to the task at hand. Out came a four-point rack of antlers, which pleased the twins to no end.

"We'll use those to practice roping later," Zeke promised them. "Those are not to be used as swords or stabbing toys."

The boys promised, but they held on to the antler spikes like handrails on the subway.

Next came boot boxes filled with cowboy boots. Used. The smell wasn't pleasant.

"What in the world am I going to do with all these?" Sophie asked.

"Sell them." Zeke shrugged. "I've seen

pairs go for good money at rodeo swap meets. There's nothing as valuable as a pair of well-broken-in boots to a cowboy."

Sophie made a mental note to order deodorizers to stick in the boots.

Heavy boxes came next, full of what looked like school textbooks.

Sophie dragged a child's school desk away from the door.

"Cool!" Alexander saw it. "Dibs!"

"Where's mine?" Andrew immediately whined. He darted up the steps to look inside. And then raised his face to the heavens and wailed, "There was only one?"

"Zip it, little man," Roy said with a chuckle. "There are plenty more where that came from. They're just buried."

"I want a desk. I want a desk." Andrew channeled a pogo stick on the porch. "I want to draw something for Mom."

"That's your cue to move a little faster," Zeke said to Sophie after he encouraged Andrew to calm down.

"Because I definitely need another love letter or work of art from my son." Seriously. Sophie loved that her boys did that.

Zeke's frown softened, along with his tone. "Let's find a desk before Andy brings the deck down."

Sophie passed out box after box, plus clusters of items. Fishing rods. Old waders. A deep-diving suit. And luckily, a desk.

"This is mine. This is mine." Andrew danced around the desk when Roy and Zeke had it on the ground.

Alexander handed his brother a math book. "Let's study."

How adorable.

"I think you've uncovered a table." Zeke pointed behind Sophie.

She turned. Homely as the table was, it had four sturdy legs. With a tablecloth—ordered online and delivered by the brown truck—it might not look too bad.

There was a bookcase with a glass front. It was filled with all kinds of odd things, like bags of bags of ping pong balls, but no paddles. These had never been opened. Treasure to the twins. She needed to find something to put all the toys in, and it wasn't going to be smelly boot boxes.

Zeke and Roy carried the emptied bookcase to the trading post, and then they moved the table. By the time they returned the second time, Sophie had uncovered another two bookcases and a few end tables. They were scarred and in need of love, but she was happy with her finds. Less happy at the thought of returning the things they'd taken out to the schoolhouse. But she had no other place to store them, especially the odorous boots.

"Look, Zeke. Another saddle." She'd found one in the rafters of the trading post. This one was propped up on a park bench on the far side of the schoolhouse.

"That's a show saddle. Look at all the silver embellishments." Zeke rubbed his fingers over the round pieces threaded through leather.

"Do you want it?" He seemed enamored with it.

Zeke shook his head. "It's small. Made for a woman or a teenager."

"What do you think it's worth?"

"Not as much as you might think. Three hundred on a good day."

Sophie frowned. "But all that silver…"

"I doubt it's high-quality silver." This from Roy, peeking over her shoulder. He belched. "Excuse me." And then he walked out the door.

"Don't worry about what that saddle will bring you." Zeke fingered a lock of Sophie's hair. "Somebody is going to think this saddle is a work of art and just what they've been looking for." Zeke's eyes were a clear green, as clear as the content of his words.

Previous protests aside, the way Zeke was

looking at her, she could believe she was a treasure to him.

Sophie couldn't move. She didn't breathe. She waited. She waited to see if Zeke was going to forget about their differences and kiss her.

"Mom, gotta potty!" Andrew jumped up and down near his desk.

"We can go back on our own." Alexander turned to run.

"Nope." Zeke put his fingers in his mouth and whistled. "Wait for me." He gave Sophie one last look. "I've got this."

She wished he'd gotten her.

"Welp, I need a break, missy." Roy waved and walked away. "I'll be back soon."

She dragged a box of license plates from several states out onto the porch, thinking it would be easy for shoppers to browse through. She tried to lift it, but didn't get her knees under it. Her glasses slipped and then her momentum carried her forward into the stack of boxes at the bottom of the stairs, through the stack and down the hill. She rolled and slid and came to a rest on the road's shoulder.

Sophie's glasses were missing. The world was a blur. And her body... Well, now she knew how a discarded rag doll felt.

Uneven footsteps pounded on pavement. "Sophie! Sophie!"

Zeke.

"I'm okay." She didn't feel okay. She felt scraped and bruised and embarrassed.

"Sophie." She couldn't make out the expression on Zeke's face but she could see his tall frame. "I'm almost there."

"I need surgery." She'd have her eyes done so she didn't need glasses. She'd been too scared to do it before, but she'd missed the sight of her cowboy running to her rescue. "Are the boys okay?"

"The boys are at the inn, but you need a doctor." Zeke stopped running and turned. "Roy, call for a doctor." And then he was by her side, wrapping his arms around her and holding her close. "I've got you. Where does it hurt?"

He was warm, and the strength of his arms was comforting.

Sophie sighed and snuggled closer. "I lost my glasses." Sophie was horrified to realize how close she was to tears. "I don't need a doctor right now. I need corrective surgery on my eyes." She pulled back, looking up into his face, his blurry face. His blurry, handsome face.

"Now is the time for something," he murmured. "Something like seize the day." And then he drew her snug against him, lowered his mouth and kissed her.

Oh.

He eased off the kissing pedal and slowed down, smoothing her hair. "What a mess. And I don't mean you. You're beautiful. It's us that's a mess, a potential pitfall."

She wished she could make out the expression on his face. It would help her choose the right tone of voice when she reassured him. "This is the only fall I plan on making."

He could certainly see hers. He pressed his thumb against the crease in her forehead. "Let me find your glasses."

"My hero," she murmured, content to let him search. "You shouldn't have run over here. Is your leg okay?"

"I'm fine. Sit here and wait for me."

"Hi-dee-ho." It was Roy. He had a distinctive smoker's voice. "Am I calling for medical or not?"

"Not," Sophie said firmly.

"Can you find Sophie's glasses?" Zeke hooked an arm around Sophie's waist, bringing her to her feet.

"I see 'em up the slope a ways. Good thing my vision is still twenty-twenty." Roy trudged up the hill slowly, making Sophie feel guilty for needing his help. "Got 'em."

"Thank you." Sophie covered Zeke's hand on her hip with her own, refusing to let him go. "If you could bring them to me, I could clean up my spill and put things back in the school-house."

"Oh, no you don't," Zeke began in a take-charge voice. "When you get your glasses, you're going to head back to the inn for a break. Roy and I can put things back."

"But—"

"No *buts*." He kissed her fast, leaving her breathless.

"You may not read so good, son," Roy said to Zeke. "But you can run good in them cowboy boots."

And he could kiss good in them, too.

But Sophie kept that to herself.

CHAPTER EIGHTEEN

"BIG DAY TOMORROW." Zeke led Sophie out on the inn's back porch after dinner to look at the stars.

The twins were asleep. He and Sophie had their heavy jackets on and he'd brought one of Odette's quilts to snuggle under. They settled into chairs that faced east and the mighty Sawtooth Mountains. Zeke covered them beneath the quilt and took hold of Sophie's hand.

It was a bittersweet time. Zeke's days as her nanny were winding to a close. Once he returned to the Bucking Bull, he'd be able to see her only on the weekends. There'd be no more stolen kisses. No more hours spent reading with the twins, which he didn't hate as much as he thought he would. He might even be learning a word or two.

"You and Laurel are opening for business tomorrow."

"When I remember what the trading post looked like inside a few weeks ago...I just can't believe it."

"I bet you have so many customers that you sell out the first day." Baby cups and bear traps would be her bestsellers.

"I don't want to talk about the store." Sophie clasped his hand in both of hers. "We're alone and I want to hear more about you, about your childhood. We never talk about that."

And with good reason. "You want to know about my reading struggles?"

"No." She scowled, the stern lines on her face illuminated by the moon. "I mean, if it's part of your childhood, yes. But...you don't talk much about your dad and I haven't heard anything about your mother."

"My mother..." Zeke stared up at the velvety sky. "She left after my grandfather died and my grandmother moved in with us."

Sophie made a soft sound of distress.

"My dad said she didn't like how hard ranch life was. And my grandmother... She said poverty didn't fit with my mother's pride."

"I'm trying very hard not to say something bad about her right now." Sophie drew Zeke's hand into her lap.

"She used to read to me every night. She left before I went into kindergarten."

"Under the Big Bright Moon," Sophie murmured.

Zeke nodded. "It was one of her favorites."

"It's one of mine now, too." She sighed, nestling her head on his shoulder.

He breathed in her scent, absorbed her warmth and tucked the moment away for a future date. A time when she'd just be a memory.

"My mom was one of those helicopter parents," Sophie admitted. "Always hovering. Always worried that I'd be the Monroe who wouldn't be hired to work in a Monroe company. Cam was a shoe-in to work at one of our hotels. Shane was a shoe-in for management anywhere. It wasn't until I was hired to manage the Monroe art collection that I felt I'd earned her approval."

Zeke's shoulder blades stiffened. "She's not going to be happy about you dating me."

"I'm not fifteen," Sophie said staunchly, squeezing his hand. "I don't need her approval. Stop worrying about what other people think."

"I can't. I've been doing that my entire life. Kids made fun of me when I tried to read. Teachers put me in special learning groups where I never learned anything. After my grandmother died, I dropped out of high school because it was easier to be good at ranching and rodeo than it was to try to fit in." That hurt to admit.

"Kids are mean." Her breath wafted across

his chest. "Were you a rodeo star? Were you ever on TV?"

"Once or twice. But I never got too hung up on the popularity stuff." He'd been too focused on making money and keeping it in his pocket. "I did well at calf roping until I worked my way up the rodeo ranks and couldn't make out what the more complicated contract forms needed." That hurt to admit even more than his being bullied at school.

Silence stretched between them.

"Sophie." It was time to face facts. He had to prep her for the end. "This... Us... It's a bad idea." He was full of painful admissions this evening. "We can spend time together until I return to the Bucking Bull. But that's it. Don't hang your hopes on me."

"You think I'll have second thoughts by the time you get cleared to ride." Not a question.

"I hope not, but it would be for the best, wouldn't it?"

"Easier for you, you mean." Sophie refused to be baited. She sounded as content as a cat who'd just had a bowl of sweet cream. "You don't date much, do you?"

"No, ma'am."

She nudged his chin with her forehead. "Save your ma'ams for my mother. She'll love your manners."

He didn't think he'd ever meet her mother. Or impress her if he did.

"When I was a little girl, I used to practice serving tea—"

"With that antique tea set."

"Yes. Practice, not play." She nodded. "I thought I'd need those skills to marry a prince someday."

"I don't think you have to give up on that dream," Zeke said softly. "You're a Monroe, after all."

She stared up at him. "Dreams change as you age. When I was a kid, I wanted a prince. When I was a teenager, I wanted a rock star. When I was in college, I wanted a man who'd tick my mother off."

She'd been a dreamer, which explained why she wouldn't listen when he said the two of them together wouldn't work. "And now?"

"And now I realize that princes are busy saving the world, rock stars flame out and men who'd tick my mother off aren't the best husbands and fathers."

Her ex-husband must be a piece of work. Zeke couldn't stop asking, "And now?"

"And now, Mr. Roosevelt, I want you." She hadn't listed his good features. Perhaps she'd known he'd argue. "It's a beautiful night and you haven't kissed me once."

Zeke stared into her eyes. He was in a precarious place. He had a beautiful woman in his arms, but he had no right to keep her. No right to whisper secrets on a back porch under the moon. No right to imagine what Sophie would look like when they were old and gray. No right to shift her in his arms and kiss her as if this kiss was their last.

"YOU HAVE A knack for this." Shane's praise warmed Sophie. "I wish I would've recognized your talent before. I would've brought you in to manage our boutiques at our hotels."

"There's more to life than art," Sophie quipped. "But I would have turned you down. I needed my independence from my twin."

The fur trading post was clean. Merchandise was on display.

Sophie had swept and mopped the floors. She'd swept the log walls clean of cobwebs. An old rag and some lemon oil had done wonders with the old counter. The wood slab on top gleamed. The windows were free of grime and cobwebs. The new window Roy had installed let in lots of warm, natural light. She was ready for business. And for love. She'd never been happier than she had these past few days.

Shane was still marveling over her shop.

"You took antique bikes and made them into porch railings."

"Which any customer can purchase," Sophie pointed out. Plus they were ideal to keep customers from falling off the porch. She'd even had Roy add railings to the steps, because no one should tumble down a hill in Second Chance. "Do you think Grandpa Harlan would approve?"

"Yes," Shane said emphatically, earning a hug. Released, he continued his perusal. "Where's that elephant bell?"

"I'm going to donate it to the Monroe Art Collection."

"No!" Shane drew back, aghast. "If anything, you should keep it."

"Here? It's too precious to be kept here." If she'd learned anything these past few weeks, it was that special things shouldn't be cocooned in a dark storage building. And that's where the bell would have to go if she kept it, because it wasn't for sale. "Look at this." Sophie pulled out a record album from beneath the sales counter. "This is one of Grandpa Harlan's albums, remember?" She flashed the colorful Hoosier Hot Shots cover to Shane.

Shane chuckled. "Back in the day that old man could cut a rug and carry a tune. No wonder the ladies loved him." He considered her for a moment. "And speaking of love…"

"Butt out." Shane was at risk of losing all his goodwill.

Her brother frowned. "Think twice before starting anything with your cowboy nanny."

"It's too late for advice." Zeke was wonderful. They spent time together at meals and after the boys went to bed. "The *Love Boat* has sailed and we're doing very well, thank you." They were doing well because a truce had been declared. They were each no longer trying to convince the other that their point of view regarding the relationship was right. That left a lot of time better spent kissing and cuddling.

Shane opened his mouth to argue, but Laurel entered before he could get in his rebuttal.

"Sophie, it's time." Laurel wore little makeup, but she glowed with happiness in her silver leggings and teal tunic.

Flip and Odette stood behind her. The two elderly sisters had their craftwork on sale in the mercantile—paintings, quilts, knitted items. They looked worried. Brows furrowed, mouths drawn, hands clasped.

"People are going to love your stuff," Sophie reassured them.

"Love." Shane shook his head, but dutifully carried the sandwich board sign Roy had made them to the highway and propped it on the road's shoulder. With a wave, he retreated to the inn.

"That sign declares we are officially open." Laurel pressed a hand over her baby bump, but her smile was out for all to see.

The sun was also out. The sky a rich blue. The air warm. All of which would have been a good omen for business if the highway hadn't been empty.

"Now what?" Flip asked.

"Now, we sit and wait for customers." Laurel sat in an Adirondack chair on the porch and picked up a pinned quilt square. "And we gossip. About Sophie, because I'm boring."

"Please." Sophie rolled her eyes. "I'm just as boring."

The other ladies begged to differ.

"If you have your heart set on that cowboy—" Odette clacked her knitting needles together "—you need to seal the deal. Do you cook?"

"No."

"That's a shame." Flip had a skein of glittery green yarn and was rolling it into a ball. "Do you ride well?"

"Horses? No." Sophie nudged Laurel's shoulder to stop her cousin from laughing.

"I know." Odette stopped knitting. "Do you dance? Gentlemen love to dance."

"Oh, especially cowboys." Flip slid Odette a sly glance.

"I have no dance skills either." Sophie sighed as if she was a failure. "I'm not athletic in any way. I guess that means I'll just have to seal the deal the old-fashioned way."

The two elderly women gaped at her.

Sophie couldn't keep a straight face. "With love and kisses."

As their laughter faded, a car pulled up in front of the inn across the road. A man and a woman got out.

"Look." Flip grabbed Odette's arms. "Are those customers?"

It took Sophie a moment to register the familiar faces. "No. That's my family." Her mother and younger brother, Camden.

Sophie hurried down the stairs to greet them. "Mom? Cam? What are you doing here?" The question was directed at her mother, who hadn't been scheduled to visit. Cam… They'd been waiting on him for months, as well as cousin Jonah, also a no-show.

"Oh, honey." Mom sniffed, sucking back tears. Beneath her jacket she wore a blue-checked blouse, white leggings and black suede booties. Her highlighted, short brown hair was carefully coifed and defied the will of the wind.

"I've left your father. I don't agree with what he's done to you three."

"Mom." Sophie hugged her. "You didn't have to leave Dad."

"Oh, yes I did. And I'm not the only one leaving. Your aunts Maggie and Rose said they're leaving, too."

Sophie stared up at Cam, her chin resting on her mother's shoulder since she was still in her embrace. "That seems rather extreme."

Cam rolled his eyes.

"Does it?" Mom held her at arm's length, taking in Sophie's blue jeans and lightweight sweater. "I'm going to sue your father for my share of community property and then give it to my children. Rose thinks it's an excellent idea."

Moving to hug Cam, Sophie shook her head. "I don't think this is what Grandpa Harlan would have wanted."

"That crafty old goat knew exactly what he was doing," her mother snapped.

A car stopped at the intersection coming from Boise to the west. The driver made the left turn toward them slowly. Rather than gaining speed, the driver pulled over in front of the general store. The occupants glanced over their shoulders to the mercantile and fur trading post.

"Woo-hoo!" Laurel hooted and waved. "Our first customers."

Mom's shoulders slumped. "You went ahead with your plan to open a store in this one-horse town? Unbelievable." She sighed. "At least I don't have to worry about Camden opening a restaurant here."

"At least," Sophie murmured, pinning Cam with her gaze. "Hey, I need to get to my store, but later you're going to come clean about what took you so long to get here."

"Are you selling Van Goghs?" Cam ignored Sophie's opening and pointed to the trading post. "Out of a log cabin with a car crashing through the front?"

A middle-aged couple approached. "Is that your store? When we saw the Edsel front end on the porch we had to stop."

"It is my store." Sophie held herself proudly as she escorted them to the trading post. "I sell oddities and collectibles. And my cousin opened a boutique in the brick mercantile."

"What's the name of your store? I don't see a sign." The woman chattered happily. "I'm in a church club. We shop thrift and estate sales. Your store looks like a gem."

Sophie had forgotten to give her business a name or even make business cards. "My Adorable Heathens," came blurting out of her mouth.

She chuckled. So much for her classy reputation. She let them enter first.

"Oh, Jim. Look at this!" The woman dived right in, setting things on the sales counter that she found interesting almost immediately. "Do you buy things, as well?"

"Yes." *Thank you, Zeke, for preparing me for that.*

Cam came to stand next to Sophie. "Wow. Impressive. I thought it'd be filled with junk and smell like my old gym shoes."

She elbowed him, thinking of all those stinky cowboy boots in the schoolhouse.

"Sophie," her mother called from the mercantile. "You should come look at this painting for the Monroe collection. The one with the roses and moon is exquisite." She turned to Laurel to explain. "My daughter has a good eye when it comes to art. She buys up-and-coming artists for the family collection."

"Not anymore." Not that her mother listened to Sophie.

"I know what she used to do, Aunt Vicki." Laurel laughed and adjusted her tunic over her baby bump. "I'm your niece. Laurel *Monroe*."

Sophie's mother gasped. "I didn't recognize you without makeup. No one would mistake you for your famous twin now, honey. Ashley's still Hollywood's number one ingenue.

But you… Was it your intention to let your-self go?"

"Yep." Laurel grinned, not rising to the bait.

A tremor of trepidation descended Sophie's spine.

Appearances. This was a reminder they were important to the Monroes outside Second Chance.

But they're not important to me.

"Excuse me," Sophie's customer called from inside the trading post. "How much for the bear trap?"

If not for Cam's laughter, Sophie might have said it was free.

Another car pulled up across the street. And then another. One carload went into the general store. The other pointed up to the mercantile before entering the diner.

"You should get a milkshake at the Bent Nickel before leaving town," Sophie recommended to her first customers.

"Do you know, I saw the funniest T-shirts in the window of the general store over there." The woman chuckled. *"If you missed your last chance, make a stop at Second Chance."*

Mack was a marketing genius. She'd taken advantage of Sophie's and Laurel's opening to stock a new line of merchandise, including kitschy items with the town's name on them.

Sophie's customer ignored the prices marked and made an offer for eight items as a bundle. Overall, it was a fair price, and Sophie hugged the woman when the deal was done.

Cam wandered down to the diner. He was a chef and couldn't resist trying the work of others. Sophie was afraid he'd be disappointed in Ivy's fare.

Meanwhile, Sophie's mother had been poking around every nook and cranny of the trading post, front and back. "That kitchen is like a time capsule. It reminds me of my grandmother's home in West Virginia."

"Thank you for being supportive, Mom. It means a lot to me." She could've come in and given her the "how far the mighty have fallen" speech.

"I'm not being supportive." Her mother tsked, picking up a sliver baby cup. "You need to get your behind out of this town. I bet kids raised here don't get into Ivy League schools." Mom glanced around. "Speaking of which, where are my grandsons?"

"Their nanny took them to the blacksmith shop and maybe fishing." Sophie wasn't sure.

The baby cup clattered into the display. "Don't you know where your children are?"

"No one goes far in Second Chance, Mom."

Sophie gestured from one end of the main drag to the other. All within sight.

Another unfamiliar car parked at the diner. The passengers took stock of the mercantile and trading post before heading into the Bent Nickel. It was going to be a busy day.

"Why don't you get a room at the inn?" Sophie suggested. Mitch had plenty of rooms, but with so many people stopping, who knew how long that would last. "You're staying the night, right?"

"That's a hotel?" Mom peered across the road. "Is it one of those quirky places? You know. Where every room has a different theme, like Western bordello or Gothic romance?"

"No."

"Is it at least a five star—"

"No."

"Four—"

"No."

"Three-star hotel?"

"Forget stars, Mom." Sophie nudged her out the door. "What it lacks in stars, it gains in charm."

"But… But…" Her mother fluffed her short hair, eyes darting to and fro. "Monroes stay at starred properties."

"You'll see plenty of stars out your window tonight." With no snow clouds, the sky would be a velvety black. And with no lights for miles and miles, the stars would be out in a thick blanket.

"You shouldn't joke about amenities. Oh, look. There are my grandsons." Her mother waved and then asked over her shoulder, "Who's the man with them? I didn't recognize Laurel. I might not recognize another of your cousins."

"That's no cousin. That's my nanny."

"Did you say nanny?" Mom pretended to have weak knees. "I don't suppose he graduated from Young's Academy?"

"I don't suppose." Perhaps she shouldn't have exposed Zeke's reading challenges to the world. It was too much to hope for that no one would tell her mother. Most likely one of her boys would spill the beans. And then...

Sophie squared her shoulders.

It wouldn't matter, because she loved Zeke. His reading would get better. And her family would love him, too.

CAM WAS WAITING for Sophie in the common room when she and Laurel closed their stores for the day.

Citing exhaustion, Laurel disappeared into the apartment she shared with Mitch and Gabby. The twins and Zeke were outside practicing their roping skills. Mom was upstairs resting. And Shane was…wherever Shane was.

"I baked you a brownie in the microwave." Cam handed Sophie the warm confection in a mug. He excelled at making comfort food with whatever ingredients and cooking implements were available. And was equally excellent at cutting to the chase. "I've been talking to Dad. He and the uncles aren't happy that Laurel decided to stay here."

"She fell in love, Cam." Sophie paused to try her brownie using a spoon. It was delectable. "It's not like Mitch is going to stay here forever. He's got a law degree and years of experience practicing. If Laurel wanted to go to New York or LA, I'm sure they'd move." But that wasn't the plan.

Camden stared at Sophie with an indecipherable look.

That tremor she'd felt earlier returned. If the family wasn't happy with Laurel, they would also be unhappy with Sophie. "Seriously, Cam. What right do Dad and the uncles have to judge? They gave up shepherding us through our lives and careers the day Grandpa Harlan's will was read."

"Dad has had second thoughts."

Sophie bet it had something to do with his wife threatening to leave him. Not that she thought their separation would last long. Her mother was a pampered, beloved princess. And Dad made sure she knew it.

"Did you hear me?" Cam nudged Sophie's knee.

Sophie nodded. "That's just it, isn't it? Dad and the uncles gave us up. So what if they don't like the choices we make now? We don't work for them anymore."

Cam wasn't talking or acting as if he was unemployed and desperate for money. In fact, he was speaking as if he'd switched allegiances to cousin Holden's develop-and-sell side of the family.

"Where've you been?" Sophie demanded, suddenly angry. "And who've you been talking to besides Dad? You were supposed to arrive two weeks after we did, and it's been two months."

"I got a job at Boca Boca in Vegas, Uncle C.R.'s place." Their mother's brother. "And yes, Holden convinced me we should sell Second Chance next January in parcels."

"No one's decided that," Sophie said firmly. The last thing the town needed was to hear that sentiment. "We need all twelve siblings and cousins to agree." And she knew four who'd vote against.

"You're defending this place?" Incredulous,

Cam turned up his nose at the inn. "Have you eaten at the diner?"

"It's a diner, Cam, not haute cuisine."

"Still…"

"And don't you dare say anything to hurt Ivy's feelings. She's got a big heart."

Cam grinned as impishly as her boys when they'd sneaked chocolate. "Too late."

Sophie wanted to slug him in the shoulder. She took a bite of brownie instead.

"You know, Sophie, you can get a job elsewhere, too. You don't have to hide out here."

The twins' laughter, followed by Zeke's deep chuckle, drifted to her.

"You want me to go back to a commute, schmoozing dinners and cocktail parties? I'm a good mom here, Cam." For once, she didn't doubt her statement.

"And when your savings run out?" Her brother didn't pull any punches. "Will that provincial store support you?"

"I'll have Frank's child support." Her gaze drifted to the windows.

"Mom thinks you're rebelling because of what Dad did." Cam held a bottle of sparkling water toward her.

No one had spoiled Sophie in a long time, not even Zeke. She set her brownie aside, unfinished. She refused his offer of a water bottle, too, thinking carefully about her words. "Grandpa Harlan thought we could be bought and sold too easily. He wanted us to find our own path in life. You don't think by going to work for family again that you've sold out?"

"Sold out? What Grandpa Harlan did was steal our lives," Cam howled. "I had it all. I was in control of my own destiny."

"You weren't in control of anything." Shane appeared unexpectedly on the stairs, a cat burglar in training. "You worked for the family 24/7. Dad insisted you get better reviews every year. You won a Michelin star, but that same night you cooked until dawn trying to design a new menu. You didn't date. You barely slept. I don't even think you ate your own food. You still look a little too thin, Cam. Still think you're in control of anything?"

"Some people have big dreams." Cam's expression darkened. "I was trying to be the best."

"Maybe you should have been trying to be happy," Shane quipped, leaning against the wall.

Sophie had never been prouder of her twin than in that moment.

Cam simmered, collecting himself. "Look, this isn't about me." His jaw barely moved as he spoke. "Mom and I are here to take Sophie and the twins back to Vegas before she makes a mistake like Laurel."

"No," Sophie said. "I make my own decisions, and I'm staying."

"We're making it on our own here." Shane came to stand next to Sophie. "I'm on the town council."

"Still running things your way." Eyes narrowing, Cam shook his head. "Still running things you don't own."

"I own a share of this town, and like any investment I'm testing all the scenarios and examining all the numbers, unlike you and the rest." Where Cam's voice had been a wounded howl, Shane's was deep and demanding of respect. "You'll just be leaving stars in your wake if you keep on cooking for someone else. That's what Grandpa Harlan recognized. I think he wanted us to learn how to deal with adversity and change, because the best CEOs, the best business owners, the best *chefs*…they know how to do just that."

"I don't have the capital to start my own place." Cam scowled. He'd lived the celebrity lifestyle and spent his salary even though he'd had a comped suite at the Monroe hotel where he worked. "That's what selling this town would give me."

"Your share won't amount to much if we

don't make this town a special destination first."

Cam sat back. "What are you saying? You're asking me to stay and open a restaurant? Here? That's ludicrous."

Shane shrugged. "I'm asking you to consider investing in your investment, just until the end of the year. How you do that is your choice."

"Where would I stay?" Cam's gesture indicated the inn wasn't acceptable.

Sophie knew exactly what to say. "Winter is over. We're opening up some cabins. You can have your pick."

"Like summer camp," Cam scoffed.

Zeke and the twins entered the inn.

Sophie welcomed her boys with open arms, but kept her gaze averted from Zeke's. She didn't want Cam to consider him a target.

Zeke hung his hat on a hook by the door, along with his lasso. After a moment's hesitation where Sophie didn't acknowledge him, Zeke went into his room.

"That's your nanny?" Cam sneered.

"He's awesome." Andrew bounced on the couch cushion.

Alexander snuggled next to Sophie. "We're teaching him to read."

"Yep," Andrew confirmed.

Shane nodded, not helping at all, but Sophie

supposed that was calculated on his part. As was his next statement. "She's dating the cowboy, too."

Cam smirked but didn't say anything. He didn't have to.

"I knew it." Mom stood on the bottom stair, grimacing, with a hand over her heart. "I came just in time."

CHAPTER NINETEEN

Two new Monroes had come to town.

The shitake mushrooms were hitting the fan. Zeke was Sophie's little shameful secret.

Just as Zeke had expected. He shouldn't feel so sick to his stomach.

After she snubbed him, Zeke hadn't expected Sophie to invite him to dinner. After the snub, he shouldn't have accepted.

"Why are we eating so early?" Alex held on to Zeke's hand as they walked to the diner.

Andy skipped ahead. "Shouldn't we wait for Grandmother Monroe and Uncle Cammy?"

"I'm not sure why I'm here." Zeke opened the door for his charges and Sophie to enter the Bent Nickel. "Mitch was making lasagna." Which was spicy and filling. "Don't sugarcoat it. Tell me."

When he'd brought the twins in after a session of roping—where he didn't get hit by a rope once—Sophie hadn't run up to kiss him the way she had been the past few days. She didn't even look at him.

He'd told her he wasn't good enough for her family. But no. She had to drag him through it, live and in person. That stung worse than any bee sting, because it hurt all over.

"You want the truth?" Sophie said tartly. "Mitch's lasagna is store bought and frozen. The noodles are like cardboard. The cheese has no taste at all." She marched through the door. "And we're eating early to avoid Uncle Cammy and Grandmother Monroe."

The twins exchanged glances, mouths forming little Os.

"Scoot." She shooed them toward their regular booth.

"It's not a bad thing to be a little less honest," Zeke said in a voice low enough the twins wouldn't hear. "To the boys, at least."

"We've been here for over two months," Sophie began her defense, talking to Zeke over her shoulder. "My brother is a world-renowned chef. My mother is a pampered guest everywhere she goes. We don't want to be here when they arrive."

Not surprisingly, Sophie's defense didn't mention Zeke's reading ability or his lack of education.

"That doesn't explain why I'm here." Zeke wanted to hear her say it.

Sophie whirled, placing her palm on his

chest, still not meeting his gaze. "I can't leave you alone with my family."

"You're embarrassed." Zeke was angry, even if he couldn't blame her. His pride was hurt, not because she wasn't standing up for him. He'd never expected her to. But because he couldn't be the man she deserved.

"I'm not embarrassed. I'm protective of what's mine." Sophie turned, and waved to Ivy. "Four specials, please."

She'd ordered for him? That was even more upsetting. "I'm no one's possession. Three specials, Ivy. I'm not staying."

"He is staying," Sophie snapped. "And, Ivy, my brother Camden is a food snob. I apologize if he said anything that was out of line."

Ivy's brows lowered. "He's not allowed in my diner."

"See?" Sophie did look at Zeke then. "My family wreaks havoc wherever they go. I'm protecting you *and* I'm buying you dinner. Try the special." She slowed down. Stopped. Swallowed, eyes suddenly filled with tears. "Please. Let me try to ease them into this." She pushed her glasses back into place.

Zeke sighed, knowing he'd stay. She had his heart wrapped around her finger. He swallowed his pride. "Okay, but I'll have the cheeseburger." He slid into the booth next to Andy. "And we should try comfortable silences."

"Are we getting another divorce?" Alex asked, brow furrowed.

Sophie's eyes widened. "Honey, Zeke and I aren't married."

Loud, shocked tone. Hurried speech. They were breaking up, all right.

"Have you looked into hiring a Young's Academy nanny? I promised Franny I'd go back to being a cowboy next week." If it wasn't for his promise to work for Sophie for four weeks, Zeke would quit being her nanny right now.

There was a haunted look in Sophie's eyes that turned Zeke's stomach. He had to look away.

Leaning heavily on his cane, Egbert entered the diner. His gaze landed on their booth. "There you two are. A word, please."

Was it too much to hope that he meant to talk to the twins?

"I'm gonna add four chocolate milkshakes to your dinner." Ivy jotted down their order on her pad, which wasn't necessary considering they were the only ones in the diner besides Egbert.

"Three milkshakes and an iced tea," Sophie adjusted their order.

"You may not *be* married," Ivy said as she

returned to the kitchen, "but you *act* like you're married."

Zeke rubbed his forehead and made a mental note to call his doctor tomorrow to see if he could get cleared to ride without having to go all the way to Ketchum for a checkup. His truck parts had yet to come in.

"I thought of another bit of history that might interest you." Egbert leaned on Sophie and Zeke's table.

"More tales of Merciless Mike Moody?" Zeke built a grin for the boys, but it felt heavier than a tall stack of hay bales.

"No." The old man gave Alex his Santa-like wink. "This is a love story, my boy."

"Perfect timing," Zeke said under his breath. The irony wasn't lost on him. Their love story was coming to an end.

"Can we start this night over?" Sophie asked Zeke, meeting his gaze squarely. "I'm sorry."

He should have refused her apology. He should have canceled his order. Instead, he nodded and slung his arm over Andy's thin shoulders.

Ivy brought Egbert a chair.

The bearded old man sat slowly. "You know, after Old Jeb survived that attack by Merciless Mike Moody, he took a good look at his life and decided he needed a wife."

Sophie made a noncommittal noise. "Could we hear this story another time?"

"Oh, there's no time like the present, eh?" Egbert fluffed his beard and eyed the community coffeepot. "Back then, women were in short supply here in Second Chance. And Old Jeb decided he'd write a letter and send for a mail-order bride. Or at least, he would have written a letter if he knew his letters."

Zeke felt heat rise from his chest to his cheeks. He crossed his arms and stared out the front window.

"Seriously, Egbert." Sophie smiled apologetically at Zeke. "This isn't the best time for a story."

For this story.

"We're all waiting on our dinners." Egbert waved off her protests by explaining he'd ordered ahead. "Now, Old Jeb wasn't sure he could trust Eldred Lee to write the letter for him." Egbert leaned forward and lowered his voice. "Eldred, that ancestor of yours, little lady, being known as something of a prankster. So, Old Jeb went to the local schoolmarm and asked her to help him pen a letter." Egbert considered Zeke's frowning face. "Imagine Old Jeb's surprise when the schoolteacher refused to write it for him. She insisted if he was sending to the East Coast for an educated bride that he be his bride's equal."

Zeke groaned and rolled his eyes. "Did you ask him to tell this story?"

Sophie shook her head and shushed him.

The unofficial town historian continued as if there'd been no interruption, "Now, Old Jeb thought this was a colossal waste of time. But he came to the schoolhouse every night to learn his letters. And during the day, he did his smithie business and worked on building a house an educated woman would be proud to live in on the very site the Clark ranch house sits today."

"Is there a movie of this?" Andy asked. "I think I'd like the movie better."

Sophie shook her head and shushed him.

The milkshake machine roared to life, bringing a much-needed period of rest from historical tales.

Sophie caught Zeke's eye. She looked as if she was fighting a smile. It was ridiculous. They'd been interrupted in the midst of an argument. Or a breakup. Or…

Zeke was suddenly grateful for the interruption.

"You've got about a minute before I start the machine again," Ivy warned.

"I'll hurry." Egbert regarded all four of them

with a benevolent smile and proceeded to talk at his same slow pace. "Now, Old Jeb, he learned his letters, but he learned something else, too. He learned about love." Chuckle. Beard fluff. "Darn if he didn't fall in love with Miss Carol. But he didn't want to ask her to marry him until the house was done, so he kept showing up for lessons even though he knew enough now to write his letter and send it off to Boston."

"Did Miss Carol marry him?" Alex preferred happy endings. "Was she Davey Clark's grandma?"

"Did Old Jeb die fighting off another robber?" Andy had more bloodthirsty ends in mind.

The milkshake machine rumbled to life again, nearly drowning out Ivy's apology.

More glances were exchanged with near smiles, this time between all four of them.

"You can finish your story now, Eggie." Ivy poured milkshakes into glasses.

"Good," Egbert said. "Old Jeb finished the house one day in spring when the wildflowers were blooming everywhere. He arrived at the schoolhouse with a bouquet of flowers, got down on one knee and asked Miss Carol to marry him."

"Did she say yes?" Alex scratched his cowlick.

"Or no?" Andy got to his knees.

Zeke tugged the back of Andy's shirt, encouraging him to sit back down, which he did.

"Well." Egbert rocked side to side in his chair. "She said, 'I'll marry you when you can write me a letter requesting my hand in marriage, the same way you were going to do for a stranger.'"

Zeke refused to look at Sophie. Not only was she out of reach in terms of marriage but he wasn't the type of guy who'd write a woman a love letter. Sure, his reading comprehension might have gone up a little over the past few days with all the books the twins had him read. But writing?

"Easy as pie, Old Jeb thought. He went back to his new home and wrote Miss Carol a letter, the same as he would've done if he hadn't fallen in love with her."

"Did she say yes?" Alex squirmed next to Sophie.

"I hope she said no." Andy scowled.

"Andrew!" Sophie frowned at him.

Andy scoffed. "Who would marry someone because of a letter?"

The kid had a point.

"Show some respect, please." Sophie tried to lighten her tone. "After all, Old Jeb learned a new skill just to win a bride."

"A bride, yes," Zeke pointed out. "But he didn't learn to write *for* the woman he loved."

That earned him a frown from Sophie.

"Can I continue?" Egbert asked, not waiting for their approval to do so. "Old Jeb came back to the schoolhouse, got down on one knee and handed Miss Carol a new letter. And do you know what she did?"

"She kissed him." Andy turned up his nose. "Yuck."

"Nope." Egbert rocked side to side. "She turned him down again. Without even reading the letter."

"But he did what she asked him to do!" Alex tossed his hands. *"Women!"*

"Listen to this, my boy." Egbert cleared his throat nearly as loud as the milkshake machine. "Miss Carol told Old Jeb she wanted a love letter and a grand gesture to prove he wasn't choosing her just because she was convenient."

"What's *con-ven-ient* mean?" Alex asked.

"Easily available. She was the only woman around," Zeke said, fighting the feeling that he was convenient to Sophie and would be cast aside.

Why does it matter when I knew this was coming?

"What did Old Jeb do?" Andy asked. "Walk away?"

"He did." Egbert nodded. "He walked back to the smithie and he didn't come to the schoolhouse for a whole week. But when he did return, he had something really special planned. He brought Miss Carol a wood-burning stove for her schoolhouse. He brought her a palomino mare for her to ride from the ranch house to the schoolhouse every day. And he wrote her a letter, this time a love letter, telling her that no one else would do, that his heart would break if she didn't say yes this time."

"She said no." Andy rolled his eyes. "She waved bye-bye."

"You wouldn't want the horse?" Zeke asked, appalled.

"Nope." Andy shook his head. "Manure."

"Well, Miss Carol got up on that horse and told Old Jeb no one had ever tried so hard to be the man for her. They got married and lived a long life...considering."

Everyone at the table groaned.

"There's more to the story?" Sophie asked.

"There's always more to Eggie's stories." Roy turned in his stool at the counter, having come in without Zeke noticing. "Why do you think we all duck our heads when we see him coming?"

"What was that?" Egbert turned in his chair to look at Roy. "You want me to join you, Roy

Stout? Why… I'd be happy to." He levered himself to his feet using his cane and sat next to the town handyman. "Tell me the truth. You missed me over the winter, didn't you?"

The twins giggled. And even Sophie and Zeke set aside their differences of opinion to exchange smiles.

But those smiles faded, as Zeke had known they would.

Because he was just a cowboy with holes in his shirts and a big hole in his education.

Not even love could fill that.

CHAPTER TWENTY

"THE TRUCK IS HERE!" Alex ran to the front window of the Lodgepole Inn.

"Truck! Truck! Truck!" Andy hopped across the room to join him.

Zeke sighed and set down the book they'd been reading. He had two more days to work and fulfill his promise to Sophie as her babysitter. Every breath felt heavy. Every look laden with longing. Every word weighed and measured for meaning. He and Sophie hadn't been alone since her mother arrived.

Thankfully, it'd been a quiet day. Sophie and Laurel were across the street working in their shops. Mitch and Shane had taken Camden and Sophie's mother on a tour of Second Chance and the surrounding valley.

"Truck! Truck! Truck!"

The brown delivery truck didn't stop at the inn. Instead, it backed up to the garage bay of the general store.

"That's what he does when he has car parts."

Gabby sat at the check-in desk doing her math homework. "Makes unloading easier, I guess."

"Car parts?" Zeke perked up. "Boys, let's go see."

They put on their jackets and sneakers with lights in the heels that flashed every time they took a step. It hadn't snowed in a week.

The twins linked arms and marched to the general store chanting, "Truck! Truck! Truck!"

Zeke almost sang along with them. The delivery was certain to contain parts needed to repair his truck.

When they spotted Mack, she said as much. "Won't be long until I have your baby running again." She examined the deliveries and checked them against the driver's manifest. "I bet that feels good to hear."

It did. Zeke would regain his independence.

The twins had each latched on to one of Zeke's hands and were trying to spin around him like he was a maypole.

Roy joined them, pounding his chest as if something had gone down the wrong pipe. "Need any help with it, Mack?"

"No." She finished inspecting the paperwork and the two pallets that held her order. "I can't start it until tonight." She jerked her thumb toward the general store. "I've got a steady stream of customers, thanks to Sophie and Laurel."

"When do you think you'll have it done?" Zeke let the boys turn him slowly in place.

"Next week." At Zeke's groan, she added, "I'm sorry. I'm just swamped."

The slow turn now represented the speed at which Zeke's life was moving, which was almost nil. "You could hire Emily Clark. She needs some space from Franny." She'd stopped by the inn the other day looking for work.

The driver closed his back door and bid them farewell.

"Or I could help," Roy piped up, still pounding a fist to his breastbone. "I may not know how to connect that newfangled steering column. But I know a radiator when I see one. That, I can do. If Zeke can help me with the heavy lifting."

Zeke stopped being a maypole and gave Mack a hopeful smile. "What do you think?" Because he was thinking: *How hard could it be to install a radiator when the old one was already out?*

"Well…" Mack was a penny-pincher, having scrabbled to earn a living for years. It probably pained her to let an opportunity to make a buck pass her by.

Despite Roy's saying he had no interest installing the new steering column and wheel, Roy bent to examine the piece.

"And…" Mack said.

The twins tugged on Zeke's arms.

A car parked in front of the store and two kids ran inside with a bathroom wiggle to their step.

Mack took a step after them.

"We negotiated on a price, Mack," Zeke said. "I'm not going to deal you down." Fair was fair.

And the sooner his truck was fixed, the sooner he'd be seeing less of Sophie. He'd be out at the Bucking Bull and wouldn't need to come into town to check on the truck or her. She'd realize what a mistake her interest in him was and going their separate ways would be that much easier.

Mack nodded. "I'll open the bay. But I'm only authorizing you to install the radiator, Roy. And you have to promise to call me if you have any questions."

Roy straightened and saluted. "Yes, ma'am."

"Yes, ma'am," Zeke agreed, standing taller. And then he knelt with the twins. "We're going to fix my truck. Which means you can each bring one toy and one book from inside for when you aren't helping." Actually, he didn't plan on letting them help at all, other than having a good look-see inside the engine compartment. But where was the fun for a boy in that?

Alex and Andy went racing back to the inn.

Mack greeted the couple getting out of the car and gave them the nickel tour of the town—diner, store, boutique, trading post. And then she escorted them inside her store.

Alex stopped at the corner of the inn. "Can I bring two books?"

"You can bring three books." Zeke shooed him off, before turning to Roy. "I'm assuming you've put in a radiator before."

"Long time ago. It was an army Jeep." Roy rubbed his breastbone and swallowed. "Pretty standard stuff. Back then, they made radiators from metal. Yours looks to be plastic."

Zeke hadn't paid a lot of attention to what went under the hood, but he realized what Roy said was true.

"Good thing about plastic..." Roy patted Zeke on the back. "It's easier to lift."

The garage door rolled up. "It's all yours, boys," Mack said, smiling. "Including bringing all those car parts here. Thanks!" She waved and disappeared inside.

An hour later, the twins were bouncing about in the cab of Zeke's truck, having read their books and lost interest in the toys they'd brought along. The garage door was down to shelter them from the breeze coming down the hill.

"Can we play with your phone, Zeke?" Andy poked his head out the passenger window.

"No." They didn't need to distract themselves with technology.

"Please." Alex leaned toward his brother from the driver's seat.

Zeke and Roy were wrestling with the brackets that held the radiator in place and had been for a good half hour.

"You have skills at fixing things, Zeke." Roy stood, rubbing his chest. "Man, this heartburn."

"Did you eat Ivy's chili again?"

Roy shook his head, brow wrinkled.

"Please!" the twins chorused, still pleading for his phone.

The old man leaned against the truck fender. His face was turning red.

"Please!"

"No phone."

"I had the turkey sandwich." Roy stared at Zeke, but he didn't seem to see him. "I've never had indigestion from a turkey sandwich."

"Please!"

Zeke handed the boys his phone absently. "Do not make any phone calls."

"What is this?" Andy flipped the phone open.

"That's not a phone," Alex said.

Roy put his hands on his knees, shaking his head. "I don't feel so good."

"It's an old phone." What use did Zeke have

for a smartphone? He helped Roy over to a stool in the corner by the workbench. "I'll get you a water."

"Is it hot in here?" Roy panted.

"This is indigestion, right?" Zeke asked. There was no doctor in town and the nearest medical clinic was an hour's drive away. "Roy? *Roy?*"

The old man slid off the stool in slow motion. Zeke barely kept him from falling onto the ground.

Roy's eyes were wide. His body tense as if he was hurting. His mouth gaped open like that fish they'd caught weeks ago, and he was struggling for breath.

"Alex! Andy! Go get help."

Roy stopped breathing. His body went limp.

"Go! Now!" Zeke began CPR.

The next few minutes were a blur. Compressions. Breaths. Feeling for a pulse. Finding none. Sweating. Compressions. Breaths.

"I brought everything." Gabby burst through the side door nearest the inn with the twins on her heels. "Phone. First-aid kit. Defibrillator. What do you…" She took one look at Zeke performing resuscitation, dropped a large box near Zeke and made a phone call on the inn's wireless house phone. "What's my emergency? Man down."

"Tell them his heart stopped and he's not breathing." Zeke didn't lose his rhythm. "Boys, go find Mack. And he's not responding to CPR."

Gabby relayed Zeke's information about Roy's condition and then their address.

Alex and Andrew stood close together, holding hands.

"Yes, we have one of those." Gabby knelt next to the defibrillator and opened it up. She stared at Zeke, eyes wide and panic-stricken. "I...I...I can't do this."

It was important to stay calm.

Zeke was cold inside, despite sweating from effort and adrenaline. "Don't you die on us, Roy."

The twins began the windup to a wail.

"Alex. Andy. I need you to go find Mack." In the back of his mind, Zeke was counting. Five more compressions before he needed to give Roy two more breaths.

Instead of retrieving Mack, the twins climbed into the cab of his truck, ducking down so they couldn't see. There was nothing Zeke could do about them now. He wasn't going to tell them to run across the street to their mother.

"We can do that," Gabby said into the phone, still staring at Zeke. "I mean, Zeke can do that." She held her phone to her chest. "They want you to use the defibrillator." She gestured toward the open unit with her hand.

Zeke paused to give Roy oxygen and then returned to the task of keeping the old man's heart beating. He stared at the machine and gulped. "I…I know how to do CPR, but that machine…"

"There are instructions." Gabby set down her phone and held up a card with words. Too many words. "Right here." Comprehension dawned. Her shoulders drooped. "Oh." She'd remembered Zeke couldn't read.

Roy might die because Zeke couldn't read. His insides knotted tighter than one of those knots Egbert used to fasten flies to a fishing line.

The concrete was cold beneath his knees. Roy's face was pale. It wasn't right that the feisty old guy was going to die here, next to a grease stain.

"I can read them to you." Gabby sat up. "I can read them to you!"

Together they figured out where to put on the two electrodes and how to operate the machine, all while Zeke kept Roy alive.

Or at least while he kept up hope that Roy would stay alive until trained medical help arrived.

"Let's hope this works." Zeke shocked him.

Roy convulsed and sucked in air. Zeke felt for his pulse. It was there. Weak and slow. The old man drew a small breath on his own.

The door from the general store swung open. "How's it going in here?" Mack gasped and then ran to them. "Roy?"

"We need a doctor," Gabby said through her tears.

"There's one about to leave." Mack sprinted off.

Leaving Gabby and Zeke to hold vigil over Roy as he fought for life.

THERE WAS A lull in business. Sophie went next door to check on Laurel.

Odette sat in a rocker in the corner, knitting. She wore a chunky beige fisherman's sweater over a black turtleneck and a blue wool skirt. "I have to admit, you two were right. People actually pay money for things I make."

"Because they're beautiful," Sophie told her.

"I must have said that a hundred times." Laurel sat on a stool behind the counter, laying out fabric in a quilt block. "She just wants to hear it again."

Odette gave Laurel a narrow-eyed glare. "If you weren't so talented with a needle and thread, I'd put you in your place."

"Yeah, yeah." Laurel rolled her eyes. "A little less talk and a lot more productivity. Notice how much we've sold from your corner of the shop. We need to restock."

Sophie became aware of a hum. Distant. Like a truck coming over the summit.

"I've sold more than Flip's pictures have." Odette cackled gleefully. "I'm finally besting her. Who'd have thought after all these years…"

The hum turned into a high-pitched whine.

Sophie went to the door and looked out.

"Is that a helicopter?" Laurel joined Sophie at the open door.

Sophie's heart lurched. "The last time there was a helicopter here, it was for Zeke." To take him to the hospital.

Laurel clutched her arm. "It's landing at the intersection. Why?"

"Because we don't have a town doctor." Sophie tugged herself free and ran for the steps leading to the highway.

CHAPTER TWENTY-ONE

"YOU SHOULD GO to bed." Sophie combed her fingers through Zeke's hair.

"Soon." Zeke kept himself from leaning into her touch.

The twins were asleep in Zeke's lap. Her mother and brother had gone upstairs to bed.

Roy was safely in a hospital in Ketchum. Alive. For now. He was going to need three stents to keep his veins clear and a pacemaker. Who knew if he'd be able to return to work as the town handyman.

"One good thing came out of today." Shane sat on the hearth, preening. "We hired a new doctor."

Dr. Shannon had stopped in the general store for an energy drink at just the right time for Roy.

"We were lucky." Mitch sat on the stool behind the check-in desk. "*Roy* was lucky."

Zeke pursed his lips.

"How's Gabby doing?" Sophie asked, not turning away from Zeke.

"Still shaken," Mitch said. "Laurel's going to sleep with her tonight."

"I think Gabby and Zeke deserve accolades from the town." Shane was still in congratulatory mode, ecstatic he'd been the one to hire the doctor instead of Mitch. "You know, keys to the town. A medal."

Zeke didn't know about Gabby, but he didn't want anything to remember the day by.

"I should turn in, too." Mitch stood. "Someone should get down the mountain to check on Roy in the morning."

"Good idea." Shane got to his feet and stretched. "It was a good day, ladies and gentlemen. A good day."

The two men left them alone. Zeke didn't say anything, because he knew if he put words to what weighed on his mind things would not end well.

He drew the twins closer. They'd been comforted by their mother at the tail end of the crisis, and by dinnertime had eaten all their macaroni and cheese with a milkshake chaser, none the worse for wear.

"Do you want to talk about it?" Sophie ran her hand through his hair once more.

Zeke shook his head. "Tomorrow's my last day."

She sat back, letting her hand drop to her thigh. "Zeke, I…I haven't hired anyone else."

He breathed in the scent of her perfume, as

if it was going to be the last time. Because it was. "I promised you I'd work for four weeks. Franny expects me back day after next."

"But...what about *us*?"

Zeke forced his gaze to hers. Her glasses had slid down and she had to tilt her head back to see him.

"You know it's better this way." His voice was gruff, already beginning to shatter.

Sophie shook her head, making her glasses slide lower. "That's not true. If you're worried about my family and their approval, don't. My mother fawned all over you for saving Roy's life."

"I almost didn't." Zeke gulped around the lump in his throat. "I couldn't read the instructions on the defibrillator. Gabby had to do it. And now... She's probably scarred for life."

"Zeke—"

"You didn't see her face, Sophie." He inched away from her as much as he could with two boys in his lap. "Gabby was horrified at the possibility that I wouldn't be able to work the equipment, that it would fall on her. Everyone knows what a liability I am. And today it almost got Roy killed."

Sophie laid a hand on his arm. "Zeke—"

"You can't change my mind about what I know is true." He removed his hands from

Alex's and Andy's backs and pressed the heels of his hands against his eyes. "You can't fix me with four-year-olds teaching me how to read. It's best if I go." And don't look back.

"You don't need to be fixed."

"That's right." He latched on to her words, lowering his hands. "Because I can't be fixed. This is the way I am. And I'm okay with that." His gut clenched at the lie. "When I came to work for you, I was in a precarious position. In fact, I still am." Because she'd gotten him to believe in fairy tales, only to make him realize stories like his didn't have a happy ending.

"We can work through this."

"Can we? The way you've worked your way through arguments to stay in Second Chance? You committed to open the trading post and ignored that little inner voice that kept wondering if you were doing the right thing. You didn't love the trading post one hundred percent."

She frowned, straightening her glasses.

"You had doubts." He cast his gaze about, not wanting to register the look on her face when she realized what he was saying was true. "You didn't know if your grandfather would want you to keep or to sell his possessions. You didn't know if this was the right place to raise your boys. And you still don't know if I'm the right man for you." He wasn't.

"That's not true." She shook her head vehemently, keeping her voice down so as not to wake the twins. "I love you."

She'd never said it to him before. Zeke took a moment for the words to sink in, for his heart to embrace them, for his mind to reject them.

"I know you love me," he whispered hoarsely. *I know I love you, too.* Those words… He couldn't speak them aloud. "But you don't love me with all your heart, unconditionally, with one hundred percent certainty."

He saw awareness dawn in her eyes, followed by guilt.

It was nothing new. He'd known it. He'd witnessed it manifest the other night on their trip to the diner.

But it hurt like a jagged knife in the back to see the truth in her eyes.

"Tomorrow's my last day." He extricated himself from her children. It wasn't easy. But neither would be extricating himself from her life.

WHEN ZEKE CLOSED the door to his room, Sophie bent over, clutching her chest as if she could hold herself together.

The boys were still asleep on the couch. The inn was quiet.

And Zeke had rejected her love.

She was colder than she'd been on the coldest days in winter when she'd first begun mining the trading post for treasure. Her heart felt as if someone had stolen it from her.

She hugged herself tighter, rolling her shoulders together.

Zeke…

He wanted to watch her kids one more day. She'd have to see him. Smile as if he hadn't hurt her. Act normal around the boys.

Zeke…

She sucked in a sob.

"Sophie?"

She straightened, sniffing. "Shane." Of all the times for him to sneak up on her. She got to her feet, turning her back on him and blinking back tears. "Can you help me carry the boys upstairs to bed?"

"Soph." Instead of doing what she wanted, her brother turned her around and enveloped her in a hug.

Sophie had to hold herself very still and squeeze her eyes shut. Otherwise she'd break into sobs and Zeke's room was only feet away.

"Can we do this later?" she whispered, loving her brother for knowing she was in pieces. "Please."

He held her at arm's length, and waited for her to look at him before saying, "I'm going to beat the crap out of him in the morning."

"You'll do no such thing," she whispered back before picking up Alexander and heading for the stairs. Her feet sounded like they found every squeaky floorboard. "What are you doing up so late?"

Shane followed her on silent feet. "The doctor I just hired? I checked on him one more time. He was racked with guilt. He admitted he's a podiatrist. He can't be our town doctor. He'll be gone in the morning and our search for a town doctor will continue."

"So much for having one less thing to worry about." Sophie's room was at the end of the creaky, slightly listing hallway, two doors away from their mother. They removed Alexander's and Andrew's shoes and tucked the boys into the bed they shared without waking them. And then she and Shane sat in the corner of the room on the forest green carpet.

"A month ago, I was looking for all the differences between Zeke and me." She knotted her fingers in her lap, keeping her voice low. "And earlier today, all I could see was how similar we are."

Zeke hadn't hesitated to save Roy. As soon as he knew Roy was stable, he'd sought to comfort Alexander and Andrew. He'd thanked Gabby profusely, until she'd told him to stop. He was kind and giving and strong and smart. And she loved him so much her heart ached with it.

"And yet, he dumped you." Knowing Shane, he'd heard the entire exchange. "For all the right reasons."

Sophie elbowed him in the ribs.

"*Oof.*" Shane's scowl was illuminated by the bathroom light. "You're only mad because you know it's true. You wanted him to learn how to read so he'd be better qualified to marry into the Monroe family."

She wanted to deny it. She wanted to denounce the idea. But the truth was…

She was the woman with two art degrees who'd interned in Paris at the Louvre. She'd attended shows at Fashion Week and worn designer clothing. She'd attended the Met Gala more than once. "I'm a snob."

Shane's shoulders shook with silent laughter. "Took you long enough."

She tried to throw another elbow, but he swatted her arm away.

"You're staring down two different paths. You're at an intersection and you can only choose one direction. I know you've been playing at being a Second Chance citizen, but if you can't commit one hundred percent, like Zeke said, if you can't embrace the education the twins will get here and know it's the right path for them, you have to go back to being one of *those* Monroes."

"One of Holden's Monroes, you mean." That world didn't appeal to her the way it once had.

Shane nodded. "If you stay here, you have to accept these people for who they are, not how much money they make. And you have to accept yourself as a well-educated woman who sells secondhand junk."

"They're treasures." Was Zeke the only one who saw that? "If I go back to the Monroe world, the boys…"

"Wouldn't see you as much every day." Shane nodded. "But they'd learn to speak French fluently. And they'd play lacrosse and know the historical significance of the master painters."

"Grandpa Harlan wouldn't have cared about that." He'd have applauded them knowing how to lasso and fish and be independent and self-reliant.

But Shane wasn't done. "And your kids would remember—*vaguely*—the winter they spent in Idaho with a cowboy nanny."

"Zeke…" She squeezed her eyes shut. "I love him." So much.

"Which part of you loves him, Soph? The worldly Monroe side? Or the run-down-cabin Second Chance side?"

"I love him," she said, not willing to qualify it.

"Fine." Shane got to his feet and helped her to hers. "You love him, but he's not going to settle for the kind of love you can give him." He shrugged. "You'll find somebody else to love."

And with that, her less than supportive, infuriating brother left her to stew about who she was and who she wanted to be and how she could make one stubborn cowboy see that both sides of this Monroe could love him. Unconditionally.

CHAPTER TWENTY-TWO

"COME ON, BOYS. Get your coats." Zeke moved toward the door of the inn. "We're going to the Bucking Bull."

His words were met with silence.

His grandmother—the ultimate believer in rainbows and silver linings—would have asked him to look for something positive in the breakup. But it was hard to be upbeat when you were trying not to say, *I told you so, Sophie.*

"Why are you going to the Clarks'?" Sophie had been throwing away their empty oatmeal bowls. She stepped out of the alcove and looked at Zeke without looking him in the eye.

This was what their relationship had come to. She couldn't bring herself to look him in the eye.

Zeke kept looking at her eyes anyway. "They need to get back on a horse." And today was Zeke's last day as their caregiver.

"Na-uh." Andy crossed his arms and scowled. "No way."

"Pandora hates me." Alex made himself as small as possible on the couch, as if trying to hide.

Sophie glanced at her children, a frown forming on her brow. "Maybe we should just end things here."

"I'm not going to put them on Pandora." He had something much tamer in mind. "Davey's younger brother Charlie has a pony they can try."

"A pony?" Andy's frown softened. "A little horse?"

"A kid-sized horse?" Alex rose back up.

"A *pony* not much bigger than you," Zeke confirmed. "We'll get her saddled and I'll hold the bridle the entire time."

"Why do they need to do this?" Sophie was staring at the floor now. "They're not going to be cowboys."

"Because…" Zeke didn't know why it was important, only that he felt compelled to take them. "Because…everyone has to face their fears." Hadn't that been what the last few weeks had been about? Zeke had faced his fears with Sophie. And she'd proved his fears were founded. A guy like him didn't belong with a woman like her. "And because they need to forgive Pandora." He pulled two carrots from his pocket. He'd bought them at the general store earlier. "I couldn't live with myself if my favorite boys held a grudge against my favorite horse."

Sophie pursed her lips and finally had the courage to look him in the eye.

Zeke wished she hadn't. Her glasses couldn't hide the pain she felt, pain he bet was mirrored in his eyes. He turned his attention to the boys. "What do you say?"

"Maybe?" Andy looked to his brother.

"Okay?" Alex shrugged.

Sophie still hadn't spoken.

"I'm asking permission this time," Zeke said softly, slowly.

He expected her to give a curt, cold nod. To turn away. To let him go with regrets. So many regrets.

Instead, Sophie approached tentatively, as if he was a stray that might bolt. "Okay. They can go ride a *pony*." She stopped within kissing distance, not nodding, not turning away, not letting him go without regrets.

Hell and damnation. He couldn't take this. He couldn't not reach for her, dropping his pride in the process. He couldn't...

She rose up on her toes and kissed his cheek. "Be careful with your carrots."

Only then did she nod, turn away and leave him with regrets pressing on the back of his throat.

Zeke helped the boys get their jackets. It may be spring and sunny, but there was still a nip in the air.

Shane appeared on the stairwell. "I hear you need a ride."

"As long as it doesn't come with a lecture." The last thing Zeke needed today was Sophie's brother making him feel guilty for breaking his sister's heart. Zeke didn't see anyone defending his broken heart.

"Didn't you know?" Shane joined them at the door. "Not only does the driver have control of the music. He also has control of the conversation."

"Too bad you're not driving." Zeke held up the keys to the Hummer.

"Hey!" Shane frowned.

"You had me move your Hummer yesterday and I kept the keys. I guess that means I'm in charge of…everything. And you aren't allowed to say a word."

There was his silver lining. All it lacked was rainbows.

"So, *THIS* is a pony." Alex peered through the stall bars at the palomino. "Uncle Bo has a dog bigger than that thing."

Andy nodded. "His name is Spot and last

Christmas he came to Grandpa Harlan's house in the passenger seat of Uncle Bo's truck."

"Seat belt and everything," Alex said absently. He stared up at Zeke. "I see manure."

"You're not going in the stall," Zeke reassured him.

Alex blew out a breath. "Good."

Zeke went inside the pony's stall to saddle her.

Across the way, Pandora paced in her stall, whinnying to Zeke. She didn't like to be left behind. Like Sophie, Pandora was willing to stamp her feet and make it clear what she wanted, regardless of what was good for her.

Which wasn't fair to Sophie. Her whole life had been upended a few months ago. Of course, she'd still be figuring out what she wanted to do with it and whom she wanted to be with.

Regardless, it was no longer his concern. In a few months he'd probably be able to think of her without a painful pang in his chest.

"Who's going first?" Zeke led the pony into the barn's main corridor.

The two boys held their ground, not looking at each other or Zeke. Instead, they stared at the palomino pony with something akin to fear in their big brown eyes.

"Come on. I need a volunteer. Davey's probably sitting at the front window waiting to see

which one of you has enough guts to get on."
Zeke had forbidden the Clark boys to come
outside to watch.

"Davey wouldn't know who got on," Alex
said solemnly, the way one does when present-
ing an idea that might cross a line or two. "We
both look the same. Same height. Same nose.
Same size feet."

"Only our family can tell us apart," Andy
said just as solemnly. "Except for you."

"And Gabby." Zeke couldn't let them get
away with that. He suspected Mitch could tell
them apart, too.

"But not Grandmother Monroe," Andy added
mournfully.

Alex shook his head. "And when you leave
us, Grandmother Monroe will be our nanny."

Sophie's mother. And she couldn't tell them
apart. This didn't bode well.

But neither did the woeful show they were
putting on, postponing the inevitable.

"Boys." Zeke wound out the word, trying to
unravel whatever twin logic was going on. "If
you're thinking only one of you has to get on
to convince Davey you both got on, you need
to flip a coin to decide who's going for a ride,
because it's not going to be the taller twin with
the bigger feet or nose."

Alex looked to Andy. Andy looked to Alex.

And then they both turned to Zeke and said, "I'll go."

Taffy swished her tail and glanced at the two boys.

"It's settled." Zeke stroked Taffy's neck.

"It is?" Alex asked.

"Yep. You're both getting on." Before either boy could stall further, Zeke plucked Alex up and set him in the saddle. "You first. Your feet go here." He guided Alex's foot into the stirrup. "Heels down." Zeke reached for Andy, but the boy backed away.

"There's no room."

"Sure, there is." Zeke held out his hand. "Don't you trust me?"

The pony shifted her weight, resting her back leg.

Alex squealed in fright. "I want down. I want down!" But he held on to the saddle horn.

Taffy's ears swiveled, but she didn't budge.

Wide-eyed, Andy backed against the stall wall.

"I've got you." Zeke moved to stand next to Alex, putting his arm around the boy's thin torso. "Sit here for a minute. Being on a horse is like being on a boat. You've been on a boat before, right?"

Alex clung to him but nodded.

If he'd asked to get off, Zeke would've put

him on the ground. For now, they rode out his unease together. "Boats move with the waves. Horses move on their feet. Whoever is on top goes side to side."

"Oh." That was a very small "oh."

"I'm going to let Taffy walk toward the door, but I'm going to stand next to you the entire time." Zeke rested his hand on the cantle behind Alex. "Are you brave enough for that?"

Alex drew a deep breath and nodded.

They walked the length of the barn and back.

"I did it!" Alex beamed. And then quickly, "I want off."

"Okay." Zeke lifted him down and turned to Andy, who looked like he was holding up the stall wall. "Your turn."

Alex slung his arm around his twin's shoulders. "It's safe, Andy."

Andy gulped and took several small, reluctant steps toward Taffy.

The pony extended her nose, bumping Andy in the chest, causing the boy to giggle.

"That's what Uncle Bo's dog, Spot, does." Andy regained some of his stair-hopping confidence. "Remember, Alex? Spot nearly knocked Grandmother Monroe over."

Good thing Spot wasn't in Second Chance. At least, as long as Grandmother Monroe was here.

"Does Spot like to be scratched behind the ears like this?" Zeke rubbed behind Taffy's ears.

"Yes." Andy reached up to scratch Taffy behind the ears. It was an easy reach considering how low to the ground the pony was. "Is Taffy going to roll over and beg for a tummy rub?"

"Nope." When it came to moving, Taffy practically didn't—not forward, not backward and certainly not down on the ground. She was a minimalist unless food was involved, and that's what made her such a great ride for a child.

"Good pony." Andy gave Taffy a tentative pat on the neck. "Okay, I'll do it."

That was all well and good, but they hadn't given the oldest Clark boy proof that they'd ridden. "Can I lead you outside so Davey can see you?"

Andy gulped and said nothing.

"Okay. We'll stay in the barn." Zeke put Andy in the saddle and helped him get his feet in the stirrups. He walked next to him the way he'd done with Alex.

"She manured!" Alex cried, pointing to the barn floor. "Ew."

Andy held on tight to the saddle horn until Zeke stopped. Once his feet were on the ground, he puffed out his chest. "I rode a horse." He stood in front of Taffy and rubbed his hand beneath her forelock.

Zeke ruffled Andy's hair. "Great job."

"I want a pony." Alex joined them at Taffy's head, reaching up to scratch her ears.

Zeke hooked a stirrup on the saddle horn and loosened the girth.

At the other end of the barn, Davey opened the door, wearing a triumphant grin. He carried a bucket and shook it.

Taffy's ears shot up and before Zeke realized what was happening, she shouldered the twins out of the way.

Zeke lunged, reaching for Andy. His boot slipped in a pile of manure and they both went down. Luckily, Zeke twisted enough that Andy landed on top of him, not in dung.

Taffy reached Davey, who had a bucketful of carrots. He handed Taffy one, and then took her by the lead rope and led her back to her stall. "Zeke, aren't you the one who always told me to tie up a horse first thing?" Davey was all smiles as he tied the pony to a ring in the stall wall.

"Yep." Zeke took mental stock of his healed shinbone. Nothing felt amiss.

"Ew." Alex pointed at Zeke. "You landed in poop."

Warmth seeped into Zeke's jeans. He helped

Andy to his feet and then stood, removing his jacket and using it to brush himself clean.

Andy stood next to him. "Are you gonna be mad at Davey?"

"Are you gonna tell his mom?" Alex peered at Zeke's face.

"Because he came into the barn looking for mischief?" Zeke gave Davey a stern look, which earned him an apologetic glance. "No. Accidents happen and being a tattletale doesn't earn you any friends."

Davey was just defending his turf. Zeke would have plenty of time to talk to the boy about his behavior in the months to come.

"Do you have clean clothes for Zeke?" Alex stood and gestured toward Davey. "Uncle Shane doesn't like horse poop."

"Nobody at my house is his size." Despite not having a hand, Davey already had the pony's saddle off.

"I'll be fine," Zeke reassured them.

"Wait until we tell Mom we didn't fall in poop this time," Alex said gleefully.

Andy grinned at his brother. "Wait until we tell Mom Zeke did."

SOPHIE HAD BEEN dragging all morning, digging through boxes and missing Zeke commenting on each find.

She entered the Bent Nickel an hour before the trading post was supposed to open, intent upon two things—a stimulating cup of coffee and some good news about Roy.

Despite kids congregating at the back corner, the diner seemed empty without the town's handyman. Somber. Sophie sat at her usual booth and stared at the empty seat across from her.

Ivy brought her a pastry. "On the house. I haven't heard anything from Mitch about Roy. Have you heard from Laurel?" She'd gone with Mitch to check on Roy.

Sophie shook her head.

"Odette came by earlier." Ivy's smile was best classified as attempted. "She's in a tizzy. Says she's going to have to run the mercantile today. I bet she scares away customers."

"I'll make sure it doesn't get out of hand." Not that Sophie's strength was managing the old woman.

Zeke could do it.

She'd come to the diner to escape thoughts of Zeke.

Sophie's mother entered the diner and called out to Ivy, "Latte, please." She claimed the seat opposite Sophie. "What's wrong? You're all blotchy and you look like you might cry."

Sniffing, Sophie righted her glasses. "It's the pollen."

"I still can't believe you've got a cowboy nanny." Mom fiddled with her large rings. "Wait until I tell the girls at the country club."

"Better phone that report in." Sophie tapped her ringless fingers on the Formica. "Today's his last day."

Ivy cleared her throat.

Mom glanced at her. "Didn't you hear me? I want a latte. On second thought, make it skinny and extra hot." She shook her head with a mini eye roll, one she used when she didn't get the five-star service she expected as her due. "Why is he leaving? He saved a man's life. What a great role model he is for the twins. What was all that mumbling my grandsons made about his reading? I suppose a cowboy like that gets a pass for not wanting to sit still and read books all day." She took a breath.

"Excuse me, ma'am." Ivy jumped in before Sophie's mother kept the conversation train going. "I don't have a steamer or a frother. I'm not one of those fancy coffee places." She took a mug from the community coffee table, filled it with coffee and then topped it off with half-and-half. "Here you go."

Staring into the depths of her mug as if looking for the answers to some of the questions she'd tossed at Sophie, her mother sighed. "How have you managed to stay here this long without a decent latte?"

"We endure," Sophie replied. "About the boys. With Zeke leaving, I need you to watch them for a few hours every day." This was a huge request. Her mother didn't like kids much. They didn't treat her like a princess.

Mom pushed the mug into the middle of the table and eyed Sophie's pastry. "How long until your next au pair arrives?"

"There is no new nanny on the horizon." Sophie didn't normally take her coffee with milk, but she needed something milder. She switched mugs with her mother and took a sip. "Just you."

Just the woman who would never be up for the mother-of-the-year award. Not that Sophie didn't love her anyway. It was just… Sophie wanted to win that mother-of-the-year award. Every year.

Mom fluffed her bangs and examined a small plastic menu that was tucked next to the napkin holder. "You never let a nanny go if you don't have another lined up."

"I didn't expect Zeke to leave me." Her words were strangled.

Her mother looked at her sharply. "You're still blotchy. And your nanny's leaving."

"Don't say it, Mom." Sophie blinked back tears. "Tell me you'll be happy to watch my adorable little heathens. Tell me you'll be thrilled to take them fishing and to the blacksmith shop or hiking up the hill to dig for buried treasure."

Mom set her menu down. "It's worse than I thought."

Sophie expected a lecture about her past mistakes in her love life. She expected Zeke's reading ability to be held up as a glaring reason why she needed to return to Philadelphia or retreat to Las Vegas.

"You're becoming one of them, just the way Harlan wanted." Mom scooted out of the booth. "Hiking. Fishing. Have you looked at your footwear? Rubber-soled boots? I'm calling your father. We are definitely getting a divorce. Hang in there, honey, I'll buy your way out of here."

"Mom. *Mom!* I don't need ransom money. Please don't divorce Dad." Sophie groaned and put her head in her hands. "I need..."

Her mother let the door shut behind her.

Sophie raised her head and sighed. Now what was she going to do?

Shane and the twins entered the diner. Her boys skipped over, full of stories about their triumphant pony ride and Zeke's fall into manure.

"He's changing," Shane explained.

Alex climbed up beside her and waved to Ivy. "Hot chocolate, please."

"Me, too." Andy slid over in the booth so Shane could join him.

Her four-year-olds were ordering in a restaurant like professional diners. That was a bit... disappointing. Teaching her children good manners was one thing. Having them order without asking permission if they could sugar-up was another. Good moms didn't do that.

Her boys chattered about someone named Taffy.

"Have you heard anything about Roy?" she asked Shane. "I don't want to sound like I don't care about his condition, but I need to move out of the inn." And Roy was the only one she knew who could make a cabin livable for her.

Shane studied her the way an art appraiser examined a potential forgery. "Why the rush to leave the inn? Zeke's moving out today."

Sophie fought the roiling that news had on her gut. "Why? My boys should be eating home-cooked meals."

"Meaning you plan to cook?" Shane sat back in his seat and took a moment to process that. And then he leaned forward with an evil-older-brother type of smile. "You don't know how to cook."

They'd never had to learn, considering they'd

had a family chef growing up and Cam was always in the kitchen cooking something.

"I can follow a recipe," Sophie said in her defense. "If I'm going to stay here, I can't eat at the diner so often." What was the working mom's definition of the number of acceptable meals to eat out in a week?

"Sister dear..." Shane whispered, grin growing. "You can't cook any worse than Ivy."

Sophie reached across the table and pushed Shane's shoulder back. "You've just ensured you won't get a dinner invitation from me."

"We won't get one from Mom either. She's leaving." Shane, the bearer of bad news.

Although she'd suspected as much. "What about Cam? He better not be leaving." Especially after the lecture Shane had given him yesterday about manning up. She leaned forward to whisper, "Is he leaving?"

"He says he's driving Mom to the airport and will return." Shane didn't look convinced their younger brother was going to honor his word.

Zeke ambled in, looking freshly dressed and showered. Worse, looking like he hadn't expected to see her in the diner. His steps slowed.

Chilled, Sophie rubbed her arms and looked away.

Zeke was moving on.

She had to accept that fact and hope someday

they could be friends, that he'd see she didn't judge him by his reading level.

Because that's what good moms who stayed in town did.

CHAPTER TWENTY-THREE

ZEKE'S LAST FEW minutes in Sophie's employ were the most painful.

"Here's your check." She handed him his pay, hesitated and then extended her hand to shake. "Thank you… For everything."

He didn't want to be thanked. He wanted a kiss on the cheek. He wanted a look of regret. He wanted to know that in the day since he'd told Sophie they couldn't be together that she still loved him.

You can't have it both ways.

He was just as bad as she'd been, trying to keep one foot in both worlds—cowboying and the high-class world of the Monroes.

"Say goodbye to Zeke," Sophie called to the twins.

They got up from a game of checkers and ran to give him hearty hugs.

"I bet you come back," Alex said in his ear.

"I bet you don't like the Clarks as much as us," Andy said in the other.

Zeke closed his eyes and held on tight, only

just realizing that he wasn't just losing Sophie. He was losing Alex and Andy. "What am I going to do without you two?"

Alex drew back, blinking back tears. "I want you to practice." He handed Zeke *Mama Duck, Papa Duck.* "Read it for real. Davey can help you."

"I told him he couldn't laugh at you when you read," Andy said, more serious than a four-year-old should be.

Zeke stared up at Sophie.

She looked as brittle as a midwinter icicle in the afternoon sun. Too much more and she'd break.

Zeke didn't want to see her break. He might collapse along with her.

There was a clattering on the porch. Mitch opened the door and held it for Laurel and Roy to enter.

Roy looked deflated and pale. He tottered over to Zeke and gave him a hug. "There's my man. My hero. Without you... I don't know what I'd have done." He clung to Zeke.

"Gabby, did you turn Zeke's room?" Mitch asked.

"Yes, I did." She came out of Zeke's room with a basket of crumpled linens.

"What's going on?" Zeke gave himself a little space, holding on to Roy's shoulders.

"I'm taking your place." Roy nodded, looking none too happy. "The doc down in Ketchum said I shouldn't be alone for a few weeks. I'm available to babysit, Sophie, if you need me."

"He can sit in the chair the way Zeke did," Mitch said firmly. "The meds he's on are making him a bit fuzzy."

"And I think—" Roy raised his voice "—that if we're doing a true job switch that Zeke should take over as town handyman. Cowboys need retirement strategies, you know."

No one said anything. Not even Zeke.

Roy squinted at the lot of them. "Unless you want Shane to take on the responsibility."

"We'll figure it out," Mitch reassured him.

Sophie and Laurel shepherded Roy to Zeke's former room. The twins followed, chattering to Roy about his favorite books and future checkers matches. Gabby hurried after them with a handful of soaps.

"So, I guess this is it." Mitch clapped Zeke on the back. "Do you need a ride?"

"No. Emily's coming to get me."

In fact, her truck pulled up in front of the inn. Perfect timing. Or it would have been if Zeke wasn't battling regrets about leaving.

"Don't forget this." Mitch handed Zeke the clown painting from the wall, a sardonic grin beginning to form. "I'm sure it's a very valuable painting."

"Actually, it is." Zeke shouldered his duffel and took the picture. "Painting on velvet is an art form." If he'd learned anything from his time with Sophie, it was that there was beauty and craftsmanship in the most basic of things.

Chuckling, Mitch held the door for him and closed it, shutting Zeke out from Roy and the Monroes and the life he'd taken for granted during his ten-week recuperation. His steps were heavy as he walked away and climbed into the Bucking Bull truck.

It wasn't Emily. It was Franny.

"It's good to have you back, Zeke." She drove slowly past Egbert's rental shop and the smithie. "I didn't realize Egbert was back in town. Has he been telling all his tales of Old Jeb?"

"Yeah. Sappy love stories about your ancestors." Writing letters to win a woman's heart? The gift of the stove and the horse alone should have convinced Miss Carol that Old Jeb loved her. What did she want? Love didn't come with a certificate to prove it was real or lasting.

The thought hit his chest, pushing him back against the seat.

Love has no proof.

"Love shines brighter with a sappy gesture or two." Franny's somber tone conveyed how much she missed her husband. "Kyle wallpapered the bunkhouse before he asked me to marry him, because he knew that's where we'd be living at first. A girl like me, who never lived in a home that had anything but round cabin logs... That meant the world to me."

Later that night, Zeke lay in the small bunkhouse and stared at the rose wallpaper, it's pattern faint in the moonlight, and wondered if he'd done the right thing by choosing his pride over love.

TWO WEEKS AFTER Zeke had left for the Bucking Bull, Sophie's life had fallen into a predictable rhythm.

Get the boys up. Sort through some boxes. Restock and stage the trading post as needed. Leave the twins with Roy before lunch and Gabby after lunch. Lunch and dinner at the Bent Nickel. Read after dinner and collapse in bed. Repeat the next day.

Who had time to think about Zeke? Her mother had returned to their family home, with daily text updates about how wrong Sophie's father was and how she'd rescue all her children financially. Soon. Very soon. And Cam? Cam was a no-show. He'd never returned after driving their mother to the airport. He wasn't answering calls or texts either. Shane, who hadn't yet received the long-awaited report from the consultant about how best to move forward with the town, was beside himself.

But today was different. It was Monday and the trading post and mercantile were closed on Mondays. Sophie refused to think about her family or how her siblings and cousins might vote regarding Second Chance's future.

"What are we looking for again?" Alexander trudged up the hill in front of her.

"Our new house." Andrew sounded cranky, possibly because he'd stumbled earlier and bruised his knee.

Roy had sent them into the woods behind his cabin. Supposedly, there was a two-bedroom cabin back there. One that Roy said wouldn't be hard to return to working condition. Sophie was staying. She'd tell anyone who'd listen that unlike other Monroes, she was fully committed to being a permanent resident.

The woods were beautiful. Sunlight streamed between pine needles. Everything smelled fresh and clean.

Zeke would have loved it.

"There it is!" Alexander ran ahead.

Sure enough, a charming cabin with a little front porch was nestled in a grove of trees. It had green shutters and a Dutch door. And there was a clearing next to it where the twins could run around without falling downhill.

Sophie unlocked the door and they all rushed inside. There was a woodstove and an L-shaped kitchen. No living room furniture, but a dinette set.

"Bunk beds!" Andrew cried, running into a bedroom, injury forgotten.

"Dibs on the top bunk!" Alexander was hot on his heels.

"There's no mattress," Andrew wailed.

The bathroom was basic, looking to have been updated in the forties or fifties with pink porcelain fixtures.

And the bedroom... The bed frame was made of wood posts for a queen mattress.

It wasn't a bed a woman looked forward to sleeping in alone.

Sophie squared her shoulders. She was staying. She was made of sturdy stock.

"Come on, boys. We have a lot to do." Ordering mattresses for one. Seeing what type of items Mack had in the general store she could use.

They traipsed down the hill, passing between Roy's place and the empty medical cabin.

"Hey! That's Zeke!" Alexander pointed to a man riding a horse past the smithie.

"And he's got ponies!" Andrew hurried down to the road.

Zeke led two ponies and a horse behind him. The sunlight glinted off the silver accent on his cowboy hatband. He stopped in the diner's parking lot when he saw them, cautioning the twins to wait for Sophie to cross safely.

She let the boys pull her across at a trot, because she was excited to see Zeke again, too.

"Hi," Zeke said simply as he got down. He looked at Sophie the way he had weeks ago before her mother had come to town.

Roy was well enough to go back to the diner. He stood at the front window, gesturing for someone to join him.

Egbert lumbered up, leaning on his cane.

"Are those for us?" Alexander pointed at the small herd of horses, his cowlick blowing in the breeze.

Andrew wasn't shy about what he wanted. "I want to ride a pony."

"I told you getting back in the saddle would make a cowboy out of you." Zeke lifted Andrew on a black pony and Alexander on a gray one. "I've got to talk to your mom about giving these ponies to you for real. You aren't going to ride anywhere until we get things straightened out. Agreed?"

"Yes, sir," they both said, making Sophie

proud of their restraint and good manners. Their ponies were tied to a rope that was tied to Zeke's saddle horn.

Zeke held on to the reins of his horse and faced Sophie. "I've been thinking—" he moved close to Sophie and tilted back his hat "—that I'm too proud for my own good."

Sophie didn't think so. She'd seen him wear a bootie knitted by an elderly woman. Seen him laugh off being hooked by her two young fishermen and take their ribbing when he'd fallen into manure to keep them clear of it. He didn't have too much pride. He had an abundance of honor.

"I was in this precarious, pathetic hole, thinking of how empty my life was because I was nearly broke and I couldn't read. And what I didn't realize was how rich I truly was. I had friends like Mitch, boys with gumption and a compassionate woman by my side. And I blew it." He drew a breath and added, softer this time, "I really blew it."

Sophie's nose stung with unshed tears. She sniffed and blinked and let Zeke go on.

"I thought I needed to be the smartest man in the room to deserve a woman like you." He took a piece of paper out of his back pocket and unfolded it. "I came into town today to tell you how wrong I was."

The ponies. The horses. The piece of paper.

All of it paled when compared with the bright, hopeful look in Zeke's eyes.

She unfolded the paper once. He'd drawn two hearts linked together and embellished it with a shamrock, a small rainbow and a pot of gold.

Sophie gazed up at him. "I love it." It was no da Vinci, but to her it was priceless.

"Open it up," he said softly.

"Yeah, Mom," Alexander encouraged her. "Read it."

She opened the card. The words were written in pencil and she could tell where one or two had been corrected. His handwriting was big and bold. And the words… They were words of apology and compromise and love.

Love.

She sniffed and blinked again.

"What does it say?" Andrew asked impatiently.

"It says…" Sophie wasn't sure she wanted to share it with anyone else.

"Go on," Zeke encouraged, eyes brimming with more love than there was on the page. "I don't mind."

"It says, 'My dearest Sophie. I'm sorry that I'm a slow learner.'" She clutched a hand over her heart and swallowed back those happy tears. "'I'm sorry that I'm not wealthy or have a PhD. But I'm not sorry I fell in love with you. How do I know it's love? Because my heart aches without you. Because memories of you and the twins fill my days to distraction.'" *Oh.* She had to pause and breathe, to gaze into his eyes and see the truth. "You love me?"

He'd never said it before, not even that last horrible night when she'd said it to him.

"I love you all," Zeke said simply. "Go on. Finish it."

She bent her head to read the last words he'd written. "'Cowboys shouldn't be distracted around bulls.'" She chuckled. "'Which is why I'm coming to you with the most important gift a cowboy can give the woman he loves— a well-trained, sure-footed horse to carry her back to his side every night. I love you more than shamrocks, pots of gold and rainbows.'" Her words drifted off on the wind.

Zeke removed a small package from a saddlebag. "Here," he said gruffly.

If he'd handed her a ring box, it was a large ring box.

Sophie unwrapped the layers of newspaper. "It's your grandmother's dolphin." It was an exquisite piece, carved with loving detail.

"She would have wanted you to have it." He added almost under his breath, *To have me.*

"Zeke…" She took his hand. "I've been

so foolish. I was clinging to the past when I should have been fully committed to the future. I talked to Eli Garland about the boys' education and I know we'll do fine here. Whatever the boys decide they want to be in life, their journey begins here. With you beside us." If that was what he was asking.

He dropped down on one knee and took her other hand, the one holding the dolphin. "I love you, Sophie. At first, it scared me how much I could love you. I would be honored if you'd be my wife. I'd be honored to help raise your boys. I love you, Sophie. Please say yes." His eyes were shining the brightest of greens.

Her eyes were leaking tears and her glasses had slid down her nose. "I love you, Zeke. We all do."

"We do! We love you!" the twins echoed, astride their ponies.

"Of course I'll marry you," Sophie said softly.

And then he was standing, and she was in his arms and there was no place she'd rather be, no man she'd rather be with, no man she'd rather kiss, no man she'd rather give her heart to.

All too soon he drew back. "Come meet your gift."

"You got me a horse?" Sophie stared at the plump horse the color of rich chestnuts.

"This—" he led her closer "—is Monroe."

She laughed. "You're so creative."

Zeke shook his head, taking the dolphin from her and wrapping it up, stowing it in his saddlebag once more. "For safekeeping," he explained. And then he helped her on board Monroe.

"I went to the livestock auction in Boise. His papers listed him as Monroe. It was a sign."

She leaned over in the saddle, took off Zeke's hat and kissed him on the forehead. "You would've had me with a bouquet of flowers and that card." She put his hat on her head. "What do you say, boys? Are you ready to ride?"

They whooped.

True to Zeke's words, the horses and ponies were well trained and didn't budge at the noise.

"Bravo!" Egbert stuck his head out the diner door, long beard and flowing locks lifting in the breeze. "Just like Old Jeb and Miss Clark."

"Nope." Sophie exchanged a smile with Zeke. "Better."

* * * * *

*The next installment of
The Mountain Monroes is coming soon from
bestselling author Melinda Curtis.
Lassoed by the Would-be Rancher
unexpectedly pairs Francis and Shane!*

*For more great romances from
Harlequin Heartwarming and
Melinda Curtis,
visit www.Harlequin.com today!*

Get 4 FREE REWARDS!

We'll send you 2 FREE Books plus 2 FREE Mystery Gifts.

Love Inspired® Suspense books feature Christian characters facing challenges to their faith... and lives.

FREE Value Over $20

YES! Please send me 2 FREE Love Inspired® Suspense novels and my 2 FREE mystery gifts (gifts are worth about $10 retail). After receiving them, if I don't wish to receive any more books, I can return the shipping statement marked "cancel." If I don't cancel, I will receive 6 brand-new novels every month and be billed just $5.24 each for the regular-print edition or $5.99 each for the larger-print edition in the U.S., or $5.74 each for the regular-print edition or $6.24 each for the larger-print edition in Canada. That's a savings of at least 13% off the cover price. It's quite a bargain! Shipping and handling is just 50¢ per book in the U.S. and $1.25 per book in Canada.* I understand that accepting the 2 free books and gifts places me under no obligation to buy anything. I can always return a shipment and cancel at any time. The free books and gifts are mine to keep no matter what I decide.

Choose one: ☐ **Love Inspired® Suspense**
Regular-Print
(153/353 IDN GNWN)

☐ **Love Inspired® Suspense**
Larger-Print
(107/307 IDN GNWN)

Name (please print)

Address   Apt. #

City   State/Province   Zip/Postal Code

Mail to the **Reader Service:**
IN U.S.A.: P.O. Box 1341, Buffalo, NY 14240-8531
IN CANADA: P.O. Box 603, Fort Erie, Ontario L2A 5X3

Want to try 2 free books from another series! Call 1-800-873-8635 or visit www.ReaderService.com.

---

*Terms and prices subject to change without notice. Prices do not include sales taxes, which will be charged (if applicable) based on your state or country of residence. Canadian residents will be charged applicable taxes. Offer not valid in Quebec. This offer is limited to one order per household. Books received may not be as shown. Not valid for current subscribers to Love Inspired Suspense books. All orders subject to approval. Credit or debit balances in a customer's account(s) may be offset by any other outstanding balance owed by or to the customer. Please allow 4 to 6 weeks for delivery. Offer available while quantities last.

Your Privacy—The Reader Service is committed to protecting your privacy. Our Privacy Policy is available online at www.ReaderService.com or upon request from the Reader Service. We make a portion of our mailing list available to reputable third parties that offer products we believe may interest you. If you prefer that we not exchange your name with third parties, or if you wish to clarify or modify your communication preferences, please visit us at www.ReaderService.com/consumerschoice or write to us at Reader Service Preference Service, P.O. Box 9062, Buffalo, NY 14240-9062. Include your complete name and address.

LIS20

THE CHRISTMAS ROMANCE COLLECTION!

'Tis the season for romance!

You're sure to fall in love with these tenderhearted love stories from some of your favorite bestselling authors!

Get 4 FREE REWARDS!

We'll send you 2 FREE Books plus 2 FREE Mystery Gifts.

FREE
Value Over
$20

Both the **Romance** and **Suspense** collections feature compelling novels
written by many of today's bestselling authors.

YES! Please send me 2 FREE novels from the Essential Romance or
Essential Suspense Collection and my 2 FREE gifts (gifts are worth about
$10 retail). After receiving them, if I don't wish to receive any more books,
I can return the shipping statement marked "cancel." If I don't cancel, I will
receive 4 brand-new novels every month and be billed just $6.99 each in the
U.S. or $7.24 each in Canada. That's a savings of at least 13% off the cover
price. It's quite a bargain! Shipping and handling is just 50¢ per book in the
U.S. and $1.25 per book in Canada.* I understand that accepting the 2 free
books and gifts places me under no obligation to buy anything. I can always
return a shipment and cancel at any time. The free books and gifts are mine
to keep no matter what I decide.

Choose one: ☐ **Essential Romance**   ☐ **Essential Suspense**
              (194/394 MDN GNNP)   (191/391 MDN GNNP)

Name (please print)

Address   Apt. #

City   State/Province   Zip/Postal Code

Mail to the Reader Service:
IN U.S.A.: P.O. Box 1341, Buffalo, NY 14240-8531
IN CANADA: P.O. Box 603, Fort Erie, Ontario L2A 5X3

Want to try 2 free books from another series? Call 1-800-873-8635 or visit www.ReaderService.com.

#303 THE COWBOY'S CHRISTMAS BABY
The Sweetheart Ranch • by Cathy McDavid
After causing a scandal to protect his family, Tanner Bridwell shocks the rodeo circuit...and loses his fiancée. Seeing her with the daughter she kept from him crushes him. But how can he betray one family to win back another?

#304 THE FIREFIGHTER'S THANKSGIVING WISH
Butterfly Harbor Stories • by Anna J. Stewart
Roman Salazar doesn't think much of becoming the fire chief to a small town, but that's before his head and heart are turned by said town and his beautiful captain, Frankie Bettencourt!

#305 HER TRIPLETS' MISTLETOE DAD
Home to Eagle's Rest • by Patricia Johns
Gabby Rogers needs help raising her triplet newborns, and marrying her best friend, cowboy Seth Straight, seems like the perfect solution. Until she's blindsided by the one thing that could ruin their safe, platonic partnership—love!

#306 HOME FOR CHRISTMAS
Shores of Indian Lake
by Catherine Lanigan
Businesswoman Joy Boston returns to her hometown to wrap up her grandfather's estate. Surprisingly, she enjoys the quaint town at Christmas—and being with her first love, Adam Masterson. But can it make Joy believe in second chances?
